Rising
Ember

Rising Ember

CHILDREN FROM SACRIFICE:
BOOK ONE

ARLETA RAE

gatekeeper press
Columbus, Ohio

This book is a work of fiction. The names, characters and events in this book are the products of the author's imagination or are used fictitiously. Any similarity to real persons living or dead is coincidental and not intended by the author.

RISING EMBER

Children From Sacrifice: Book 1

Published by **Gatekeeper Press**
2167 Stringtown Rd., Suite 109
Columbus, OH 43123-2989
www.GatekeeperPress.com

Copyright © 2022 by **Arleta Rae**

All rights reserved. Neither this book, nor any parts within it may be sold or reproduced in any form or by any electronic or mechanical means, including information storage and retrieval systems without permission in writing from the author. The only exception is by a reviewer, who may quote short excerpts in a review.

The cover design, interior formatting, typesetting, and editorial work for this book are entirely the product of the author. Gatekeeper Press did not participate in and is not responsible for any aspect of these elements.

Library of Congress Control Number: 2022934209

ISBN (paperback): 9781662926167

To my family.
Thank you for being my rock.

Contents

Chapter 1	5
Chapter 2	15
Chapter 3	27
Chapter 4	29
Chapter 5	47
Chapter 6	63
Chapter 7	85
Chapter 8	99
Chapter 9	111
Chapter 10	133
Chapter 11	145
Chapter 12	165
Chapter 13	181

Chapter 14	189
Chapter 15	197
Chapter 16	211
Chapter 17	219
Chapter 18	229
Chapter 19	239
Chapter 20	241
Chapter 21	245
Chapter 22	259
Chapter 23	265
Acknowledgements	271
About the Author	273

Chapter 1

*A*nything can happen in a silent moment. Tragedy will wield its brutal blade, leaving only sorrow and broken pieces behind. It will scar the mind and soul like a forest fire upon a growing tree, etched in its rings forever.

The eerie stillness of the old-growth forest is numbing, the only sound coming from the occasional caress of summer's gentle winds as it dances in the canopy of the tall, white pines and spruces. It is in the silence like this that memories long stashed away flood my thoughts. Sometimes they are welcoming. But other times, they can be debilitating.

Looking down at the sketchbook on my lap, I curse at the doodles my wandering brain let my unsupervised hand create, covering the lines that would have created the dark forest around me. The towering pines stand like guardians of the wilds, the wind as their weapon, cast aglow like warriors of fire in the setting sun. An omnipresent force of natural determination. The woody giants surround a smaller pine with withering branches as if they were protecting it from an unseen threat. My untrained hands would never do this moss-covered scenic beauty justice.

I shift uncomfortably on my sitting rock in the silence, combing my fingers through my long hair—a habit of anxious tendency, I've realized. Upon discovery, the forest was blooming with the sounds of scurrying and singing animals and the sun shone on this rock like a spotlight. An artist could not wish for a more perfect spot. Now, however, the birds and squirrels have departed, plunging me into a landscape frozen in time. Even the stream has quieted.

When people learn that I prefer sound over silence, they are astonished—as if that is such an unusual preference. Maybe it is.

Over the past year and a half, I have created a series of art pieces to capture the most stunning and desolate places the wilds have to offer. I scroll through my many sold pieces on my phone for inspiration.

The nudge of a soft nose on my elbow creates an unwanted line on the page with the pencil in my hand. My cat purrs into the silence as his orange eyes stare up at me.

"I know, I know. It's dinner time." He blinks slowly at me, placing a paw on my leg. "When I found you, you were perfectly content being starving. Now you can't be late for dinner by even a second." Another bump on my arm.

I go to close the sketchbook, but the sight of a doodle in the top corner catches my attention. A set of eyes. Not just any eyes, but those of the stranger who lives in my dreams, like a light in the dark. They swirl like mist over a serene pool in the early morning. I have frequently woken up to the same dream—one where I find myself in darkness, surrounded by the silent hauntings of howling winds. At the peak of my fear, this stranger emerges, offering safety with a gentle, warm smile. He appears like magic when fear digs its claws into me.

Helios nudges my arm again, pulling me away from the mesmerizing drawing and lets out an inquisitive meow. His voice has broken the silence spell that has fallen upon the area. The birds start singing their gleeful songs and the distant sound of the burbling stream chases the unsettling quiet away.

I stand, shaking off the tension from sitting in a single position for the last three hours. Helios jumps down from the rock and stretches in sync with me. Buttery sunlight filters through the branches and shimmers on his orange coat like sparks from a flame. I store the image of the melancholy forest with its viridian trees and needle-covered ground in my mind so that I can draw it later. I don't think he would be willing to put off dinner to finish what I've started so that I could create that art piece now.

Neither could I, in fact. My stomach grumbles as we turn to exit through the narrow pathway, created to reach this sitting spot. We—mostly me since tiny Helios couldn't care less—carefully step over the vast amounts of delicate maidenhair ferns and purple trillium. Crickets chirp their evening melodies as the sun continues its descent. The narrow dirt path snakes in the underbrush, and I focus on my feet so as to not trip over the protruding roots and rocks, hidden within the veil of dusk.

Out of the forest, Helios darts toward the RV to wait at the door. A spike of fear that he would change course when a chipmunk crosses his path floods through me. My breathing hitches as I watch Helios ignore the creature and stay true toward the vehicle. Well behaved, as usual.

That same eerie quiet from earlier settles over the small clearing that the silver airstream trailer is parked in. The setting sun is well below the tree line now, covering the space in a blanket of shadowy hues. The dirt road ahead is swallowed by the darkening of the forest. I quicken my pace to the safety of the trailer. As I reach for the door handle, a few loose papers slip out of the sketchbook in my arm. I contemplate leaving them there just so I can get inside quicker. Instead, I grab them hastily, crinkling them as I clutch my work tightly.

Helios darts inside as the door opens just enough for his body to squeeze through. That is when I feel it. Eyes on my back. It causes the hairs on my neck to stand on end. I tense and scan the area, seeing no one. A chill runs down my spine, forcing a shiver. An impatient meow from inside has me swiftly squeezing through the door myself, locking it once inside.

The lightness of the trailer soothes my tense mind. The curtains are already closed, leaving Helios and me to ourselves. Helios sits patiently beside the dining bench, waiting for his bowl of food. I toss the sketchbook on the dining table before crossing the narrow, tan-tiled center aisle to open the refrigerator. "We are going to have to stop at a store before hitting the road tomorrow, bud."

Tomorrow starts the eight-hour trek back to my hometown, the city of Inbery. In a rare phone call the other day, I told Sarah that I wouldn't be home until her birthday toward the beginning of

September. I will surprise her and her mom, Valeria, quite a few days early.

While Helios graciously chows down on his food, I prepare my own quick meal and sit at the dining booth with my computer. Looking at a map, I plan to stop in a city about halfway to Inbery so that I can upload my latest drawings and monthly blog post. Not that I have too many people who read my posts, but for those who do, I like to keep them updated. They could be potential clients after all.

After dinner, I curl up on the soft corner couch with my current novel and a blanket as small rain drops drum against the roof of the trailer. I have been mostly lucky with nighttime temperatures not getting too chilly as we slowly approach the end of summer. Tonight, however, there is a chill in the air. I pulled on all the warmest clothing I own and the chunkiest blanket. Helios adds another layer of warmth as he gets up on the couch and snuggles onto my lap.

Two chapters into the book, and that prickly sensation of being watched washes over me again. My nerves beat in my ears over the sound of the rain. Helios lifts his head and meets my gaze as his ears swivel toward the door. He moves from my lap and sits at the edge of the couch as I check the locks for the third time. I sigh and run a hand through my hair before deciding to head to bed.

~

The golden, morning sunlight beams through the thin floral curtains, stirring me awake. My eyes peel open, reluctant to face the day. A night of haunting dreams of unidentifiable shadowy figures had me checking my windows and door more times that I can count. Songs of early rising birds' lilt in a soothing melody. I find Helios curled up at my feet. He lifts his head when I stretch, his eyes still full of morning sleepiness.

"Good morning, boy." Flipping the blanket off of me, I run a hand down his soft fur.

He responds with a yawn before stretching and trotting to his empty food bowl.

I feed the needy feline before changing into my exercise clothes and head out for a bit of early morning jogging to calm the lingering unease from yesterday evening. My mother used to always tell me to go seek nature when life fails you. It has always been the long-needed remedy for many stressors. A place to get pleasantly lost in. I stop first to admire the small creek that runs past the trailer and parallel with the road. A lovely moss-covered fallen tree rests perpendicular to the creek with large mushrooms growing on top. Across the water were some Lion's Mane mushrooms growing on upright trees and I thought about crossing to pick some. Mornings are my favorite times to witness the natural world as it yields to a new day. Sunlight flickers between open branches, birds dance and sing merrily from tree to tree, and everything stills as the forest slowly awakens. Even the wind hardly stirs, only brushing along the highest of branches, allowing for the serenity of the forest to fill my senses.

The crisp air and rhythmic sound of my sneakers hitting the dirt path energizes my body into a steady pace. Helios is never too pleased when I leave him behind in the mornings, but he prefers sitting amongst the trees and sunbathing.

The sound of a large branch cracking to the right has me pausing to catch my breath. I stretch while looking around, thinking that it is an animal. I have been out for almost an hour already.

In front of me sits a dilapidated fence post worn away from years of abandonment and weathering. A decaying vine tried claiming it at one point in time but has since only left a thin skeleton if its former self. A lone black beetle crawls up the side of it, flying away once I get too close.

A sudden hush has fallen over the forest on both sides of the path. The uneasiness I felt the night before slams into my chest. The steady pounding of heavy footsteps echo in the silence and I turn in their direction, ready to flee. I know that there are other camping sites here, maybe it is a jogger. With nervous footing, I turn around to run back toward my trailer. I clench my jaw, forcing all the old self-defense movements my father has taught me into the forefront of my memory.

The steps come closer. Closer. My mind raced to what it is. A deer? A bear? And just as my breath dwindles, around the curve of the dirt path comes a jogger. My lungs inhale with an explosion of oxygen and a release of relief.

After a few steps, I look behind me again and notice the jogger had changed his own path and turned back around. I slow my pace, having pushed myself more than usual. I wonder if he realized that he had startled me and decided to turn around because of it.

A light wind picks up and curls around my chin, cooling the sweat on my skin. I take a deep breath of the chilled air to further calm myself. My favorite scent—that of pine—fills my lungs. A sparrow leaps from a branch to my left and flies across the path, startling me a bit. I exhale, placing my hand on my stammering heart. "That's enough excitement for today," I say to the forest.

Luckily, the forest listened and resumed its usual tranquil melody of sounds as I continued back to the trailer, reaching it after almost another hour has passed. The rising sun peeks just above the tips of the trees. Helios waits impatiently on the bed that sits toward the back. A smile tugs at my lips when I notice the aggressive flap of his tail as he watches me approach through the window.

I feel a set of eyes on my back as I reach the threshold of the trailer. This time, I don't pause to look around, I just scurry inside and lock the door.

"Let's get out of here." I say to the four-legged furball rubbing at my ankles. "No amount of art is worth this paranoia. Plus, you get to finally meet Sarah and Valeria."

~

Helios sits in his car seat next to me as we begin our journey, watching the world whirl by. The coniferous forest transitions into open fields before reaching the bustling highway. I was hoping to get back to that sitting spot from yesterday before leaving, but I guess the rest of the drawing will have to come from the pull on my memory.

After a few hours of steady driving, I find a coffee shop in a small town to stop at. Leaving Helios in the trailer, I grab my laptop and sketchbook and head in for something to eat and a cup of caffeine.

The aroma of ground coffee beans and freshly made pastries wafts around the café, causing my stomach to grumble. The place is quaint. Brown painted walls and photos of coffee bean plants hung in various locations. A handful of small, circular tables dot the wooden floor with only a couple of them occupied. I place my things down at a table on the empty side of the building and stand in line.

I order a croissant and the specialty latte and take the number the barista handed me. A black-haired man takes the table next to mine. He is holding a mug and reading a book. It makes me wish that I could also be reading, but this blog post won't upload itself—nor will the photos of my art.

As it uploads, the barista comes over to my table with my order. I graciously take the purple ceramic mug and smile as she places the small plate down before grabbing the number and retreating back to the counter. The lavender latte, though steaming hot, dances on my tongue and I enjoy the heat as it warms. Floral notes melt heavenly with the bitterness of the espresso.

As I tilt the mug away from my face, the feeling of being watched shakes me again. I stare into the white bubbles of the foam, feeling the prickling sensation of another's gaze on my skin. I feel it roam across my body before landing on my face. I do all I can to not slump in my chair and run for the exit. A lump form in my throat as sweat tickles the back of my neck. Steeling a glance, I notice the man next to me looking in this direction. His sculpted, diamond-shaped face is angled slightly down, his alluring lips curved subtly. My heart skips a beat as my eyes meet his.

Chapter 2

A large, green signpost with big white letters reads "Welcome to Vermont!" I blink at it, stupefied. I crossed an entire state before reaching this one and don't remember a moment of it. In fact, I don't remember anything after entering the coffee shop. After that man with the striking gray eyes looked at me. Helios curls up in his seat. Gripping the steering wheel with white knuckles, I try to recall the last few hours. Memories of going back to the trailer and getting on the road are lost.

I clear my throat and swallow nervously, wiping one sweaty palm on my pale jeans. An ache subtly pulses behind my eyes as I try and recall what happened at the coffee shop, subsiding only when I stop trying. I thrust a hand into my hair and realize that it is shaking when it comes back to the wheel.

The sun shines behind slate-colored clouds, beams lighting up the familiar painted rock of Inbery that sits amongst a semi-circle of trees at the city's borders. A few crows sit atop it, pecking at the old artwork.

The chime of my cell phone startles me out of my disturbing thoughts. My phone, perched on the dusty dashboard, reads Sarah's name. Still shaken with the memory loss, I consider ignoring her call. She would undoubtedly be able to tell that something was off. However, ignoring her might activate her overactive protectiveness. "Hey, Sarah," I say into the cab of my truck.

"Hey, sis!" she exclaims, sounding extra excited. "What glorious sights are you seeing today?"

Another reason I was hoping to not have to speak with her was because I wanted to surprise her, and I am absolutely horrible at keeping things a secret. "Nothing spectacular. I'm just on the road."

"Obviously, smart-ass. Where on the road?"

Helios picks up his head and stares at me with an irritated look at having woke him. The strap that keeps his car seat in place is not secured like it normally is and I furrow my brows. What was I doing that caused me to unsafely put him there?

"Thea?" Sarah's voice chimes in, her tone raising an octave.

"Yeah, sorry. I'm driving." I flinch at remaining vague. We tell each other everything, so not divulging my current worries with her is hard. But, with this, I feel like I need to figure it out on my own before stressing her about it.

"So you said." Her voice picks up its excitement again. "A little birdy told me they saw a shiny silver trailer entering the city."

The city isn't too big, but large enough that you would think you could sneak into it without being spotted. Unfortunately, my apartment building is rather close to the university that the majority of the locals attend, so a lot of the people know my trailer. Sarah and I were close to students from more than just the environmental department. I let out a sigh. "I was trying to surprise you."

The sound of clapping echoes through the line, and I receive more glares from my cat. "Oh my goddess, I can't wait! How much longer?"

It is impossible not to share in her enthusiasm. "I'm almost home. I just want to unpack a little and shower before we meet up." I pass by a small restaurant with outdoor seating and receive a wave from an old classmate. "Don't tell your mom, okay? Maybe I can surprise at least one person."

Sarah chuckles. "All right. I'll be out of work in a couple hours, so come by the house as soon as you can. I've missed you so much."

"I've missed you, too. I'll see you soon."

"See you," she responds and we both hang up.

I look to Helios who fixes his attention on me again. "Aren't you excited to meet her, boy?" He flaps his tail slowly in response and I laugh. When I park the trailer at the back of the apartment building, he sits up and looks around, most likely excited to be able to move.

I stretch as my feet hit the pavement, glancing up at the six-story building. My parents owned the entire thing and the whole first floor was where my father had his gym. When they passed, the building was given to me. Valeria helped keep it in my possession until I was old enough to handle it. One of the few apartments on the top floor was where I moved into after leaving Sarah and Valeria's care. It was hard to come back to. In fact, I didn't set foot around the building for a few years after their deaths. Every Saturday and some evenings during the week, I would spend my time here with my dad, doing homework or taking lessons.

I grab Helios and put him in his carrier, which he expresses his disinterest in quite vocally, and head up the back stairs. I pass one tenant on the way to the top floor, an older woman who simply smiles and nods her head at me before continuing downward.

I open the door to the apartment and am met with the familiar calming scent of rose. The floor plan is open and spacious, complete with high ceilings and a balcony. To the left is the kitchen, outlined by white countertops with a matching island in the middle. The entire opposite wall from the front door has enormous windows. They look out onto a small balcony where you can watch the bustling city below.

To the right is the living room. It is kept simple with a cozy brown couch that sits against the wall of windows and an old coffee table. Scattered around are plants on the floor, including my two favorite rose bushes by the balcony door, and paintings on the walls. The stairs across from the couch lead to the bedroom, which is also separated by a banister, and beach-themed bathroom.

I set the carrier down and open the door. Helios cautiously steps out and inspects his new surroundings. "It is our stationary home for a while, bud." As if he understands, he trots over to the windows and looks out onto the world beyond. I smile and turn to retrieve more things from the trailer. "Be right back."

When I get outside, the afternoon sun is now completely blocked by an endless stretch of gray clouds. Knowing that the weather can change dramatically quickly here, I mentally ask the rain to hold off until I get back inside. The forest behind the apartment building glows as I round the corner of the trailer. So much of my spare time has been spent on the trails within that forest that it is practically my second home. I can walk the whole thing with my eyes closed and never step off the trails.

Inside, I throw all my necessary items into a tote, including my computer, sketchbook, clothes, and toiletries. Just barely fitting through the doorway, I stumble back out onto the pavement. A few raindrops sizzle on the hot parking lot as they fall from the sky. Cursing aloud at the impatient clouds, I lock the door and turn to hurry back to the building. I freeze at the tail end, feeling like there is someone within the trees watching. My body tenses and screams to run as a cold shiver slithers down my spine. My eyes scan the array of maple and birch trees. I don't know if I would prefer to see something or not.

To experience this in the middle of a foreign forest is one thing, but to feel it across from my home? An uneasy sensation rises in my gut. The clouds above blacken even more, blanketing the world in an unnerving darkness. A violent gust of wind blows at me from the trees, knocking me off balance. I feel exposed to the gaze of whatever lurks in the void of the once peaceful woods.

Images flash in my mind, as fleeting as a snowflake on a hot surface. Grey eyes, purple flowers, a crimson stone on silver paper.

"Thea!" a familiar voice rings out as a set of hands land on my shoulder. I startle, turning to see the vibrant brown eyes of my best friend, a worried expression on her flawless, maple-toned skin. The wind flees from her presence. "Are you all right?"

I clear my throat, shoving the passing sensation and memories of those images away. "Yeah, sorry. I was daydreaming."

"You look suspicious while staring into the forest, holding a heavy tote, and in the rain," she asks skeptically, though her focus is on the surrounding trees.

"Can you help me carry this in?" I ask to defuse the conversation.

Her eyes flutter to mine. "Of course."

We climb the stairs with the tote, and I answer all the typical questions one receives after a long trip away. When we enter the apartment, Helios greets me with a flurry of meows.

"Oh my goddess, he is adorable," she squeals, helping me put the tote down on the kitchen floor. Helios trots over to her outstretched hand and nudges her fingers.

I laugh. "Watch out, he is a vicious watchdog."

She snorts. "Yeah, I can tell." He rolls onto his back, allowing her to scratch his stomach. The apartment echoes with his loud purring as the rain outside pelts the windows and balcony. The cement flooring darkens with each drop of water.

Sarah and I finally reunited in a hug before we sit at the island counter with cups of freshly brewed coffee. "I thought you had work for a few more hours?"

An impish expression dazzles across her face. "I did, but I couldn't stay at work and *not* tell my mom about you coming back. I had to leave before I completely ruined your surprise."

I arch a brow. "Did she not ask why you wanted to leave?"

Sarah's shoulder rises and drops. "It was super slow. She didn't even argue when I asked. I'm sure she's comfortable selling all her tinctures, salves, and herb mixes on her own."

"Good, at least my visit home will be a surprise to someone. I know how horrible you are at keeping secrets." We share a laugh as her gaze breaks to the cup in her hands. "Thanks for taking care of my plants by the way."

She lifts her eyes back to mine, a renewed sparkle in them. "It was my pleasure. I know these are your babies." She looks to the roses. "I know I have said this before, but those roses are the most fragrant I have ever smelled. I hope you don't mind if I took a flower," she says shyly.

"Not at all."

"Any romances on your travels?" she inquires, taking the last sip of her coffee before shoving the mug away. The rain outside has transitioned to a drizzle, and the sky has already lightened to a soft gray.

I scoff, picking at a chipped piece of paint on the old white mug. "Please, you would most certainly know already if there had been."

She sighs then pouts with a longing in her eyes. "You were supposed to live out our fantasy by meeting a mysterious stranger while traveling and fall in love."

Grey eyes. Purple flowers. A crimson stone on silver paper.

The images pour into my mind like the sound of a bell in the most silent of nights. A slight throb pulses in my head and I wince.

Concern flashes across Sarah's face. "Are you okay?"

"Just a small headache."

"I'm sorry. I think I have some peppermint oil in my coat pocket. Do you want some for it?"

I shake my head. "No, thank you. Its already subsiding." As powerful as the oil is for headaches, the lingering fragrance stings the eyes. I prefer to use it only when a nap follows.

Something on her phone catches her eye and her expression changes to one of excitement. "My mom just let me know that she's home." She turns her childlike happiness toward me. "Can we go surprise her?"

I tap my fingers on the counter as if in contemplation, which only makes her eyes go wider, a playful plea on her lips.

I chuckle. "Of course. Let's go. I miss your mom." With a squeal of excitement, she pulls my hand, leading me out the apartment.

~

"Is your headache gone?" Sarah asks as we walk up the steps of her family's Victorian style brick manor. It is set a distance from the road with gardens on each side of the stone walkway and a pool near the backyard. Two pyramidal turrets sit on either side of the slim, double-panel front door. Stone friezes line the spaces between each of the three floors. A high-peaked gable roof sits above the front door where white lights twinkle across and down the two columns. Valeria put them up for the holidays one year and they have been there since. They'd just have to switch the batteries here and there.

"Yeah, thanks." The headache vanished the moment we stepped out into the fresh air at the apartment building.

We don't even make it in the doorway before Valeria is embracing me in a tight, comforting embrace. Herbs and incense wafts from her clothing, and I breathe it in deeply as I melt into this woman who took me in when I was alone. Her dark brown hair smells of the salty sea.

"I missed you so much, dear." She pulls away though still holding my shoulders, her hazel eyes gleaming into mine. "I hope your journey has been all you hoped it would be so far."

I nod and smile warmly at her. "I missed you too." A glossy twinkle forms at the corner of her eyes and I swear it is a tear, but she pulls me into another hug before I can be sure. I have only ever seen her cry when her husband, Sarah's father, passed away years ago.

"Come. I'm so happy you stopped by," she says as she closes the door behind us. "I am making your favorite dish for dinner."

My eyes widen. "Ratatouille?" My mouth waters at the thought. "I haven't had that since the last time you made it for me." Almost two years ago.

"Actually," Sarah chimes in, "I was hoping we could go to the Archer for drinks tonight? Zach, Mike, and Alice are taking me out for my birthday tonight."

"Well, it is a good thing that dinner is almost ready, then, isn't it?" Valeria winks.

I look to Sarah. "One shouldn't drink on an empty stomach, right?"

"Very true," she agrees.

Valeria finishes dinner while I shower in their upstairs bathroom and change into some of Sarah's clothes. After months of using a cramped trailer shower, showering in an actual home bathroom feels like heaven. The aroma of my favorite meal entices me to hurry downstairs.

"That was probably the quickest shower you have ever taken," Sarah observes with a crooked grin. She sits at the narrow island, set with three dishes and cutlery.

"No, I think that trophy is reserved for that evening she was determined to go out with that 'yellow-shirt dreamboat from eleventh grade math class'," Valeria utters quickly.

"Ha-ha," I say through a snort.

We eat and help Valeria clean up before marching upstairs. Sarah and I help each other get ready for the night at the local bar.

When I lived here with them, Sarah and I would use the bathroom that our bedrooms shared. Tonight, Sarah colored my eyelids in a subtle golden shadow with black liner that define my hazel eyes. She kept my light brown hair simple with a few waves as it drapes over my shoulders. It all ties in with the daffodil-colored cropped tee and black pants that I found while rummaging through the back of her closet. For her, I decide to go with lavender eyeshadow, to match the dried petals she weaves in her hair, and plum colored lipstick, two colors that I've always said complement her skin tone quite well.

When my gaze catch the sight of the woven pale petals, those haunting images flash through my mind again, persistent and vibrant. My hands still while applying her makeup, a small pain pulsing in my head.

Sarah's eyes flutter open, noting my hand clutching the utensil. "Are you okay?" Concern filters in her expression.

"Yes." I clench my teeth, forcing those images away, and take a step back from my friend. Nerves prick my skin, an uneasiness settling over my body. "I think I might skip going to the bar tonight." The words spill out before I can stop them. Though a good idea, my gut wrenches for suddenly ditching her during a birthday celebration. "Let's get drinks together a different night."

She narrows her eyes at me. "Are you sure you're all right? Is your headache back?"

I blink at her. "I'm just tired from all the traveling. I promise, we will celebrate soon," I say, twisting a lock of hair around my fingers.

She watches the movement momentarily before rising to her feet. The stool she sits on wheels backward from the sudden force. "Sure," she says, her voice clipped.

I swallow the guilt growing in my chest, contemplating telling her about my worries. She looks at herself in the large, gilded mirror, a small contempt smile pulling her lips. Her earlier excitement about going out with friends stifles any more thoughts of sharing. How could I burden her with this when she is happy and eager for a fun night?

Tomorrow. I will tell her then.

"Don't be a stranger," Valeria says to me as we make our way to the front door.

"Never," I respond. "I'll be back for leftovers." As we get outside, I shiver at the night's chill touch, wishing I grabbed a jacket.

A running, dark blue sedan idles at the front of her driveway. "You can take that car back if you are okay with it," she says insipidly. "It's my cousin's boyfriend, James. He was going to be our driver." I search her face for any anger or disappointment.

"What about you?"

She shrugs. "I asked Zach to pick me up. He'll be here soon." A light breeze rustles by us and I shiver, rubbing my hands along my cold arms. Sarah's eyes soften and she pulls me into a hug. "Get some rest," she whispers in a comforting tone. "Call me tomorrow. I can bring over some pick-me-ups from my mom's store."

"Thank you," I answer as we release each other. I feel Sarah watching me as I make my way to the car, her gaze full of worry. I shove that gnawing guilt of hiding this from her away. Her sisterly concern tickles my back, subsiding only when I reach the vehicle, my body tensing. It is taken over by that thorny gaze of the fearful unknown setting itself upon me again.

Chapter 3

I sit in the front seat and am pleased to feel the heat of the seat warmers spreading into my chilly body. The drive to my place is not too long. Ten-minutes of winding back roads does nothing to ease that tense feeling. Luckily, the soothing instrumental playlist coming from the speaker eases me...and the images. My body sinks into the cushion of the seat.

"So, how is it that you had lived with Sarah for most of your life and we have not met yet?" he asks, his fingers tapping on the steering wheel to the light drum of the music. Sarah said his name earlier, but it went right out my ears.

"Were you there for her last Samhain party?" he continues. "My boyfriend and I dressed up as Genevieve and Arthur." The house party that I intentionally missed. I had so much studying to do that night and didn't want to be tempted by all the goodies downstairs. Sarah was unhappy about it, but she understood all the same. I had helped her choose the cleopatra costume that she looked absolutely flawless in. The playlist ends plunging us into silence. He reaches for the play button on the dashboard display.

I open my mouth to respond only to be consumed with terror as a massive black truck on the other side of the road veers toward us. Time moves painfully slow as its wheels careen off the other side of the road and onto ours. Underneath the light of the lampposts, I can make out an etched triangle on the hood of the offending vehicle.

Memories of the car accident all those years ago flash in my mind and I see my parents in front of me. My mother turns to look at me, a strangely solemn worry in her face. I have always wondered if she knew that she and my father would leave me that night. The driver turns the wheel of the vehicle sharply—too sharply—the sound of rubber burning on concrete rings in the air. The guard rail gives in and we smash through it, continuing down the side of the hill. Nothing stands between us and the dark forest below.

Chapter 4

I watch in horror as we speed too fast headfirst toward a dark forest. Pines and towering deciduous trees stand in an unbreakable line at the edge, their silhouettes so obscure that they blend with the black clouds above. In the space between their enormous bodies, an ebony curtain stretches far across. It watches with a hungry awareness. Some *thing* watches, waiting within the shadows. Figures leap from the path of the vehicle, their movements fluid and swift.

The thud of the driver's foot as he attempts to stomp on the brake echoes in the cab and in my head, the sound a somber symphony to a daunting theatrical horror. The car continues on, despite his efforts, speeding up on the steep grade downhill. Unable to do anything, I grip the seatbelt nestled across my torso. I want to close my eyes, as if that will magically make it better, but they are frozen open. It is like the dreaded downward release on a rollercoaster. Except this is much, much worse. The forest charges closer, like soldiers marching in war.

Silence is broken by the sharp, thunderous sound of glass and metal shattering and folding. The car was stopped forcefully by a gigantic, unmoving tree that stands like a sentinel in front of the others. Like a needle through paper, one of the tree's thick, low-lying branches poked a jagged hole into the windshield. It did not break, not when it hit the glass, and most certainly not when it punctured my upper chest. The metallic tang of blood slips into my mouth, coating my tongue. My limbs turn numb and shake. I look to the driver and my eyes widen in fear.

His head, smothered in blood, rests motionless on the inflated airbags. Shards of glass from the windshield cover his body. He lies facing the driver side door, so I can't see his eyes. I hope they're closed, and he is just unconscious. I attempt to lift my arm when all the pain that was somehow nonexistent decides to explode within my body. A searing, sharp throb erupts from my arm when it moves. That, however, is nothing compared to my burning chest.

I choke back a scream as I roll my head, nausea and dizziness replacing the adrenaline. With my right hand, I shakily search my pockets for my cellphone. I peer down at my feet, past the blood-soaked branch, and see the phone resting on the floor. Confined in place from the branch, I am unable to lean forward to get it.

Out of my reach.

Blood cakes my clothing and stains my tongue.

Tears run freely down my cheeks, my body shaking violently.

The irony of being spared in the accident that claimed the lives of my parents is not lost on me. Nature's sick sense of humor.

I grab the branch with my uninjured arm, hoping that maybe I can break it and get to my phone. A groan escapes my lips as I do so, the vibrations causing more pain. Slowly, my eyelids feel the pull of gravity.

Movement in the passenger side mirror catches in my blurring vision. Maybe the driver of the truck that veered into our lane stopped and is coming to help. I turn and see someone aiming to break the glass with their elbow. No, that's impossible. The person must have a tool or stone. I quickly look away. A rush of the cool air floods the car as the door rips open instead. Darkness creeps further into my vision from the edges and every movements creates lingering mirages. Somehow, the stranger crushed the tree branch, releasing me from my imprisonment. Black hair falls around the hard features of his face as worry seeps into his shadowy eyes. Everything in my sight is tainted with darkness. He picks me up and carries me to the grass next to the accordion car. I wince, moaning at the pain and gasp for air. My lungs inflate with staggering breaths, a thick liquid erupting from them with each exhale.

"Thea, hold on. It'll be okay." The soothing, muffled voice comes from the dark-haired stranger.

I blink at him, his features becoming a bit clearer. His comforting eyes are a dark grey, like the clouds on a stormy day. I do not recognize his voice, though it sounds familiar all the same. Like the gentle melody of the winds that sing on a warm summer day. The sound lulls me to a place of peace, the pain almost imperceivable to my mind. Blackness swallows my vision and I close my eyes, resting into the thought of sleeping. I hear the stranger frantically say something else, though I can't make out the words.

My attention is drawn to a euphoric sensation on my neck, covering the last bit of discomfort from my wounds. Slowly, I feel myself sinking into the earth below me like an offering, the cold grass caressing my skin. An orange flare of fire emerges in the blackness of my eyelids. Its warmth consumes and welcomes me as I let go of my hold onto the world.

~

My eyelids peel open, revealing a dimly lit, unfamiliar room. I furrow my brows and blink the tired ache in my eyes away, confusion seeping into my mind. I lie on a dark wooden couch with forest green cushions and am covered in a green plaid throw blanket. Books rest on a matching wooden coffee table which sit in front of the couch, and at my feet is a roaring fire in a small stone fireplace.

That car accident. All that blood.

I swiftly move my hand to my chest. There is no wound, no blood. An unfamiliar black sweatshirt covers my body that smells of wood smoke. My eyes widen as my gaze falls onto the window. Blackness covers the glass, an indication that it is still nighttime.

A pinprick of nerves builds up. The sound of a foot scuffing on a tiled floor startles me and I freeze, unable to move from fear.

Maybe I am dreaming. A dream within a dream. Surely, I would be in a hospital if that car accident actually happened, right? A log in the fireplace cracks, sparks flying up into the chimney. I jump at the sudden noise, sweat beading on my forehead. Across from the couch is a green door with a small semi-circle stained glass window at the top. Most likely it leads to the outdoors. I can try to run. But where? I have no idea where I am.

"I know you are awake," that familiar, soothing voice comes from behind. It is the voice I heard as I was being pulled from the car.

Images of the truck's headlights and the splitting guardrail race across my mind. The car hurtling toward the gigantic tree with its branch that—

I shove the memory away, my limbs trembling, and swallow as I nervously lift myself slightly to look at the man behind. Surprisingly, nothing hurts as I do so. I peer over the back of the couch with green cushions. My eyes find themselves staring right into those same ones that rendered me frozen at the coffee shop. I blink, still trying to determine whether or not this is real or in my head.

"How...?"

He just stands in the small kitchenette, leaning against a counter. There is no lamp on in the house, the only light comes from the flickering fire.

Something in my gut reaches out, telling me to trust him as it soothes a bit of the fear.

The playful curve of a smirk lifts his lips at the corner. "Where are you? How are you even here?" He watches me as I slowly lift myself up some more, my gaze falling on my unscathed body. My breathing hitches as I run a shaky hand over my body. I observe my left arm, noting the pain I felt when moving it before. I trace that familiar circular birthmark on my palm. "Why aren't you in pain?" he mocks, reciting my thoughts out loud.

With a quivering voice, I look to him, "What happened?"

All pleasantries disappear from his face, replaced with a solemn expression. "You were in a car accident. A nasty one, at that."

I shake my head, running a hand through my disheveled hair as I clutch the stranger's sweatshirt. "No—no that was a dream." Even as the words leave my lips, I can feel that they aren't true. Some part of me, hidden deep in places of my soul knows the truth.

And it is fearful.

And angry.

Everything was real. My hand falls to my mouth, stifling the explosion of emotions threatening to escape. Everything I felt, everything I saw, was real. The encroaching forest, the tree branch that stuck into my chest, dangerously close to my heart, the blood. So much blood. And the pain.

I stare at him. "I remember," my voice comes out in a whisper. "There was a tree branch." I trace the spot where the wood protruded from my abdomen, shivering at the thought. As I recall the incident, I remember that I wasn't the only one in the vehicle. My heart beats faster, afraid. It was my fault that we took that road. If I went to the bar with Sarah, would any of this have happened? "The other person in the car," my voice cracks. "Is he...?"

The dark-haired stranger inclines his head. "He will be okay. He was badly injured, and I was able to give him just a little bit of my blood before the authorities arrived."

I frown at him with mixed emotions of confusion and disgust. "You did what?" I want to pretend that I didn't hear that. Or I would just like to wake up from this weird, realistic nightmare.

His smile reappears, a knowing one, suggesting that I know too. "I gave him my blood. Vampire blood heals mortals."

I move so fast off the couch, all thoughts of trust vanishing. The blanket falls to the floor in a heap as the fire spits another burst of embers. The back of my calf smacks into the coffee table and I move around it, stumbling as I keep my eyes on his.

Vampires? This man is clearly delusional.

Or he is a murderer.

Or maybe I really am dreaming.

I swallow a lump in my throat. "Where am I?" I ask as I slowly creep toward that green door. The stranger makes no move toward me, his face a masterpiece of calm.

"My house." He cocks his head slightly. "But you are asking the wrong questions."

My heartbeat echoes in my ears and reverberates throughout the entire house. Adrenaline pumps through my body as I contemplate fighting or fleeing. "I'm leaving," I say with wavering confidence.

With inhuman speed, the stranger vanishes from the kitchen and is in front of me. I gasp and take a few nervous steps back, unintentionally pinning myself against the wall. His eyes change from gray to a deep shade of red as they scan my face, moving from my eyes to my lips before returning back. "Do you believe me now?" Holding my breath, I ever so slightly jerk my head down in a nod. He seems to have noticed because he smirks devilishly again. "Now ask me."

As close as we are, I can see all his features. The perfection of his symmetry. His diamond-shaped face is outlined by a dark stubble of hair, curving around his angular jaw. It matches that of the shadow underneath his narrow nose. I rip my gaze from his lips and bring it back to the entrancing vastness of his eyes. "Did you save me with your blood too?" Waves of nausea turn in my stomach.

Silence stands between us as he takes a moment to answer. His eyes flick between mine like thoughts bouncing in his head, determining the best way to respond. His lips turn down, as if disappointed in the question I asked. "Yes. And no." He takes a step back and I release the nervous breath that I was holding. "You were much worse than your friend was. Even vampire blood would not have healed your human body." He emphasized the word *human*, and I'm not sure I want to know why.

My legs feel weak and the world around me spins viciously. I clutch my stomach as tidal waves of nausea roll in. I tremble, nearly falling over, but catch myself with a hand on the doorframe. I didn't realize that I am this close to the exit. He reaches out to steady me, but I shove him away. Glaring, I say, "What did you do?"

Still, he remains unaffected with my reactions—reactions that are more than warranted. "It was the only thing I could do to save you. I turned you." His brows turn up slightly. Painful cramps pound at my insides and I mindlessly clutch the sweatshirt. "You need to feed."

The world stops spinning. I hear him talking, but it is just a random combination of sounds. I silently will whoever is listening to wake me up from this nightmare. To wake up to the sunlight filtering through my window. To find the inevitable text from Sarah who regrets either too much alcohol or spending the night with someone.

"Thea..." I snap my head back to this person—no, this *vampire*—standing next to me as my hand falls to the doorknob. His gaze follows my movement. "What are you doing? It isn't safe out there," he warns as his hand moves to mine with extreme speed, causing me to startle.

"Clearly! A vampire kidnapped me. Let me leave," my voice wavers. The world is starting to cave in. Everything that has happened, all the heavy emotions start to rumble from the deepest parts within me like a volcano echoing its only warning with a devastating earthquake. My skin feels hot, like the lava that's preparing to burst from the earth. The forest has always been a place of peace, and right now, it might be the only thing to prevent an explosion. "Let me leave," I repeat, this time with an unwavering tone.

His jaw tightens, as if in contemplation. My knuckles are white from clutching the doorknob so hard when he finally releases his hold. He lets out a sigh, but I don't wait for him to say anything before running out of the door.

I let my feet guide me, the sound of them stomping on the forest floor as I run is the only thing that I focus on. The beat of their drumming sings in between the chorus of crickets. Trees part the way as I move hastily away from that cabin, as if they sensed the fear planted in my heart. I am not sure how long I run for, but when I finally stop, my breathing is ragged, and I have to lean against a tall pine tree to keep from falling over from dizziness. Nausea roils in my stomach, causing me to double over with dry heaves.

My fingernails scrape against the tree's rough bark so hard that blood trickles out of scratched skin. An unpleasant feeling washes over me. It is like all the emotions one can experience are hitting me at once—anger, grief, regret, and sadness scream the loudest. They intensify the pounding headache and intense stomach pains. Every part of my body is tense. My clothing, and even the air, feel like sandpaper rubbing against my skin. Moving hurts. Standing still hurts too, as if my soul wants to jump out of its fleshy cage.

I should have just joined Sarah.

My eyes widen, a thought distracting me from the unpleasantness.

Sarah. I should find Sarah.

An explosive sharp pain erupts in my stomach and I double over.

"A little lost, are we?" an unfamiliar, gruff voice says behind me.

I swirl around, wincing at the sharp pain that the movement causes. A tall, slim man stands almost three meters away, shrouded by the darkness of the forest. All the insects have ceased their songs, waiting for this engagement to be finished. I have never seen this man before, but the way his body stands so unnaturally still, I would bet that he is not human. Something I find strange for even noticing.

He cocks his head. "Not human, but not quite vampire." He steps forward, illuminated by the silvery light of the moon peeking through a hole in the canopy. His light-colored hair is half tied up and half down, touching his broad shoulders. I catch the glimpse of rosy irises changing to a dark, more natural color. "It is insufferable, isn't it? The pain that drives you to your first feeding." Slowly, he takes another step forward, and I find myself caught in the intensity of his gaze. He wears a linen shirt with ruffled sleeves and black pants. He stretches a hand toward me, palm up in a friendly gesture. "I can help you. Join me and my clan." He flashes a brilliant smile at me. Sharp, lethal fangs wipe away the softness of his expression, knocking me out of my stupor.

I blink at him and take a step back, ignoring the burn of moving.

The man's face twists with irritation.

"Get away from me," I demand.

He plasters a smile on his lips, masking the annoyance. He takes a step forward, his hand still outstretched. My body screams to run, nerves building in my gut. "You will need help with your transition. We can be that for you."

I shake my head, my nails digging into my palms as anger rises in me. My skin burns and I want to tear off the clothing I wear. "I am no vampire. Leave me alone!"

His lip curls, and he shrugs. "Then die, I suppose." He pulls a dagger out of thin air and plunges it toward my chest with impressive speed. All those trainings with my father in his gym has never prepared me for fighting with a vampire, who's speed is unnatural.

Or has it? My body remembers the lessons long forgotten since his passing. With surprising speed of my own, I raise a palm to block his forward movement. My defense catches him off guard, but he recovers quickly. His other hand reaches upward and grips my throat hard. I fight to swallow a scream at the pain of the physical contact. His pale skin is like pure fire.

With one hand clutching his weapon arm, my other grabs hold of his wrist that has my throat. His grasp tightens and I struggle to breathe as he pushes harder against my grip with the dagger. "There are no second chances with us," he snarls.

"I don't even know who you are!" My voice comes out garbled against his suffocating hold. The longer I struggle for air, the weaker I become. A drop of a clear liquid drips off the tip off his weapon as it gets dangerously close to my chest. His grip fires tendrils of icy pain down my body.

A subtle heat spreads into my palms.

The vampire looks at my hand, an intrigued expression momentarily crossing his anger ridden face. He flashes his unnatural teeth at me. "You have no choice. You have something that belongs with us. I can smell it all over you."

"Screw—" The words are cut off from his tightening grasp on my throat. Hardly any oxygen is making its way to my lungs. Dots of darkness creep into the edges of my vision. If I let go just a little, his weapon would find its mark. I don't know if it would be a quick death. But I could see my parents again.

The entire forest is silent, holding its own breath as it watches.

Images of the car accident flash in my mind—both accidents. The one that just happened and the one with my parents. The crunching of metal and breaking of glass. The car tumbling off a road, flipping as it goes. The last look my parents gave me from the front seats, a knowing look that still baffles me. Then I see that forest hurtling toward the driver and I. The branch that stuck itself in my chest. The soothing voice of the stranger who saved me.

Saved.

I nearly laugh out loud. To almost die only to be saved and turned inhuman. Just to die again by this hateful vampire. All in a... actually I don't know how long it has been since the accident.

A second chance, thrown away because of the fear of what was given up for it. Not that I had a choice.

Sarah's face flashes in my mind. Helios next. Then Valeria. I grip the vampire's arm tighter and he snarls. "I don't know what the hell you're talking about, but when I say leave, I mean it." Despite his hold, my words come out clear and laced with venom.

A vicious wind picks up around us. Leaves rain down from bending trees. The vampire takes his eyes off of mine, a worried expression on his face. A sharp wooden dagger explodes through his chest. His eyes widen and the grip on my throat weakens, allowing air to flood its way back into my lungs. He releases me and I drop to the ground, gasping for more air.

When I look up, the vampire's skin turns a sickly white as the weapon is pulled out of his chest. A deep crimson, almost black, liquid spills from the wound. I watch as he crumples to the ground, blood coating his blueish lips. The gray-eyed stranger who saved me before stands over the lifeless body of my attacker.

A brief flash of anger is replaced with worry as he kneels beside me. "Thea, are you okay?" With uncertain movements, he lifts a hand toward my arm but refrains and keeps a space between us.

I shake my head, my gaze moving from his to the body. His eyes, now black, stare up blankly at the canopy. Crickets resume their song in the sudden peace of the forest. Their ignorant, mirthful sounds rupture the thin hold I have over my quivering emotions as tears streak across my cheeks. "I died," I admit through sobs. The forest hushes to a low melody as if it was feeling my pain. We sit there in silence for a while, listening to my sad breaths and the mournful song of the crickets and wind-shivering leaves. The dried tears on my face crack as I move, and I can still feel the vampire's lethal grip on my skin.

I died.

But I also survived.

"Thea, I'm sorry," he whispers softly, a sadness to his voice.

"How do you know me?" I ask with sudden irritation in my tone. "You said my name when you pulled me from that car too. I don't even know yours." My nails dig into the ground, the cool earth a contrast to my heated limbs.

He sighs and runs a hand through his black hair. "Cole. My name is Cole."

Like the flip of a switch, sorrow floods my emotions like a bursting dam. Tears well in my eyes and threaten to escape. Some do, and I don't try to wipe them away. Cole sits next to me on the ground, his arm brushing against mine. I tense, waiting for that fiery sensation of touch. Strangely, his closeness is comforting and elicits only a feeling of warmth and safety. I rest my head on the trunk of the tree behind me and close my eyes.

With a gentle voice, Cole speaks up, "I'm sorry I brought you into this. And I'm sorry I couldn't ask your permission to turn you. You were fading quickly." He brings a hand over to my leg but again hesitates when it rests just above before pulling it back to himself. "I understand how you are feeling right now. On edge. As if moving will break you, both physically and emotionally."

I roll my head to face him, wincing at the movement, and he meets my gaze. I just stare into him for a moment, searching for something unknown. He doesn't say anything, letting me sit in my thoughts.

"You have something that belongs with us." My attacker's words slice into my mind. What did he mean? I've never met him before, but he acted as though he knew something about me. Could Cole be after the same thing? Something in my heart recoils at that, but I ignore it.

I swallow the dry lump in my throat. "I didn't ask you to save me."

He flinches—a movement so subtle it was hard to be sure of.

I squeeze my eyes shut, wishing that all of this really was only a dream. I would wake up and share it with Sarah. She always loved listening to dreams. "But thanks," I mutter as I open my eyes. Though this is not the ideal way to be alive, it is better than the alternative. Had I died, I would have left Sarah, leaving her to mourn a friend—a sister. Her mother would mourn me too.

"Why did I wake at your place and not the hospital?"

Cole stands, holding out a hand to help me. "Let's talk where there isn't a decaying vampire corpse beside us," he muses.

I am in no mood for amusement but agree. I stand slowly, using the tree as support. My movements are shaky and standing sends a new wave of nausea through my body. "What if someone sees it?" I gesture to the dead vampire and regret looking at it. The skin is already sunken, giving him a skeletal look. The image does not help the sick feeling in my stomach.

Cole shakes his head. "Vampires decay quickly. He'll fade into the earth within the next hour."

"Got it," I say turning away. We walk in silence for a bit before I am too tired to keep moving. Every inch of my skin feels as though it was hit with a hammer, wielded by someone with superhuman strength. Even my bones ache as they carry me. The pounding in my head has increased, the sound of the insects only magnify it. I lean against a maple tree as the green and brown landscape swirls around me and slide slowly to the cool earth. Various ferns and late summer flowers perk as the sun starts to ascend in the sky. "Tell me," I say through heavy breaths.

Cole's brows turn up in a worried expression. "You really need to feed."

I swallow, grimacing at the scratchiness of my throat. "Tell me first."

He blows out an exasperated breath. "To maintain your human cover, I went into the minds of the first responders and convinced them to create a report that you were in the hospital but was released already."

I lift an eyebrow and curl my lips at the thought of invading a person's mind. Or at least I think I do since my body feels extremely weak. "You can do that?"

He nods, his brows turning up with his growing concern. "And your friend called." My heart drops. If she called and talked to Cole on my phone, she would definitely know that something was wrong. Aside from the fact that I didn't leave her house with a stranger, she has always been protective over me. After my parents died and Sarah and Valeria took me in, I tried with all my might to be anywhere else. I snuck out to parties, bars, the park, just to get away or to forget. "I didn't answer but sent her a text as yourself. I told her that you are okay and needed some rest and would call afterward."

"How long has it been?"

He is quiet for long enough that I roll my head to the side to look at him. His expression is soft. "Almost two days. You were... unconscious all of yesterday."

I inhale sharply, stiffening at the pain it causes. I pull out my cell and motion to dial her number, but Cole places his hand on mine, this time without hesitation. "What?" I ask, my voice hoarse and clipped.

"You need to feed before you do anything. It'll make you feel better and will finish the transition."

"And if I don't feed?" I ask inquisitively. Somehow "you'll return to being human" doesn't sound likely.

He looks at me stoically. "Then you'll lose control and hurt someone you might not want to hurt." Those gray eyes of his hold my hazel ones. The light caress of a gentle wind blows a few strands of my brown hair into my face, tickling my chin. I hardly have the energy to push it away. "And if you manage to seclude yourself from humans, you'll wither and die. For good."

A rock drops in my chest as his words sink in. Either live the rest of my life as a blood thirsty vampire or cease to exist. I glance down at my hands, examining the scars from when I had surgery after the accident that killed my parents. Like this recent accident, we swerved off the road to avoid a head on collision. I was told that my parents died instantly upon hitting an unforgiving wall. The EMT's and doctors weren't even sure how I survived. Shrapnel from one of the vehicles exploded inside our cabin and stuck themselves in my skin. Most of the scars are gone, a few on my hand and right shoulder remain.

I'm never getting in a car again.

But...

I survived that night, and I will survive this too.

"I'll feed," I say in a declaration of survival. Cole tries to hide his joy in my decision by keeping his lips pressed together, though I see the ghost of an upward twitch on his lips. I don't know where he came from or why he has an interest in my life, but that nagging gut of mine still says to trust him. And if there is one thing that I have learned in life, it is to trust your instincts, and the more you do, the easier it is to hear. That, and I don't see how anyone else can help me with this newfound life problem.

Just because I try to trust him, doesn't mean I have to like him.

Even if he is breath takingly gorgeous.

Cole stands and offers me another helping hand, "I was hoping you would say that."

Chapter 5

The door creaks as it is opened, the fireplace still lights up the interior. The warmth of the cabin is soothing, my entire body shakes—from the chill of the early morning air or for what is to come, I am not sure. Cole closes the door behind me, and I stand to the side uncomfortably. He offers a kind smile and gestures to the couch, the blanket still in a heap on the floor in front. "You can sit, if you would like."

I probably should. Walking here took what little energy remained in my body. "Can I use your restroom?" I ask instead, my voice breathy.

He nods, the curve on his lips softening a bit more as he leads me through the living area and kitchen.

My legs feel like liquid as I follow him. Around the corner of the L-shaped space is the dining room with a slightly open door by the table.

"There you are," he gestures to the restroom. "Take your time."

I close the door and let out a deep, shaky exhale. A wave of absolute exhaustion washes over me as more tears threaten to escape, though this time I don't let them. Not yet. I run my hands through my disheveled hair and step up to the mirror against the back wall that sits above a small ceramic sink. A toothbrush, bar of soap, and razor is all that is in this bathroom aside from the shower, toilet, and washer and dryer. My complexion is startlingly pale, eyes are rimmed in red, the hazel irises dull, and my pink lips are cracked. Underneath the sweatshirt I am wearing is my bloodstained torso. Though Cole must have given me clean clothes, he didn't wash the once fatal wound. He left that for me. He was right to. It proves more that this is not a dream. Now it is nothing but dry blood. I trace a finger over the spot where the branch was before grabbing the towel to my left and vigorously scrubbing it away with water.

When it is mostly gone, my hands are shaking, and I am breathing heavily again. I close my eyes and picture my parents. Their unyielding strength and courage will forever be held within my memories.

When I exit the restroom, Cole is leaning against the counter again, his face a display of worry. "Are you ready?" His tone is gentle.

I nod, unable to form words for fear that I will decide to not finish the transition. He pushes off from the counter and hands me a bag filled with blood. My stomach turns at the sight of it. I hesitate to grab it, stopping just short of his offering. Am I doing the right thing? What if I hurt someone? I would never forgive myself. Would I be able to control any urges afterward? Or will I just live with constant fear of becoming a monster? I've seen enough vampire movies and read enough books to know that something bad generally happens.

"Your human thinking will be the death of you if you continue to listen to it," he warns. "It doesn't take long to wither away or to lose control."

I swallow hard. There is no going back after this.

Hesitantly, I grab the bag out of his hand. The liquid swirls as I hold onto it. "Whose blood is this?" I inquire, my stomach churning like the sea in a hurricane.

"Believe it or not, there are humans who donate their blood to vampires." He gestures to the bag. "That came from the hospital. Older blood that would have expired. Freely given."

I manage a light bob of my head and pull the top off. Ignoring that gnawing combination of pain, nausea, and hunger in my stomach, I close my eyes and draw some of the liquid into my mouth. The moment it touches my tongue, I regret it. A thick, metallic tang coats my tongue. Cole places his warm hand on my back as I heave and gag.

"Don't. Don't fight it."

Fight it? I just want to spit the repulsive contents out of my mouth. How did I even consider this? I turn quickly to use the sink in the bathroom, but he is faster. His square frame blocks the doorway, his arms crossed. Instead, I reach out to grab the water glass on his dining room table. Without a beat, I spit out the abhorrent liquid, shaking my head between gags. "I can't."

"Thea," he says, his voice sympathetic. "I know it tastes absolutely repulsive right now, but," he puts a hand on my arm, forcing me to turn and look at him, his gray eyes soft, "I mean it, you will die if you don't drink it." Is that trepidation etched in his tone?

I clench my jaw, pushing down the wave of nausea wreaking havoc on my insides. This...vampirism is a second chance at life—albeit a scary and unnatural one. If what he said earlier was the truth—and I believe it was—then I would have died in that accident. I shudder at the thought of leaving this world, leaving Sarah, Valeria, and Helios. At not being able to see my favorite places again or read my favorite books an absurd number of more times. To not be able to visit all the state parks like I have slowly been doing. I sigh. "How much do I need to drink?"

"Enough for the transition to finish. You will know when that is."

Helpful. "Will the taste get better at least?" In all the vampire movies and books, I have never come across one where the character hated the taste. Those are just fiction though.

Real life tends to be less forgiving.

He nods. "It will. Trust me."

Trust.

He reaches out a hand for the glass. With shaking limbs, I hand it to him and return my attention to the bag, the contents swirling inside. When I was little, I couldn't even look at a paper cut without feeling queasy. That lessened as I got older, though I still don't enjoy looking at blood. I bring the bag back to my mouth and close my eyes as I take in another small sip, bracing for the metallic horridness. During my time regretting the first sip and taking this second one, the taste changed to something sweet. My eyes widen in surprise, and I drink more, feeling a wash of relief flood my body as I do. Tension I don't know I hold onto releases in my entire body, leaving a pleasant euphoria in its wake. Halfway through the bag, a subtle pain pinches at my gums. Entranced by the honeyed taste, I ignore it and continue until it becomes unbearable. I rip the bag away and hold my hand over my mouth, wincing as the pain grows more intense.

Cole stands there, still blocking the bathroom. After a few seconds of excruciating torture, I look up at him.

"Invite the pain in. It's your new teeth," he states.

I can feel my teeth shifting beneath my gums. It is strange and mesmerizing all the same. The pain is gone when I let myself get intrigued, forgetting the agony. I run my tongue under the sharp point of my new teeth, the feeling as they rest on my bottom lip is foreign. I become all too aware of all the stimuli competing for my attention: my new teeth poking my lip, the irregular drip of water from a pipe under the bathroom sink, the incessant song of a lone cricket beyond the other closed door off the dining room, the flow of air between Cole and I, and his scent of cedar. His erratic heartbeat matches mine. The invisible electricity that jumps from our bodies to the other. I look to Cole and lose myself in the gray of his eyes. It is like the clouds during a summer thunderstorm. Intense and enigmatic. We stand there, compelled to stillness, though something calls for us to touch. It feels like an intoxicating eternity that we remain still before he rips his gaze from me and nods back to the bag. "Finish that."

Graciously, I do, the honeyed taste distracting me from whatever is occurring in the space between us. Love has never been for me, as it has never ended well. Someone with his sculpture would be no different. As I take the last mouthful, I feel invigorated. I feel anew. Like I could climb the tallest mountain in one continuous trek.

The sensation is addictive.

The glass on the table catches my eye. My body craves that last bit, like what I just drank was not a full meal because the rest is right there, which is absolutely gross considering that it is technically backwash. Cole cocks his head, leading me to believe that he knows exactly what I am thinking. Especially because in a blur, he moves into the bathroom and back like a yo-yo, the sound of the toilet flushing follows.

"Do you believe me now?" His question from earlier. I think he just likes hearing me prove him right.

"Yes," I huff.

"Good. I will get you more. Your phone was ringing by the way."

If Sarah is calling again and I miss it, she is going to kill me. I take a step back and stop, looking down at my feet. The softness of the socks I wear feels exquisite, more so than they ever did before. Curling my toes, I feel every fiber hugging my skin. I want to wrap my entire body with this velvety sensation. The sound of a clock ringing above the fireplace mantel startles me and I jump. Cole laughs beside me.

"What?" I seethe, annoyed that my jumpiness amuses him.

He holds up his hands in surrender, the pull of a smile still tugging at his lips. "Sometimes, I forget all the adjustments the kindria have to go through."

"Kindria?"

"Newly turned vampires," he clarifies. "What you are experiencing are heightened emotions..." he pauses, observing my scowl. "You should know that vampires feel and experience everything on a higher level. Our senses are heightened, our emotions stronger. They can be glorious, or they can be debilitating."

"Great," I say flatly.

He takes a step forward and casts his eyes downward, gazing to his right. "I wanted to tell you that now, so that you can learn to recognize when your emotions are taking over before it becomes too hard to come back." His tone is soft as he rocks back and forth on his heels with his eyes on the ceiling, and I wonder what memories haunt him about this. Has he succumbed to these debilitating emotions? Or maybe it was someone he knew once in the past. "Bloodlust will take over," he adds quietly. "And then no amount of human blood is enough."

I open my mouth to defend my ability to control my own emotions, but my phone buzzes again. "Hey, Sarah." I watch Cole as he walks to his couch and sits down, folding the blanket and placing it on the armrest.

"Thank the goddess. Thea, are you okay?" she asks, her voice shaky.

"I'm fine," I respond gently.

"James got out of the hospital yesterday evening. He told us what happened and was wondering if you were okay. We all were. When we called the hospital, they said that you were fine and was released already. You didn't call," she notes warily.

My heart breaks for my friend. For having to worry while I was... unable to talk, wondering just how okay I was. Cole's text message to her must have been somewhat of a relief, though I'm sure her worry is still skyrocketing. "I'm fine, really. Just tired." Curiously, that isn't a lie. One would think that waking from a literal dead sleep would make you feel ready for the world.

"Can I come over and do anything for you?"

"Y—"

Cole shakes his head.

I scowl at him in response and almost decide to say yes anyway. "No, that's okay. I think I might get some more rest. Maybe later?" The thought of keeping this a secret from her turns my stomach.

"All right. But call me if you need anything, okay?" Her tone falls, disappointment ringing in her words. For as long as I have known her—and that is almost our entire lives—she has been a healer.

"I promise. How is your cousin's boyfriend?"

"James is doing a lot better. The doctors seemed baffled at how you both are so okay." Her tone is inquisitive, though laced with relief.

"Likewise." I glance at Cole, suddenly wondering what he did with the branch that impaled me like a spear. He watches me intently, a picture of impassiveness.

"Well, I'll let you get some sleep. I love you, girl."

"Love you too," I respond, choking back some stray tears. I wait for her to hang up first, not wanting to be the first to let go. After she does, I stare at my phone momentarily, watching the photo of her smiling at the music festival we attended two years ago blink and fade away. I feel like a liar and a horrible friend. But how do you tell your human best friend that you died and came back as a vampire?

Sighing, I plod to the couch and sit down next to Cole. A small part of my being wants to still be angry at him, as if this whole mess is his fault. I just need someone to blame, and I don't know who that truck driver was. There is no face, just a monster vehicle ramming us off the road. I can't get mad at a truck. The memory of the sound of the guardrail breaking makes me shiver. If it weren't for Cole, I wouldn't even be sitting here. Loosening a breath, I let all the stressful emotions expel with my exhale.

"You really should get some rest, Thea," he says softly. He places a hand on my leg before standing up. The touch is like a blazing fire during a snowstorm.

"Cole?" My heart drums as questions swirl in my head like a tornado. I need answers, and he is the only one who can give them to me.

"Yes?" His grey eyes pull me in. They gleam, even in the lack of lighting.

I suck my teeth, chewing on my lower lip, realizing the lack of elongated points. "How did you find me out in that car?" The image of seeing him in the coffee shop flashes in my mind. I questioned myself afterward for seeing the imaginary. Now, I am less sure that it wasn't real. I can't even give thought to seeing him in my sleep. Not yet.

One bizarre thing at a time.

He clenches his jaw before sitting back down. For a minute or so, we sit in silence. Then, giving me his full attention, he turns his body to mine, his messy hair falling over his eyes. "Thea, I promise I will tell you. But, for now, you really need to get some rest." He steals a glance at the window. The sky is a dark blue now, awaiting the ascension of the bright star. "Please, trust me."

Every time he uses the "T" word, my gut echoes it. *Just trust, Thea.* Easier said than done.

"Why not tell me now?" There is that part of me that knows he will stay true to his word. Perhaps all those life lessons from my mother about leaning on your intuition is to blame. A wave of exhaustion washes over me. It could just be from the warmth of the crackling fire, but my eyelids feel heavy and my body weary.

He rubs his palms on his pants. I watch his movements, the sound of the friction is loud and rough in my ears. "There is a lot to this world that you don't know. To tell you now, after everything that you just went through, it could be a lot. Too much."

"Shouldn't I be the judge of that? I'm stronger than you think."

He chuckles. "I don't doubt that."

"Then why?"

His lips are pressed into a thin line. "Sometimes, when we push for knowledge, the treasure we seek is not quite ready to be discovered and it becomes unfavorable in the moment to an unripe mind."

To know without knowing, having patience that what you seek will offer itself to you in the right time, is the key to life. Something my mother used to say to me frequently when my curious child's mind prodded for information. She has said it so many times that I memorized it and would say it in sync with her. I blink at Cole, his words so close to her lesson.

"Okay," I say with a sigh. "I trust you to tell me when it is right." My fingers idly twirl on the rough fabric of the couch. "But don't think that I won't keep pestering you to tell me."

He plasters a solemn smile at me. "Deal. I can walk you back to your apartment if you would like. It is only a ten-minute walk or so. Or you can stay here."

My cheeks flush at the thought and I stand to hide it. "I should probably go back to my place." Keeping my back to him, I take a few steps toward the door. "Helios is probably hungry."

"Helios?" Cole stands and follows me out the door.

"My cat." I stop abruptly. "Wait, is he safe around me?" Anxiety pulses through me at the thought of harming my companion.

"He is safe. Animal blood does not taunt us like that of humans. We can feed on them, but it does not sustain us nearly enough. The smell is not very tempting. Nor does their blood taste good," he grimaces. "I would suggest staying away from your friend for a while, however. That could turn out bad," his voice is hard, a warning.

The early morning air is cool so far. It's the only indication that summer is coming to an end. All the trees still hold onto their green leaves, not even tips of older trees have begun to turn yet.

Before we enter the worn dirt path leading north into the forest, Cole looks toward the slowly brightening sky, a worry creasing his forehead.

"Will I spontaneously combust when the sun comes up if I am awake?" I ask in a weary tone. All his sky gazing is making me suspicious.

He stares momentarily before a soft laugh escapes his lips. The sound wraps around me like a cashmere blanket on bare skin. "No, not unless you walk out into the sunlight. Make sure to close your window shades before you go to bed."

The sun. Something that I didn't even think about. Sarah and I had hoped to hike to a lookout tower on one of the mountains on the outskirts of town to watch the sunrise before the cold weather comes.

The air within the forest gets even cooler the farther we continue on. Pines stand tall, creating a barrier that the colder air can't escape through. Even in the middle of summer when the sun is high above, you can feel the difference. I narrow my eyes at him. "The sun is already coming up. Are you staying at my house, then?"

Please say no. I need some time alone.

He shakes his head. "No." He pulls out a large silver coin from his pocket and holds it in his palm so I can see. "This is a sun totem. It protects its owner from the sun." My eyes widen, and he laughs. So, the sun is not lost to me after all. I couldn't hide that excitement if I wanted to. "We will get you one, don't worry. But for now—"

"Yes, yes. Stay out of sun," I mock.

A smirk pulls at his lips. "Right."

"How do you get one? Do vampires really catch fire if they are in the sun?"

He places the coin back into his pocket and looks at me sidelong. "There are other supernatural beings out there other than vampires. A witch needs to perform a sun spell on an object which will protect its vampiric owner from the effects of the sun. And yes, we do."

I swallow a nervous gulp. Stay out of the sun. Right. "Vampires, witches. What else?" Do I really want that information? My head hurts from what little he has told me already. Have patience, my mother's words ring again. "Are werewolves real, then?"

He contemplates for a moment, his hand scratching at his neck. "Yes. Although they have not been seen in this area for a few centuries."

I stare moon-eyed at him. "What else?" The ache in my head intensifies. I ignore it, eager to learn more as it reminds me of stories I was told as a kid. My father delighted in telling bedtime stories, I hardly ever had to ask.

Cole snorts, brushing his fingertips against the rough skin of a birch tree. "Well, those are the only ones that I have ever met. There are stories about fae and dragons."

That's...a lot. To think that a human can go their entire life without knowing any of this, with all that is out there, is mindboggling. I wonder how many creatures I have walked by, thinking that they were merely mortals like myself. Like I was. Or am I? "Are supernatural creatures immortal?"

"Some. Immortal in the sense that we won't die of old age. Vampires and werewolves, for example. I've heard the same for fae and dragons. Witches will live and die from natural causes, but they live longer than humans." Cole glances up at the sky through a break in the canopy as we walk through a thicket of tall ostrich ferns. A few sparrows flutter between branches above. His angular face is set with soft features. "How are you feeling?"

I shove my hands in the pockets of my jeans. "Okay, I think. My head hurts a bit."

"You'll feel better with some rest," he assures.

We reach my apartment building while the sun still has not shown itself. Cole walks me to my door upstairs, insisting that he help with the shades. I assure him that I am capable, that the sun is not hiding inside, and I am fine. When we reach the top floor, I notice the lack of feeling winded from climbing the stairs. He gave me his number in case I needed him and a blood bag to keep in my fridge for the morning. Luckily, the bag was safely hidden inside a small airtight container that blocked both the sight and smell.

As predicted, Helios was waiting for me by the door and he promptly started his meowing the moment I stepped foot inside. I am thankful that he cannot sense the transition and that his affection has not changed. I reach down to pet him as he weaves around my ankles. The silkiness of his fur tickles my skin. He nudges my face as I bend to kiss the top of his head. He smells of cotton, warm and comforting. The quick, steady beat of his feline heart bounces in my ears, lulling me into a state of calm.

Outside, slate-colored clouds begin rolling in, bringing the promise of rain. I feed Helios before closing the shades and running upstairs to get ready for some much-needed sleep. I stand in my restroom looking at myself in the large mirror with only the small flickering nightlight on. The overhead lights were too bright and caused the throbbing in my head to increase. Already, my skin has gained color back and my eyes are their bright mix of brown and green colors. My father's eyes. The only physical trait I inherited from him.

The squeal of the old faucet as I turn on the cold water sends shivers down my spine like nails on a chalkboard. The headache only worsens. I wish I had some of Sarah's peppermint oil. Maybe she can bring some later.

Cole's warning to stay away from my friend rings in my ears and my heart sinks. Shoving the thought away, I fill my palms with water and lean down to splash my face. When I straighten, the faint glow of red eyes outside the bathroom window startles me. I jump backward, nearly knocking the towel rack to the floor. My heart hammers against my ribcage. I squint and flick the lights on, wincing at the intensity. There is nothing outside, save from the air conditioning unit on the roof. Still, my nerves tingle all across my body.

A soft touch at my ankles makes me jump again. Helios lets out a tiny meow, his sandy eyes resting on mine. "You scared me," I say to him as I bend down and run a hand over his soft fur. He runs to the bed and curls up at the edge, waiting for me to cuddle. I go to the bathroom window and glance outside, my mouth dry. With shaky limbs, I close the shades before joining my cat.

Chapter 6

Eyes of swirling smoke peer through the veil of thick, dancing darkness. Thin white mist slithers on the ground. An invisible force tugs me forward, like an elastic tether stretched for too long. My feet move on their own, entranced by the call of the person in front of me. Step after step, colors appear from the blackness. Skin of golden hues reflect a light that forms behind me, my shadow dancing in the flickers of auburn flames. The stranger reaches a hand toward me, and my arm, a magnet, follows. Our fingertips touch gently like too much force would break the connection. At that same moment, the light behind me explodes. I see his face—Cole's face in front of me, a tender smile on his lips—before everything goes black again, and he disappears.

I want to scream his name, but a loud, sudden noise from behind forces me to turn around. Red, dangerous eyes now stare at me from across a blazing fire. They are not the same shade of red as Cole's. Even from this distance, I can see the gold specks that dot the irises. A sinister energy washes over me and I freeze in terror.

"Thea!"

The shrill of my name rips me out of the nightmare and I burst out of the bed, my heart pounding against my ribcage. Footsteps slam up the stairs and I see the head of a disheveled Sarah running up them. I place my hand over my heart and am stunned to feel nothing, though it was just pounding like an all-out percussion band. There is no beat. Not even the slightest thump. Another indication that the past couple of days actually happened.

I shift on my feet as my friend takes the last step upstairs. I offer her a tired smile which turns into a straight, pressed line as I behold what she is clutching in her hands. The blood bag from the fridge. "Thea. I've seen these bags before. Please tell me this is a Halloween prop."

I consider the lie. Even though it is only August. The silence of my contemplation after her question was enough of an answer for her. Tears welled in those honeyed eyes. "Thea...did you...did you die in that accident?" Her voice cracks and she waves the bag as if it were no more than a plastic bag carrying water.

I blink at her, my mouth agape, unsure how to answer.

Here I was concerned about keeping this a secret from her when it appears, she has some knowledge of this world beyond human.

But how?

A hole in the clouds outside give the sun a chance to shine, lighting up my apartment. I squint at the sudden brightness, noticing a beam of sunlight that stretches halfway into my bedroom from a window downstairs. I'll have to close that later. In the kitchen, my clock chimes to signal a changed hour and I jump.

"I..." My brain and voice don't connect, words vanish from my tongue the moment they are conjured by my frazzled and overwhelmed mind. I swallow nervously as she continues standing with her arms at her side, lips turned down. Somberly, I nod.

Sarah presses her eyelids closed, water flowing down her cheeks.

I want to comfort her, but I don't know how. Not as this. For all I know, she would be angry or terrified. I don't know which I would prefer. So, I stand frozen next to my bed.

A single, trembling sob escapes her lips before she opens her eyes again. She wipes her wet face with the sleeve of her pink sweater. Instead of running or yelling, she gently walks closer and embraces me.

I tense at her closeness, Cole's warning still fresh in my mind. Though her heartbeat pulses by my ear, there is no desire to bite her. No gnawing hunger or lengthening of my teeth. Her heartbeat sings melodious tunes, soothing the hunger rather than igniting it. I slowly hug her back and she tightens her grip. A stray curl of her floral-scented hair tickles my cheek. I get lost in her calm.

"I'm so sorry," she mumbles through cracks of staggering, sorrowful breath. Water drips on the skin of my back exposed from the tank top I changed into before sleep. The protective and invisible mental wall that was reinforced by my stubborn protective mind while I was dreaming of this impossible new life breaks a little and I follow suit. We stand there, comforting each other until the clock rings its quarter mark.

When she pulls away, her eyes are pink and puffy. "What happened?" she asks tenderly.

I reach into the drawer of my nightstand and pull out a small box of tissues for our sniffling noses. I tell her everything. From seeing Cole at the coffee shop to the truck running us off the road to being saved. The only details I leave out are Cole's name and those of the pain and blood. She doesn't need to know any of that.

Before she can respond, I ask her a question. "If you've seen these bags before, does that mean...are you a vampire too?"

She looks down at her hands, avoiding my gaze and takes a deep, shaky breath. I sit down and pat the side of my bed next to me. She sits, a sullen look on her face and scoots closer. Resting my head on her shoulder, I inhale her calming scent of lavender and note the absence of dried petals in her hair. "I'm not. Thea, there's something I haven't told you before. And it isn't because I didn't want to or didn't trust you, but because I wasn't allowed to." The quickening of her heartbeat echoes in the silence of the apartment. Clouds roll over the sun again and I hear the patter of raindrops hitting the windows and balcony. The pulsing sound of her nerves under her skin is emphasized with the tapping of her fingers.

"Okay," I respond skeptically, unsure of what that even implies.

She sighs while playing with a thread of her jeans. "You obviously know now that there are supernatural beings out there. You are a vampire." She hesitates at the word as if it were dirty. Maybe it is. "I am a witch," she adds timidly. I raise my head and stare at her in shock and confusion, not expecting the conversation to go that way at all.

Actually, I had zero expectations for this conversation since the whole thing has just been more craziness.

A voice in my head whispers about the secret that she has hid from me for our entire lives. I ignore the gripping pain on my heart.

"The reason I never told you is because as a part of a coven, I wasn't allowed to. Humans can't know about us." She scoffs, "Even if they are family or best friends. But since you are part of the supernatural now, it's okay."

I think back to all the times when we hung out and she would randomly remember that she had something else that she had to do. Or the times when I lived with her that she would leave to go someplace at super late times. When I would ask where she was going, she would say there was an emergency at her mom's apothecary downtown and Valeria needed assistance. If I offered to help, she would always tell me not to worry. There was always a nagging feeling that I shouldn't press her for information, even though what she said felt untrue, so I didn't.

I think of how hard it has been to not call her and tell her everything for only this short while. Keeping this secret for years, decades, must have been torture for her. Had she not found the blood bag first, I might have never told her, nor she me. I let a genuine smile spread on my lips. "Is that why you refused to be the witch sisters from that movie for Halloween?"

"Partly the reason." She laughs.

We both sit more comfortably. I rest my head back on her shoulder and we sink into the fluff of my bed, relaxing into each other's company. She wiggles her toes in her shoes, the sound scraping inside my head. The blood bag she placed on the banister glistens in the beam of sunlight. I take shallow breaths, not wanting to risk smelling its contents. A thought pours into my head, distracting me from the sight. I look up at my best friend. "What were you doing in my refrigerator?"

Her gentle hand slides down my arm. "I brought you some of my mom's ratatouille. I noticed the box and don't remember it being there the morning you came back." When she checked on my plants. I gave her a key long before she agreed to become my plant-sitter.

Tiny footsteps sound on the wooden stairs. Helios rounds the corner and jumps up onto the bed, demanding cuddles. Or food. He crosses the comforter and sits at my side, orange eyes gleaming at me expectantly. When I lift a hand to him, he nudges it with his nose. Soft vibrations echo into the room and shake the bed as he rolls over.

"So, you can do magic?" I ask as Sarah pats her lap, gaining the cat's attention. He doesn't hesitate to step on me for more love.

I feel the tug of a grin on her face. "Yes, I have magic." She pauses briefly before intaking a gasp of air that causes me to lift my head. "You know, vampires have magic as well," she exclaims excitedly.

My mouth hangs open. "What...how?" is all I manage to get out.

She lifts a shoulder. "Magic is given by the Earth. The first vampire was a witch who dabbled into forbidden magic in order to defeat her enemies. She somehow kept most of her powers after her transition. Vampires are the only ones who can create more vampires, and in that process, magic awakens in the newly turned." Kindria, the new vampires, Cole had called me that. "Once the magic is developed, vampires tend to one type or another."

Cole didn't mention this. "Do all vampires have magic?"

"Yes."

Was this what that vampire who attacked me meant? Suspicion churns in my mind. What if Cole really is after what that other vampire wanted from me? A small part of me tries to subdue any ill thoughts toward Cole and his lack of information. I look down at my hands, examining them as if for the first time. "You said one type or another? Is that magic or vampire?"

She clears her throat and twirls her fingers in the sheets. The sound is like crumpling paper to my ears. Helios rolls on her lap exposing the soft fur of his stomach. "Both, I suppose. Though vampires don't choose their magic. The types of vampires are the Essites and the Brais, though it never used to be that way." In the hall, a door nearby is slammed closed and I jump at the sudden sound. Sarah just squeezes my knee. "The difference is a matter of life choices and preferences, really."

I take a minute to think about all of this. There is a whole world out there that I, and most other people, have no idea about. "This is crazy."

"Yep." She nods. "There are not that many vampires, honestly. It is risky to create one. Even if the vampire who is creating a new one succeeds, there is no telling whether or not that new vampire will survive the transition." A shiver runs down my spine as I recall the horrible sensations I endured, the excruciating stomach pains and the gagging. Maybe that is what Cole meant when he said not to fight it.

"So, what is the difference between the two types? And which one am I?" I ask, changing the subject, not wanting to dwell on what could have happened.

"You are an Essite," she answers without any thought. "There isn't much of a difference between the two. Both have magic, but the Brais tend to use theirs for more... diabolical means. They wouldn't mind if humans knew about vampires because they want to be in control of them. Like they want all humans as slaves basically." I feel her shudder. She grinds her teeth, the sound like nails on a chalkboard in my ears. "And they would declare war on other supernatural races as well."

I raise my eyebrows. "That's frightening."

Sarah nods.

"Movies and television just make you think that all vampires would be like that," I say as I recall a movie that I used to watch frequently as a kid.

She shakes her head. "No, not all of them, thankfully."

"Not that I want them to, but why haven't the Brais done anything? What stops them?" Shadowy figures with pointed teeth flash in my mind, destruction and chaos surrounding them. I shake the conjured images of the Brais from my head.

"The Essites. They are the only reason the Brais have not actually been able to hold true to their threats. Any time the Brais try to wage war against the humans, the Essites are there to keep humans safe. Both sides have lost countless lives from the centuries of fighting." A chunk of fur from Helios floats in the air as she continues petting him. It flutters in the stagnant air, seemingly in slow motion, making its way to her sweater. I reach out to grab it before it lands and Sarah jumps. Her heartbeat thunders against my ear.

"I'm sorry."

She laughs, placing her hand on her chest. "You just moved so quickly."

I frown. "I didn't think that I was moving fast at all."

"Vampire speed," she states, a hint of distaste laced in her words.

I readjust myself, leaning on the pillows instead of her. "Do you not like that?" I toss the fur over the side of the bed.

She blinks at me. "No, I'm sorry that it came off that way. It's just..." she chews on her lips. "Vampires and witches don't particularly get along. We tend to stay out of each other's business."

I lift a brow. That didn't quite answer the question, but I don't prod for more. "Would the witches help the Essites fight the Brais?"

She winces. "No. Old ways of thinking and doing things. We keep our lives separate. If I were the leader of the coven, alliances would be the first thing I would aim for."

I squeeze her hand. "So, what are the Essites like?"

She flicks a piece of lint from the cuff of her sweater. "The Essites want peace and believe in co-living with humans and other supernatural races. They have a monarchy that keeps them in check and tries to keep humans from finding out about you. I guess you could say that the Brais are rebels. They broke free from the Essites hundreds of years ago. They have a king too, a terrible, old and powerful king. All he wants though is to have the Brais as the only vampire race."

Vampire kings and vampire wars. I bury my face in my hands and shake my head, swallowing the overwhelming sensations. "I don't want to be a part of any of this." Yesterday, my biggest thoughts were how long I would stay in town and who to visit. Now, I have to worry about this secret, dangerous world that I have been thrust into. At best, I know a bit of self-defense that maybe I could protect myself. Never, in all my life, have I had to use anything that my father taught me. I wonder if it is like riding a bicycle—would I remember the moves if needed? Would human self-defense moves even be useful against a vampire?

They were this morning.

The image of that vampire's rotting corpse claws its way into my mind. I rub my eyes and blink it away.

Sarah puts a comforting hand on my neck, the warmth from her skin seeping into mine. "I know. I wish none of this happened to you."

I look at her, a flickering smile on my lips. "At least we can share everything with each other now."

She loosens a quiet, amused breath, "There is your immortal optimism that I love." Emphasis on the immortal part. "Yes, and it's pretty cool that you have magic."

My eyes light up as excitement courses through my buzzing body. As if in answer, an electrifying sensation, so subtle in its appearance, stirs in my gut and underneath the skin in my palms. "Could I practice it now? What kind of magic can I do?" The words practically meld together.

"Elemental," she says nonchalantly. Magic may be an everyday thing to her, but its existence is absolutely mind-blowing to me. "There is water, earth, air, and fire. Each vampire specializes in one of them." I stifle a laugh, picturing myself as an anime character from my favorite television show as a kid bending the elements. "Some can also specialize in some other type of magic along with their element, like psychic abilities or invisibility, etcetera. Though, that type of magic takes a lot of their power, leaving the vampire weakened. Those abilities can't be done often, or for very long." She looks at me with a studious, hopeful gaze. "I can help you learn. From what I hear though, it takes a couple weeks for a vampire's magic to manifest. It signals the end of their transition from mortal to immortal." My shoulders sink. She must have noticed because she places a gentle hand on mine. "Don't worry, I'm sure it will be worth the wait." She offers a smile.

"Thank you, And yes, please. I would love to have you as a teacher." Having Sarah as a mentor calms my nerves. I know her and know how well she is at teaching. Cole, on the other hand, I know nothing about him. Something in my chest tightens at the thought and I ignore it. I nudge her arm. "And I would like to know more about your secret life."

"Of course," she says, a smile crinkling her eyes. Her face then returns somber. "Thea, the Brais are ruthless, the king especially so." Her face pales. "I have never met or seen him, but the stories I hear..." she swallows nervously and shakes her head. "They use their magic and strength for terrible things. They kill and destroy and...if you find out that the vampire who turned you is one of them...please get away as fast as you can, okay?"

"Okay," I promise. The thought causes me to shudder. Cole seems to be of the good kind—not a Brais. But I can't help but keep her warning in the back of my mind.

~

*S*arah left after several warnings about the dangers of being in the sun and using too much of my magic. She assured me that she would help get me a sun totem. She just needs to find the correct spell for it in her mother's grimoire. Our conversation ended with some frivolous laughter and reminiscing. She said that she needed to help her coven prepare for some ritual later tonight. We were both in better spirits after being able to express our secrets. Even though the secrets are new to each of us, it felt like there was never anything hidden. After just an hour of talking, it felt like we have always known these parts of each other. I'm thankful to be able to share everything with her, as I'm sure she is also. Aside from being open with my best friend, having someone other than a guy I just met to talk about this with is comforting.

She also gave me a talisman that she had on her. I trace the contours of the wooden figure resting in the drawer of my nightstand before tucking it away inside. It is a protection emblem. She will always know where I am when I have it, and since it belonged to her, I can always find her with it. When I asked, she said that she has always carried it on her, though the accident made her decide to give it to me. I think she still holds onto the regret for not coming with me. I wonder if a witch could have stopped the accident from happening.

Sarah let herself out and I decided to nap a little more since the sun was still out. Now, I sit on the edge of my bed, my toes caressing the soft, white rug. The intensifying, sharp pain of hunger burns in my stomach. I let out a sigh, allowing my shoulders to slump. This is what I will have to deal with for the rest of my life, however long that will be.

I tread to the bathroom, stopping at my wardrobe for a change of clothes and settle with a comfortable outfit of jeans and a blue t-shirt. The moment I round the bed my bare leg is swallowed by warm, glorious sunlight. Cole's warning rings in my ears, and in a flash, I retreat back toward my bed, cursing myself for forgetting that the shades in the right window weren't measured correctly. There's a generous gap between ceiling and cover. I examine my leg. There is no pain, no smoke or burns. My eyebrows raise with intrigue.

I creep toward the soft sunbeam, stopping only a foot from the line of light and shadow. Particles dance in the stream of golden sun, beckoning me to join. I shift my gaze to the window and take a deep breath, shakily moving my arm out and into the beam. As soon as the light hits the tip of my middle finger, I yank it back, again examining my limb. Still, nothing has happened.

Interesting.

This time, I stick my whole hand into the light, not even a tingle happens. With surprising confidence, I walk into the sun, my entire body engulfed. It feels as though each cell is hungrily soaking up the warmth. The light is invigorating as it wraps around me. My eyes, on the other hand, still don't enjoy the intensity of the sun's bright gleam.

The sun won't hurt me. I beam. The outdoors is no enemy of mine. Not even in undeath.

Happiness turns to anger. Why did both Cole and Sarah lie? Did they think that I was going to run away? *Maybe Cole is a Brais*, my subconscious warns. I shake my head and dismiss the thought. Should I call him or Sarah? She mentioned being busy until later.

Cole it is, then.

Downstairs, darkness engulfs the area, and my sensitive eyes are thankful for it. I walk into the kitchen and pull my phone off the charger, it reads 12:52 PM.

"Good morning," Cole answers chipperly after the second ring, an audible smile in his words. My heart stammers in my chest.

Focus. You called him for a reason. I curse at myself.

"Thanks for lying to me," I say.

"What?" He sounds offended.

I stride to the blinds in the kitchen and open them slightly. Like before, no harm comes to my skin, the only sensation is that of the enveloping warmness. It is as if I stuck my limb in front of a winter's bonfire. My hand tingles pleasantly as it embraces the light of the giant star. "I forgot that I have broken shades in the living room and the sun shone on my—"

He inhales sharply. "Did something happen? Are you okay?" His tone rises, masked by worry.

I laugh aloofly. He can really keep a lie going. "Yeah, I'm fine." A sigh of relief comes from his end of the phone. "I'm standing in the sun now, in fact."

A brief silence. "What?"

"Yep. I'm standing right in the sun, skin exposed and everything." Annoyance creeps into my voice. "If you didn't want me to leave my apartment alone, you could have just said so."

If you don't trust me.

"Thea, I wasn't lying. The sun will kill vampires," he explains gravely. "I'm coming over. Be there in ten minutes."

I shrug, put my phone in my pocket, and turn the coffee maker on. My eyes fall on the appliance holding the blood bag. The gnawing at my stomach returns, pushing my feet forward. I open the door, revealing the bag Sarah put back before she left, a small note stuck to the top with a heart. The words "I'll always have your back" are scribbled in her handwriting. My heart warms at her message, feeling full for the love of her friendship. I pull the top off the bag and feel my teeth elongate into their lethal points—the sensation as they slide out of my gums, over the teeth I have had almost my entire life is strange, though already feeling natural. With the bag halfway to my mouth, I pause, blinking as my eyes catch the teal travel cup sitting on the counter. The color...it shines brighter than usual. I lift my gaze to the living room and stumble backward at the sight. Everything is more vibrant. The ruby colored roses almost twinkle in the dim light. Images appear sharper, more in focus. On the other side of the apartment, I see a tiny jumping spider crawling along the banister. I blink and rub my face before turning around, a headache forming behind my eyes.

The instant the contents touch my tongue, I am filled with a euphoria so great that I feel like I am floating. Like a raindrop released from its tether to the cloud, descending gloriously to the ground in a free fall. My body relaxes and buzzes all the same. It is like taking a gulp of ice-cold water on a scorching summer day. Or jumping into a lake after hiking to a mountain's summit. In this moment, I am consumed by the addicting rapture of the power it gives. The enticing sweetness flows from my tongue to my toes, revitalizing all parts. All too suddenly, the bag is empty. I feel energetically charged with all that is within me, but also utterly disappointed at having finished it.

Already, my body craves more.

If this is how I feel after finishing only a bag... I shudder at the thought of harming a human for this liquid—my elixir of life.

Pointed teeth recede, hiding from sight. The color of the travel cup on the counter dulls.

My apartment door swings open and I turn to see Cole letting himself in. His dark hair is tousled and falls to his eyes, giving him a wild look. The stubble that lines his jaw and upper lip appears darker today, a contrast against his olive skin.

"Oh hey, come in," I retort. He looks at me but doesn't respond, placing his black coat on the rack. "No more blood bags?" I tease, my anger having already dissipated since our call.

"If you wanted it, you could have asked," he says, taking a few steps into the apartment and shoving his hands in his pockets. His grey eyes pierce mine.

I lean against the island counter. "I *always* want it."

He furrows his brows. "Is that why you really called? Did this window thing actually happen?"

I narrow my eyes. "Watch." I move to the window by the balcony door and grab the string. I feel tension radiate from Cole as I do so, a thick strand of energy hangs in the air between us. It clings to me like an invisible limb, forcing me to turn around and face him. I shrug off the strange sensation. "Trust me," I assure him.

He blinks at me, a stunned look crossing his face before quickly disappearing.

Some of the tightness loosens and his shoulders relax. As I pull the shades open, the bright, early afternoon sun shines onto my skin. Like before, nothing happens.

I look to Cole through squinting, stressed eyes. "See?"

He stands there, his mouth slightly agape, dumbfounded into silence. "How—this is impossible." He slowly walks to the window, examining the pane. "Maybe the windows themselves are UV protective?" He pulls something out of his pocket and puts it down on the kitchen counter. His totem. The coin clinks on the marble.

With a nervous swallow, he raises an arm into the sunlight. His skin sizzles to a burn, a sickly sound accompanied by a charred, putrid smell. My sarcastic expression fades as he winces and yanks his hand back.

Regret washes over me. He never lied. "Cole, I'm sorry." I watch his hand mend itself back to health as if nothing happened. The burns turn pink as new skin stitches itself together over the top of them. "I'm sorry for calling you a liar." My chest tightens again.

He walks to his totem and puts it back into his pocket. "Don't worry about it. I probably would have had the same reaction." He peers up at me and offers a reassuring look. The light reflects off of his smokey eyes, reminding me of early morning mists that settle over the nearby pond as the sun rises in the sky. It would be easy to stare into them and get lost.

"Okay." I smile back sheepishly, tucking my hair behind an ear and looking toward the kitchen. "So, why doesn't the sun burn me like it does you?" I ask as I stare at my hand fully engulfed in the sunlight again. It hugs me, warming from the outside in.

I watch his shoulders slump as he sighs. "Thea, there is more to being a vampire than what meets the eye," he says through an exhale. "We have elemental magic, specializing in one of the four." I raise an eyebrow, as if hearing this for the first time. Sarah's warnings ring in my head. I shouldn't tell him that Sarah, my witch best friend told me. Not yet anyway.

More secrets.

"So, earth, air, fire, or water?"

He nods. "Yes."

I purse my lips. "So, what does that have to do with this?" I gesture to my hand, still enjoying the heat.

"Well, it is rumored that some vampires who specialize in fire aren't harmed by the sun. It's rare though, like, myth-worthy rare." He walks away, leaving me speechless. In the kitchen, he pulls out two coffee mugs from the drainer and pours coffee in them, gesturing for me to take one.

Finally finding the words to speak, I say, "So, I am going to be a fire bender?" I can't hide the disappointment in my voice, even when adding the reference to that childhood show. To me, fire has always represented hatred, anger, and destruction. None of those are me. His eyebrow quirks up as I walk over to him and grab my cup of coffee, the heat filling my already cooled hands. "Water or air would be cooler," I add, laughing at my own unintended pun. Water is an element of healing, of fluidity and stamina. Air is calm, uplifting. Each can be devastating if they wish, but their qualities are not generally seen that way. At least not to me. Those elements and their peaceful qualities are how I prefer to live.

Cole shrugs, the hint of a smile forming and vanishing quickly. "Maybe, I can't say for sure though." He keeps his eye contact with me long after he finishes.

"What?" I ask, moving to the island.

"I just can't believe it. I never would have imagined that this could happen, I guess. I just thought it was a myth." He takes a sip of his coffee. "I guess you won't be needing a sun totem after all."

"No, I guess not." My mind flashes to the talisman that Sarah gave me. Could that somehow be protecting me from the sun? I run a hand through my long hair, fixing a small knot that formed while sleeping. "Do you have to have it on to be protected?"

"Yes."

The totem still sits in the drawer of my nightstand, so it can't be the reason why the sun isn't burning me. "You said before that a witch can cast a spell on an object to make a totem?"

"Right. You need two things. First is an object that is tied to you emotionally." He pulls out his totem again, the large metallic coin glistening in the light. "My mother gave this to me when I was young. She passed away sometime after and I had always carried it with me." His eyes remain fixed on the coin, his mind far away. Sadness tugs on my heart, the pain of losing a loved one all too familiar.

"I'm sorry you lost her."

He shakes his head, his attention returning to the present. "Don't be. It was a lifetime ago." He slips the item and the memories back into his pocket. "Step two would be to find a witch who could put a sun protection spell on it." He looks at me sidelong, his hands wrapped around the steaming mug.

Pretending to be ignorant, I respond, "Yeah. Sounds easy."

Cole chuckles. "It isn't. Witches tend to keep away from us. And we would do well to stay away from them. They may look and smell human, but they are strong. Some can kill a vampire with the snap of their fingers."

A shiver runs down my spine despite the heat from the coffee.

"Well, good thing we don't have to try to find you one." I twirl a finger around some hair to keep my focus busy, biting back the urge to tell him about Sarah. I can't help but wonder if he can see through the deception. If he can, he doesn't let on.

My eyes gleam. "So, I can go outside today?"

Cole mimics my exuberance. "Yeah, actually."

"And learn some magic?" I sound like a child staring at a stack of gifts on their birthday.

"Perhaps. For most, it takes a couple of weeks for magic to manifest." The same thing that Sarah had said.

My chest deflates.

"But we can try." An impish grin cuts across his face. "Wielding magic is the best part of being us."

Enthusiasm rushes through me. "I'll be the first to master it on day one." As excited as I am to get outside and see what I have only ever read about in books, I am equally as nervous.

No risk, no reward. My father's old mantra echoes in my mind.

Cole chuckles and pushes off from the counter, placing the mug in the sink. "Second, actually. According to the stories, the first vampire was able to master her vampiric magic hours after turning."

Sarah said she was a witch first. She already had an affinity for magic, so that sounds like cheating to me. I huff.

Another laugh escapes his lips. "We'll start off with the small, easy stuff. And, for now, we are just going to assume you specialize in fire," he says as he makes his way to the door.

"Okay." I start after him but hear my phone ring. I pull it out of my pocket and look from the screen to Cole, who shakes his head.

"You don't need to answer," he states.

Sarah is calling and I want to tell her about the sun immunity. "It's my best friend. I have to take this." My thumb hovers over the answer button, hesitating. There are secrets I am keeping from both of them and taking her call would most certainly reveal those. I reevaluate my decision. "On second thought, I'll just call her back later."

A sigh of relief escapes his lips. "Thank you. Let's go test out your magic."

Chapter 7

Cole leads us to the forest behind my apartment building. Experiencing the sun outdoors as a vampire is a whole new experience. As a human, the sun plays on the skin, warming it with its touch. As a vampire, the warmth holds me like a pool of water and flows from the outside in, leaving its heat in every single cell. Above, a beautiful clear, blue sky stretches far into the distance—something rarely given in Inbery. An old friend of mine would call it a "bluebird day". It shines more vibrantly than I remember it usually looking. I spot a smile painted on Cole's lips as he turns from me and continues walking toward the forest.

When we enter, a strange feeling washes over me, like I just walked through a giant wall of spider webs. It is so overwhelming that I immediately stop in my tracks.

Cole turns and looks at me when he realizes that I stopped following him. "What's wrong?" he asks, concern etching in his expression.

"I don't know." I take a few more steps forward and notice the strange feeling growing more intense. Soft, invisible tendrils caress my skin, beckoning forward like a dance partner during a waltz. "As soon as I walked into the forest, I got this unfamiliar vibe."

An intrigued look fixes itself across his face. "Good or bad?" He looks around, his eyes scanning everything from tall pines and maple trees to the small forest ferns, as if looking for something or someone.

I close my eyes and slowly take in some fresh air, inhaling the scent of the forest. The feeling reminds me of when you watch the sun set over the mountains or hear the song of a bird in the early morning light. The smell of a freshly printed book in your hands and the crackle of leaves under your feet in a serene forest. I hear the secret sounds of dancing and laughter from beings unseen, exuberance melting away distress and uncertainty. The forest is welcoming me. "No," I say, shaking my head. "A good one. It's... It's hard to explain. It feels like—"

"Life?" he finishes for me. My eyes fly open to meet his.

The perfect word.

I dip my head. "Yes. That is exactly it."

"I used to get the same feeling when I was a kindria. It lessens as time goes on," he responds, disappointment ringing in his voice. "I think it's because of the magic. We get it from the earth and since you're new, the connection is more intense."

"But I like it. I don't want to lose it." The tug of a faint, broken energy pulls my attention to a sugar maple sapling on my left. The closer I stalk toward it, the stronger the feeling gets, becoming unbearable as I stand in front of it. Pain fills my chest, and I can't help but wonder if it is mine or if it is emanating from the tree.

Cole shrugs. "I don't know what to tell you then."

"Maybe you pushed the feeling away," I tease. "You may not have embraced it." I say the words as a joke, but secretly hope it to be true. To lose this ability that allows me to feel the aliveness of this serene place would be painful. The spirits of the forest dance across my skin like a bubbly drink on the tongue.

He laughs. "I don't think that's how it works." I feel his gaze on my back as I raise an arm to touch the tree in front of me. When I do, another alien sensation washes over me. I feel as if I am not in my own body anymore, but in that of the tree, my woody flesh digging into the soil beneath. I reach for nutrients, only to be starved dry by my own, aching roots.

"What are you doing?" he wonders, his voice pulling me back to my own body.

I close my eyes. "I don't know. I can feel something coming from this tree, something like pain."

He scoffs. "Pain? I didn't know trees could feel that, much less communicate."

I shake my head and look at a withering branch that stretches overhead. Its pale leaves droop over the sides. "Not like 'ouch I stubbed my toe' pain, but like an illness or something. It's hard to put into words."

Cole steps closer. "Well, it happens, I guess. Let's go."

"Hold on." I hear him sigh quietly as he walks a few feet away, the sound of leaves crunching beneath his boots. Still gently gripping the tree, I close my eyes again. My soul joins with that of the tree. We are one. I am aware of myself touching the bark, but at the same time, feel the touch of a human on my woody skin. The sickly feeling of an illness creeps from my toes—my roots. To combat it, I envision health. Happiness and love, warmth and laughter. Memories of the love between my parents. The nights that Sarah and I stayed up too late, our cheeks burning from laughing. I focus on the merriment felt throughout the forest and the tingling warmth of the sun on my neck. My hand tickles and a faint, white glow emanates from it and into the tree. It travels down and into the ground, soaked up by roots, earth, and hyphae—all that aids the plant. They take it in hungrily but graciously. After a few moments of this blissful experience, I open my eyes. The branch that was once withered is now a vibrant brown, lush with the greenest of leaves. I receive a sense of gratitude from it as I release my hold, my eyes widening as I step back.

"How did you do that?" Cole is beside me again, admiring the branch. "How did you know you could do that?" A subtle ginger-colored aura encircles him. I blink and it is gone.

There is enough of a silence after his question that he looks at me. "I didn't," I reply, still amazed at what I had done and confused at seeing the flash of color around him. "I just wanted to help it, and I guess I did." Dizziness washes over me and I lean against the birch tree to my left.

"Wow." Cole reaches for the branch and examines it like it is a foreign object, unaware of my abrupt case of light headedness.

I beam. "I guess that means I'm not going to specialize in fire." My body relaxes with excitement.

Without a glance to me, Cole says, "What makes you think that?" He lets go of the branch and walks in the direction he was first headed.

I put my hands in the pocket of my sweater and follow behind him, the buzz of magic still tingling in my arm. "Well, fire is an element of destruction, and that," I point in the direction of the tree, "was definitely not destruction."

He shakes his head. "That doesn't mean anything. I specialize in air, but I have psychic abilities. Many vampires can have second abilities, which we call beta abilities, that are completely separate from their main elemental one. Everything is not always connected, Thea." He says my name like a mentor teaching their pupil. I lower my head in disappointment. I don't want fire. "Listen," he continues, "I'm not a hundred percent sure that you are going to have fire as your element. But, given your sun immunity, it is just really likely." I don't respond and we keep walking, the only sound between us is that of the forest and her creatures.

My thoughts move to a more personal topic. Images of the accident flash in my mind and I squeeze my fingers into a fist. "Can I ask you a question?"

"Of course," he answers, his eyes still locked forward.

I take a deep, calming breath. "Why me? How were you there so fast the night of the accident? Were you watching me?" Unless I have some guardian-angel looking out for my well-being, there would only be one reason he was around at the coffee shop and again at the site of the accident. A shiver runs down my spine.

Coming to a slow stop, he inhales fresh air and exhales loudly out of his mouth before turning to look at me, his jaw clenching then loosening. He stands still, pinching the bridge of his nose before rubbing his face. "I'm sorry that you feel uneasy about this. It makes sense. I am also sorry that I haven't yet given any explanation." His words are laced with sincerity. "I promise I will answer your questions better, but I would rather not do that here."

I stare at him for a moment before nodding, again listening to that nagging voice in my gut that tells me to trust him. I just hope that it isn't leading me astray.

He looks around. "This is a good place."

I mimic his gaze. "Good for what?" All around us is leaf litter, trees of all sizes, moss, small ferns, and a rotted log on the ground. "I am not setting a tree on fire. Or anything else that is living for that matter." I cross my arms.

Cole bends down and picks up a medium-sized dead log with ease—something that a human could not do, I note. "Burn this then." He clears a spot of decaying leaves on the ground and places the log down. "Considering that I am not a fire user, I will try my best to teach you."

I move my eyes from the log to meet his, my lips curving up. "Isn't this considered nature abuse?" I tease.

A laugh escapes his mouth, a hand on his stomach. The heartening sound vibrates in the air, penetrating my senses and coaxing my own amused laugh. "Sorry, I just wasn't expecting that," he says with one last giggle leaving his lips. "Come." He leans his head, gesturing for me to get closer to the log. We stand about ten feet from it. "All right, I'm going to try a few different approaches."

"Okay," I reply nervously. In all my life, I never would have imagined myself setting fire in the middle of a forest. I shake out my hands and any lingering nerves.

"I'm going to try the easiest first. Close your eyes." Cole moves to the other side of the log, so he is facing me. I do as he says and close my eyes. "Now," he resumes, "keep the log in the center of your focus. Think of something that made or makes you furious. Relive that memory and be in that moment. See it vividly and focus your anger on the log."

I search through my memories. At first, matters that aggravated me briefly pop into my head, like when I failed a test my first semester in college or accidentally broke one of Sarah's family heirlooms. I pull forward the images and emotions of those incidents. A subtle heat pools in the centers of my palms, like a stray ember from a flame.

I crack my eyes open, peaking at the log. It sits, unaffected by my efforts. I close my eyes again. Perhaps the emotions from these memories are not strong enough.

My mind then recalls the car accident that killed my parents when I was thirteen. I was so grief-stricken that my personality changed. To the outside world, I was a rage filled teenager lashing out. And I was angry—actually I was downright wrathful. After years of being someone I never used to be, I swallowed that anger. Locked it away deep within myself so that it wouldn't control me anymore.

I can still feel it poking its mutated head at me. It reaches for the key that sits too close to the cage.

I shake my head, salty tears threatening to beak free. "Not those memories." My mouth is dry and I realize I said that out loud.

Cole watches my stoically. "Whatever it is, it'll work. Just keep concentrating."

I shake my head aggressively, avoiding his gaze. "I can't."

His lips are pressed into a thin line, his muscular arms crossed at his chest. "You have to face old emotions, Thea." Again with the life lessons. "Keeping them bottled up will only ever cause an explosion later. Often, those are catastrophic for vampires."

"Not now, please." I cast my eyes downward, focusing on a bare spot on a tree. The bark was likely scrapped off by a deer or bear some time ago.

"Not now, then. But soon. Promise me."

"I promise." Hopefully he can't read through the lie. I'm not sure when—or if—I'll ever be ready to face those emotions again.

I return my gaze to his. He watches intently, silence hanging in the air. I expect him to reprimand me for lying, but he continues. "All right, then. How about the other night when I turned you without your consent? I killed you. Were you not angry then?" His question appears to be more out of hope than to bring up an angry memory.

I shrug. "Not really. I was, but...you said it yourself, I would have died otherwise." Memories of the sound the car made when it slammed into the tree echo in my mind, followed by the sight of the branch in my chest. "And plus," I continue, "I can't change that situation now. So, no. It won't help."

His shoulders relax, and he looks relieved. "Well, that's good," he says, a half-smile dancing playfully on his lips, crinkling his left eye.

I feel heat rising toward my ears and quickly turn away to observe whatever is not him.

My eyes land on the peculiar dark blotch on a tree trunk to my right—more specifically, an oak trunk. Recalling one of my classes, I remember that oak trees are fairly resistant to forest fires and actually revel in the fresh, nutrient rich soil that follows a blaze. My favorite college professor, Mr. Esposito, the fire lover that he was, frequently advocated for the use of controlled burning. He would sometimes lose himself in his lectures, blabbing about how "fire is pure energy.

It is energy and life combined into one, beautiful force". Though I appreciated the element's usefulness in some situations, like forest regeneration, I always scoffed at those particular beliefs of his. When I was a freshman, he told me that he and my father were good friends. Together, they always talked about becoming firefighters. I carved his stories about my father into my mind, his words forging an image from a perspective I have never known.

In this, there is a tether to my father.

"Hmm," I murmur quietly, if only to myself, my brain churning with ideas.

"What?" Cole asks.

I return my attention to him. "I think I just thought of my own approach." He waves a hand, gesturing for me to continue. Turning back to the log, I plant my feet in place and shake out the nerves gathering in my hands. I take a steady breath in, close my eyes and exhale, stretching my awareness out toward the decaying log. Like before, I reach out and create a connection to the material in front of me. The sensations that arise aren't like the ones that came from the sick tree. These feel dull, barely a hum of anything other than death. Once I feel confident in my attention's placement, I fill my thoughts with that of energy. Of motion and heat. Cole thinks fire is related to emotions—to anger.

Maybe he is right.

I go back to Mr. Esposito's lectures. In my head, I hear him describing flames and their consuming desire for growth. "Fire is not malicious," he would say. "It is nature's way of starting anew."

Breathe in, breathe out.

No risk, no reward.

I imagine myself in the clouds, watching as a darkening sky roars for a show. Brilliant flashes of purple and white dance in between each puff of gray. One of those streaks twists out of its canvas and hurtles for the ground beneath. It strikes the surface, erupting in a marvelous display of light as the drums above cheer on. Bright auburn and buttery flames simmer on the surface of the earth, collecting more fuel. They consume both dead matter of the earth and oxygen of the air—willing participants eager to witness a wonderous spectacle. Within moments, heat bursts from the ground like a water dancer would from the sea. I stand amidst the flames, the fire licking at my skin. It beckons to me, calling to my blood. I open my palms and it rushes my hands, seeping into my body. I flinch at first, expecting pain but gasp instead as euphoria envelopes me. The warmth quickly spreads, traveling throughout my entire body and igniting my cells within. It hugs me, swirling underneath my skin like a protective shell. I look up to the willing crowd of tall, dark pines, ready to participate in creation. Between them, a faint pair of glowing reddish-gold eyes peer at me inquisitively. I squint to see them better, shifting nervously on my feet. The sun breaks through the black clouds, shining down around me in beams, blinding momentarily. I place a hand over my brows and search for those eyes. Above, the angry clouds push against the light as more lightning streaks across the sky in violent displays of power.

That locked cage rattles deep within my bones.

"Thea," Cole's wavering voice whispers from far away. "Thea," he says again but with more urgency. When I open my eyes, I smell it before I see it. The smell of a wood stove burning on a chilly night.

Fire.

My eyebrows climb with widening eyes, my mouth quirking up. "I did it!" I exclaim, unable to hide the excitement. Small flames creep from the middle of the log toward the edges. Though they reach the underside, they don't appear to be jumping to the ground.

Even Cole seems enthusiastic. "You did." He strides over to me and puts a hand on my arm, his expression unchanged. "What was your angle?"

I shrug. "I just thought back to my fire ecology lecture from a class in school. My professor was a bit obsessed with fire." I wonder what he and my father would say if they knew about vampires and their ability to control their favorite element. The pair of eyes and the darkness of the looming clouds in my vision unsettles me, but I push them away. "Then I thought about forest fires and lightning and envisioned a bolt starting a fire and…" I cease my rambling when I see Cole's attention wavering. "What?"

He grins. "Sorry, I am listening, just not paying attention."

I scowl at him, sending a fist into his arm.

He laughs, clutching his arm. "Ouch." He turns away from the log, his eyes fixed on mine, a lightness to them. "I really was listening," he repeats mirthfully.

"Just not paying attention," I mock.

He places a rough hand on my cheek. His features soften. "I heard everything. It is pretty amazing that you figured out how to call your magic by yourself. And only days after turning."

I fight with myself about slapping his hand away. The gesture could mean nothing, but the miniscule sparks dancing between our skin says otherwise. My brain wants nothing more than to shoo him away, though the rest of me devours the invisible electricity between our bodies. A heat churns in my center, my entire focus split between his touch and the swirling depths of his eyes.

A sudden, loud crack alarms us both.

Before either of us can turn around, we are sent flying backward, an invisible force exerting pressure on us. We land past the oak tree, my shoulder scraping against its trunk. I sit up and frantically look around, adrenaline coursing through my veins. A dissipating heat in my hands distracts me and I look down to examine my cooling limbs, my eyes widening in realization. I stand and trudge to the spot where the log was, a black scorch mark the only indication that it was here.

"Wow," I whistle, amazed at the power. My thoughts are quickly interrupted by Cole's grunt.

"Thea," he says, his voice a faint groan behind me. I turn to see a piece of the exploded log sticking out of his back, dread washing over me.

"Oh no," I cry as I frantically run over to him. Blood runs down from the wound, caking his shirt.

His chest rises and falls in shallow, forced bursts. "I can't reach it," he mutters, wincing as I pull the wood out without hesitation and throw it far behind us. It splinters on impact, pieces disappearing into the brush of ferns and saplings. He rubs his back, the wound slowly mending itself.

I extend my hand to help him up. "C'mon, I don't bite," I say with a smirk. He lets out a small laugh and grabs my hand for support. "Doesn't wood kill vampires?" The image of that vampire who attacked me after fleeing Cole's cabin floods my thoughts.

"Yes, it can. If that was a fresh picked branch, things would have been a lot worse." He runs his hands on his face. "We can get incapacitated by stakes made of dead wood if it gets us in the heart. Live woody plants will poison us if they're exposed to our blood, so like in the instance of being stabbed." He points to the middle of his chest. "If the poison reaches our heart, we die."

Good to know. "Is there an antidote?"

He studies his blood-stained shirt. "More or less. The blood of a sire can heal." He continues when he notices my blank face. "So, your blood will heal me, and mine will heal you."

"Ah." I raise my eyebrows before lowering my head in shame. "I'm sorry," I say, regret glowing in my eyes. My disdain for fire returns, the excitement was fleeting.

"Don't be," he orders reassuringly before moving to observe the empty space where the log was. "That's amazing." His face lights up as he walks to the charred earth. I follow behind him, not sharing in his sense of awe. He clutches his jaw and shakes his head. "It is also really bad."

"Why?" I ask, puzzled.

He glances from the ground to our surroundings, his gaze darting from the various oaks, pines, and maples. Decaying leaves and moss litter the forest floor and bases of trees. "It is a long story."

"Well, lucky for you," I nudge him with my elbow, "I've got plenty of time." An eternity, in fact. I watch as his eyes continue to dart around, the gesture becoming unnerving. "What is it?"

"I'll tell you when we get somewhere safer." He finally stops scanning the trees around us and brings his attention back to me.

I swear they were red as he looks at me, though when I blink, they are their usual smokey color. "First, let's get something to drink. I can hear a couple people over in that direction." He points to our left. Shakily, I nod, nervous about feeding on humans. He takes off out of the blue and I follow after him.

Chapter 8

Everything moves in a blur, though appears stationary all the same, as if we are moving too fast for time to see. My body tingles at the liberating rush of moving this fast. Maybe I could run around the world instead of drive or fly, though I don't think Helios would enjoy being strapped to my back. We startle a squirrel who scurries down a tree as we pass by. He leaps off the trunk and nose-dives onto the ground, little feet pounding as quickly as possible.

We come to a stop once we can see the humans, remaining out of their ear shot. Two hikers are taking a break from their excursion. A tall, brunette male leans against a tree while drinking from his water canteen while a blonde female stretches in front of him. The sounds of their laughter reaches my ears, though not the sound of their conversing voices.

Cole glances at me, noticing my concentrated, furrowed brows. "It takes a while to learn how to use your heightened senses. You'll get it under control though," he assures me. "So, lesson number two. Not every vampire has advanced psychic abilities, but all have the capability to control a human's mind briefly. It allows us to coerce them to not be afraid or to not run. When we get what we need, we can heal them by supplying some of our blood. In turn, this allows us to further tap into their mind and erase the memory of us being there."

I crinkle my nose at the invasion, but keep my mouth closed, only nodding to signal that I understand. I suppose that is how humans have remained ignorant of the existence of vampires. "How do you do it?" I ask eagerly. My mind is splitting between human and vampire. The human in me still clings on to life, desiring to protect those who still own a beating heart. The vampire in me, however, seeks to consume. A sliver of that gnawing hunger pushes to devour until there is nothing left, and that is terrifying. My limbs buzz with the enticing thought. Rubbing my hands on my pants, I swallow and mentally lock those frightening ideas away.

"I'll show you." He starts toward the humans but pauses and turns to me with his hand outstretched. A captivating half smile dazzles across his face, stopping me in my tracks. I scoff to myself, not wanting to do as he says. But no one told my hand that. Like on autopilot, I place my hand in his. "Just follow my lead, okay?" I nod in agreement, all too aware of our skin touching as we make our way down the unmarked path. My hand, basking in the warmth of his, tingles delightfully. I want to rip it out of his, but it remains, and I am acutely aware of those sensations between our palms. As we get closer, the girl sees us, her body stiffening slightly as she stands from her stretch. The closer we get to them, the more my nerves pulsate under my skin.

Cole squeezes my hand and leans in, his voice a whispering wind, "Relax. I will be here the entire time." We reach earshot of the hikers and they watch us with narrowed eyes. Cole releases my hand, leaving an empty coldness in his absence.

"Hey," he says to them.

The male pushes away from the tree, his arms crossed, and glares at us with piercing blue eyes.

The woman watches Cole, her gaze roving from his face to his feet and back again. "Hi." She beams. Her blonde hair is tied tightly back and smoothed against her scalp. Dazzling blue eyes sparkle in the filtering sunlight. Despite the chill in the air, she wears a thin, white long-sleeved shirt and black running shorts with matching sneakers.

Cole looks at her, a kind expression on his face. "So, we," he gestures between himself and me, "were out walking and took a wrong turn somewhere and got lost." He looks around. "You two wouldn't happen to know how to get out of this maze, would you?"

At this, the guy relaxes, his arms dropping to his side. "Just follow that path," he says, pointing behind us. "It is about a ten-minute walk to the entrance of the park." Cole's gaze follows the male's arm.

"Thank you," he replies.

"You're welcome."

"Just one more thing," Cole says as he steps closer to them. The female hiker becomes stiff, her eyes pinned on Cole's, a glaze covering them. "Do not say anything and do not move," he commands, slowly glancing from one to the other. Both of them freeze in place as he finishes the sentence. A slight chill runs down my spine and I have to remind myself that the compulsion was not used on me. His gray irises change to that glowing ruby as his elongated, lethal teeth become visible. The girl's facial expression changes, her eyes widen and her nostrils flare. In a split second, Cole is embracing her, a hand tipping her head back while the other clutches her arm. The honeyed smell of fresh blood dances in the air around us. I close my eyes and inhale deeply, slowly taking in the grounding scent of the pine forest around us.

Calm.

This fresh aroma is even more enticing than that of a blood bag. In it, I note a second, new scent mixed in. Its spiciness is enticing, willing my body to move.

Fear.

It taunts that caged part of me that wants to break free so terribly. Deep inside, it roars with anger, shaking and thrusting against the fragile bars. I shiver at the intensity, panting at restraining myself. The heightened emotions drag that part of me out. The part that I never dare to face. My nails dig hard into the flesh of my palms, the pain keeping me still.

The cage clatters in the roaring of my mind.

When I open my eyes, they lock with those of the male hiker. His expression matches that of his partner's. His short brown hair sticks to his face with sweat from their exercise and the fear. At his sides, his fingertips tap against his grey pants in an uneven rhythm.

Tap tap, tap tap, tap tap.

The sound vibrates through my body, synching with the drum of my heart.

The man swallows, the muscles of his throat tightening and releasing. Under the skin of his neck, a pulsating beat chants, drowning out the melodies of the forest. My foot moves on its own accord, spellbound by the sound of his blood pumping.

Cole releases the girl, the movement pausing my steps. The girl stands there, in shock, with her eyes staring straight into the wilderness, her mouth slightly agape. He looks to me, his expression surprisingly calm for having just fed, a vast contrast to the shakiness of my own body. "I'm surprised you haven't moved yet."

"I want to..."

Cole shifts on his feet so that he is mostly blocking the female.

I tear my gaze from her blood which is remarkably not dripping down to her clothes. Twin pinpricks of pooled blood sit on her neck, a slow drip heading toward her shoulder. "I needed to wait until you were done."

That and I am just terrified.

I don't want to kill a human.

"Okay." He places a hand on my lower back and guides me to the other hiker. Every ounce of my focus pinpoints to the spot of our touch, and I struggle to keep an even breath. "Just concentrate on not killing him and you'll be fine. You'll want to, but don't." When he stops guiding, I step away, embracing the chill of the air.

"Sounds easy," I retort.

The frightened guy watches me, standing stiffly as I slowly walk closer. With every step, I fight the urge to lunge at his neck and rip into him. Standing so close, I can hear his staggering breathing and thumping heartbeat that competes with mine. The sound of his nervous swallow bounces into my ears as if I were wearing headphones. I mimic Cole, using my left hand to gently push his head to the side and my right to hold his arm. By the time my mouth is at his neck, my teeth are already prepared to break the vibrant tanned skin. As I drink, I focus not on the taste or sensations—which are decadently addicting—but on not killing him, as Cole advised. Every time my mind turns toward the vampiric, hungry, and power-crazed, I have to remind myself that he is a human with a life. And with each reminder, that vampiric urge gets louder. Slowly, but easily, the human thoughts give way to the physical relief that washes over me. I can feel my magic taking in the nutrients like a lake welcoming the rain. Shadows locked inside the cage within me whisper to keep drinking. The lock slowly twists as the desire becomes harder to ignore. Fear mingles with the taste of his blood. Honey mixed with cinnamon.

Intoxicating.

Addictive.

My grip on his arm tightens and I feel him wince underneath, causing another surge of that fear to blend in further with the flavor. My sips become gulps as my limbs loosen in a refreshing burst of renewal.

"Thea," Cole's firm voice and hard grip on my neck pull me away. "Release him."

I shrink under his grip and do as he commands, releasing the human gently. His eyes lazily remain open. Regret washes over me. "I'm sorry," I say to both him and Cole. I add another lock to the cage, which angers those trapped desires and emotions more.

"It wasn't bad," Cole says, oblivious to my internal struggles. "I could sense your control for the most part. It will take time. Bloodlust is dangerous. We will always have to fight that intoxicating desire to keep drinking."

"Why is it dangerous?" I wipe my mouth with my fingers and see a smear of crimson on them. My body screams for just that little amount. The thought of wiping it on the ground or my shirt in self-discipline crosses my mind, but my hand moves on its own. I clean my fingers, relishing in that last taste.

Cole watches my movements. "Because it pushes our predator desire to kill. If we give in, we will never be satisfied, regardless of how much blood we consume."

I shiver. It would have been easy to give in to that desire. If Cole wasn't here...

"It becomes easier to push away with more experience." Cole walks to the female, who is now holding her neck. "Now, to finish, we erase the past few minutes of their memory." He pulls a small pocketknife from his jeans and cuts into his palm. She fights him weakly when he brings it up to her mouth. Again, her eyes glaze over when they meet his. "As soon as we are gone you will forget that any of this happened to you. You were just out on a hike and two people asked for directions." When he finishes, her eyelids close.

"All right, your turn." He points to the guy and tosses me the knife.

"Okay." I copy everything that he does, wincing when I drag the blade across my skin. A crimson pool fills my palm. The guy takes my blood with ease. The sight floods my body with a lust for more.

More blood.

The feeding did not leave me satisfied. A need deep within craved to pull every last drop from the human's body. Only then could I be fully satiated. A euphoric pressure in my mouth causes me to shiver and I take a step closer to the man.

I tense as Cole's voice breaks through the whirring in my mind. "It is only our unsustainable primal thinking that tells us to drain a human."

My head whips to Cole, who stands closer to me than he was, his arms crossed at his chest. "Can you read minds?" I ask, my nostrils flaring. I tear my arm from the human and clench my fists.

Cole shakes his head. "No. Your jittery movement gave everything away." He clucks his tongue. "That, and you couldn't take your eyes off of him. Your *red* eyes."

"My blood healed him. I could drink a little—"

"No, Thea." Cole's unyielding voice startles me. I've never heard him use this tone before. My hair curls around my neck as a strong gust blows through. "That is not how we do things. He is a *human*. You've taken all you need."

It feels like a rock in my gut. My teeth slide back into my gums, the sounds of the forest replacing the pounding in my ears. "I-I'm sorry," I confess again.

Cole releases a breath, his shoulders loosening a bit. "It's okay. Just remember that, always. They are humans. As we both were, once."

I swallow a lump of shame.

"Now," Cole continues, "finish altering his mind."

I turn back to the male. The wound is gone, though his drying blood still remains on his neck. Cole was much neater with his feeding.

A smear of blood the size of a golf ball sticks to his skin. Two drips had made their way to the top of his shirt. I force him to lock eyes with me while I repeat Cole's words. A strange connection links my mind to his. I can feel his consciousness in mine, sitting at the edges like a block that doesn't fit in a puzzle. It lingers for the duration of the compulsion. The image of the splinter of wood in Cole's back streaks through my mind and I add a little extra command for the jacket the hiker wears around his waist. Once I finish, he closes his eyes as well. I turn to Cole who is gesturing for me to walk away.

"Smart, thanks," he says as I toss him the jacket to cover his still blood-stained shirt. I wonder how the humans would have reacted if they had noticed his soiled shirt. "Let's go, the faster we get away, the quicker they can get back to their lives." I follow him, and we vanish from the dazed humans.

~

Almost a minute later of blurring brown and green, we find ourselves at the tree line separating the forest from the small public park. When we stop, I am left panting, my hands resting on my knees. Cole holds up a finger, unfazed by our run. "Using our speed like that can drain our energy reserves. So, be careful when doing so." He notes my heavy breathing. I respond with an aggressive thumbs up.

Ten feet to our right is the main path into the state forest. The park is small and simple. Picnic tables and wooden chairs lay sporadically around an obscure kidney-shaped pond. A young couple strolls the stone bridge that crosses one side of the pond to the other, connecting the two open spaces. The single set of metal swings are occupied by a few young, laughing children. Their parents watch closely from the benches next to it.

Nostalgia slams into me like a bus. "I used to come here with my family all the time when I was little," I tell Cole as we exit the forest. "I haven't been back here in years." Purposefully, I avoided this place.

Cole brushes my back with his hand. His touch brings me out from the emerging memories and back into reality. "I'm sorry you lost them at such a young age."

"Thanks." I notice that his eyes, though they meet mine, will often move to our surroundings, scanning like he had back in the forest as if he were paranoid. "You've been looking around like that a lot. Are you searching for something?"

He walks in the direction of the park's entrance, toward the town.

I follow after him.

"Just precautions."

I narrow my eyes at him and snort. "That sounds like half the truth." We cross the stone bridge and pass by the young couple who sit on the ledge holding hands and conversing, their gazes set on each other in a sort of longing, loving way. A pang of envy bubbles in my chest.

Hopeless romantic, I scoff.

Cole continues walking with his head facing straight, unaware of the couple. I sigh, not sure why his lack of romantic awareness annoys me so much.

Yeah, don't even think about falling for the guy who killed you, my subconscious sneers.

The guy who saved *me.*

Right.

We continue walking toward the town without saying a single word to each other. I quicken my pace slightly so as to walk beside him instead of behind. Stealing a sidelong glance in his direction, I notice that he is deep in thought about something, his attention wholly on the path straight ahead with those dark, full brows furrowed. I wish he would tell me what is going on. I'm in this life now.

We reach the end of the park boundaries, indicated by a four-foot brick wall. Across the street are some local businesses ranging from a pharmacy, to a bakery, some clothing stores, and cafés. Some street vendors have set up small stations along the wide sidewalk down the length of the strip. Here, there is more foot traffic than vehicles. Once we are out of earshot of anyone around us, I decide to break the irritating silence. "What is going on exactly? Why do I feel like you are gearing up to fight?"

Cole stops at the side of the road and loosens a breath. "All right," he says as he rubs his hands on his face. "Let's get a burger and I'll tell you everything."

Chapter 9

I open my mouth to rebut what I thought would have been another avoidance answer but snap my lips closed. Of all the things he could have said, I wasn't expecting that. An excuse is what I was waiting for. I blink at him, "Yeah, sure."

He points to a brick building across the street. It is a fairly new, locally owned restaurant that I haven't been to yet. "There is a burger joint right there. It is usually pretty busy and loud in there, so we can talk freely." He crosses the road before finishing the sentence, eager to get moving.

The interior of the restaurant is industrial in style with high walls of exposed gray brick and a ceiling made into a grid of dark wooden beams. It is a fairly open space with tables and benches made of the same wood mixed with planks of silver metal. A decent width walkway in the center is the only part of the floor covered in a gray rug, the rest is bare, ashen wood. Black and white paintings, blueprints, and mirrors decorate the walls. A sleek, modern bar in the back separates the customers from the kitchen. Signs with various beers and mixed drinks are written in chalk on a blackboard.

Almost every bench is taken by other hungry citizens. Dozens of different conversations crash into my ears like a flood. Some are gossip, others are work related, and some booming with merriment. My head pounds from all the noise and I stumble back a step.

Cole's warm hand lands on my lower back, his lips to my ear. "Thea, block it out." I pinch my eyes closed, trying to create a barrier between the sounds and me. The cacophony of noises slam into the barrier, creating ripples that blend together, each a pinprick of a headache. "Look at me," he says. "Listen only to my voice."

I do as he says, slowly opening my eyes. Gray stares back at me, like the clouds before a summer storm. When the trees sway in different directions and leaves race across the sky and land, but all you can notice is the swirling beauty of the darkening clouds. "Breathe," he says. "Close your eyes and focus on your breathing, hear it fill your nose and travel to your lungs. Then exhale out through the mouth."

I take in a deep inhale of air through my nose, feeling it fill my abdomen. There sits a jumbled sphere of whirring tension, strings of hunger and fire wrap around it. Slowly, the tightness releases in my chest as it fills with soothing oxygen. Holding the breath momentarily, I focus on the warmth of Cole's hand. It seeps into my skin and spreads throughout my body. I open my eyes as I exhale through my mouth. All the different voices have muffled to a normal tone.

"Thank you," I whisper, still rubbing my temples. The throbbing in my head subsides quickly and smoothly, like ice melting under hot water.

"Of course. When getting used to our senses, they are like dials with a mind of their own."

A young red-headed male in a black apron uniform leads us to a lone table in the back corner, gesturing for us to take a seat before handing us the menus and vanishing in the kitchen. Cole sits in the chair against the wall and I sit in the one opposite of him. A subtle sliver of pain pulses in the back of my neck and I rub it as I sit to massage it out.

I keep my eyes on Cole's face, studying his chiseled features. His gray eyes hold a tiredness to them that I haven't noticed before, like they have seen a lot during their existence—and they most likely have. His hair has become ruffled from the wind, sticking out in some spots, though he still looks like he should be on television. A bit of facial hair lines his jaw and creeps up to his ears. I envision my hands following the line to his hair and twirling my hands in them.

Stop, Thea. I scold myself before any telltale sign betrays my thoughts.

Finally, he speaks, "So, what is it that you would like to know?"

I stare wide-eyed at him, blinking. So many questions, he will definitely regret letting me choose the topic. All the curiosities, half-thoughts, and pieces float around in my head. It is like listening to all the other people in here talking again, but this time all the voices are mine, and they are inside my head. "Why were you so on edge today?"

He opens his mouth to speak, but a brunette, bushy-haired waitress approaches our table. She places two mugs of coffee and a small glass pitcher of cream down on the table. She takes us both in and offers a smile. "Good afternoon, my name is Lyla and I'll be your server today." She takes out an order pad from the pocket of her black apron. "Are you ready to order?"

"Yes, I think we are," Cole responds. "Thea, you're first."

Lyla turns her attention to me, her big, brown eyes warm. I wish I actually was ready. I quickly look at the menu and order the first thing my eyes land on. "Um I think I will have the Bleu, please."

"Sure thing, hon." She jots my order down in a few scribbles before looking to Cole. "And for you, chap?"

Chap? I bite back a laugh.

"I'll have the House Burger, please."

She scribbles his order down before taking our menus. "Thank you. Those will be right out for you." Her heels click on the floor as she walks away.

I look to Cole, a grin emerging on my lips. "Chap?"

He smirks in return. "Some people like me." We both laugh and my shoulders relax as a wave of relief spreads throughout my body. His mood after we left the hikers earlier and entered the park dramatically changed from loose and kind to cold and rigid. "So, to go back to your question." He takes a sip of his black coffee, his two fingers inserted in the hook of the handle.

I nod to show that I am listening while I prepare my own hot drink.

"I'm sorry if I seemed a little stand-offish earlier. I was actually a little bit tense."

"Why?" I take a sip of my coffee, the flavor and warmth spreading into me as I swallow. I feel it spread into other parts of my body. The bitterness sticks to my tongue.

"Well, remember how I told you that our magic is elemental?" His voice lowered an octave as he said the last part of his sentence, his eyes scanning the surrounding people.

"Yes, I do."

I watch him as he takes another sip and sinks into the cushion of his seat, clearly enjoying the heat from the drink as well. "All right, well, there are two different races of vampires. They are the Essites and the Brais. We are the former." Relief further washes over my body at his proclamation. "The Brais are a cruel race that wish to extinguish anyone who gets in their way of basically world domination. This includes us, the Essites, as well as the humans, witches, and other supernatural creatures."

"Wonderful," I say flatly.

Sarah had mentioned that the Brais were not kind. With every experience of my new, heightened senses and always lingering hunger, I am painfully reminded that this is now the real world. It is not a story in one of the many books I have read. "And, while we were in the forest," he continues, "I had a sense like we were being tracked." He looks around.

My eyes widen, brows pinching together. "By the Brais? Why would we be targets?" I bite my lip, unsure if I actually want the answer for that one.

"Kindria emit a sort of energetic wave—especially when they unlock their element. Some vampires have the ability to trace that. However, in the moment that a new vampire unlocks their element, depending how strong it is, nearby vampires of that same element can 'feel' it," he says, using air quotes. "And, unfortunately, fire is the main element of the Brais."

Behind the bar, a glass is dropped, shattering on the hard wooden floor. I startle at the noise. "More wonderful news," I respond with an eye roll, my voice low. "So does that make me a Brais?" Sarah said I was an Essite, but she didn't know what magic I possessed then.

He contemplates for a moment, placing the coffee cup down on the table. "Our element does not determine if we are an Essite or a Brais. Vampires of all elements are on each side. We choose which side we are on." He inhales deeply. "You are free to choose which side you want to be, Thea. Just know that I am an Essite."

I didn't miss the hint of warning in his last sentence. The Essites and Brais are enemies. "I would prefer to be with the Essites as well, I think." I take a slow breath to calm my growing nerves, which allows for a bit of anger to seep in the cracks. My left hand, resting on my lap underneath the table, tightens into a fist. "Why were you there that night?"

At the coffee shop. At the accident site.

His gaze is intense, so piercing that it feels like the swirling clouds within could swallow me whole. "For a couple reasons actually." He sighs, exhaling slowly. I imagine his mind struggling to put together his thoughts. Underneath the table, I hear one of his feet tapping the floor. When my mother was anxious about something, she would often do the same. "The Essites are losing the war, Thea. The Brais are generally successful in cutting our numbers, either by killing or converting." For the first time since we arrived at the restaurant, his eyes are cast downward—in either embarrassment or sadness, I am not sure—to his hands clasping on the glossy surface of the table. "I'm very sorry for bringing you into this war." When he lifts his gaze to meet mine again, I see the sadness. It twinkles in the colors of his eyes, reflecting what I feel in my own. "It is very risky to create one of our kind, and for that I am sorry as well. Unfortunately, more Essites are also crucial in defeating the Brais, and you were already close to death."

I pull in a breath of air, contemplating his words that are echoing in my head. He wants me to fight in a war. Sure, I have some self-defense training, but I am no warrior. No soldier. When I graduated college last year, I made a promise to myself that I would travel the world. It was a dream, and now it is withering away. I don't want to be a soldier in a supernatural war. Cole's warm hand on mine snaps me from my spiraling thoughts of carnage and death.

"Thea?" he asks cautiously.

I look to him, then see our waitress walk toward our table with two plates in hand. I quickly pull my hand from his as she places the plates down.

She walks away and I look back at Cole and ask the one question I have had since all this began. "So, why me? I mean, anyone would have that question, I suppose. But you could have let me die." Cole stiffens then nods.

He clenches his jaw, taking a moment before answering. "I was very conflicted about turning you. Mainly because one would see it as selfishness, I suppose."

I lift an eyebrow.

"Let me start from the beginning," he says, taking a sip of coffee to chase away the crumbs. "My good friend, Eero, was the King of the Essites. He was elected to the position and was very good at what it entailed." He stares at the food on his plate, lost in whatever thought followed his sentence.

The bartender shakes a metal mixer filled with ice and the mixing of some type of alcoholic beverage. She pulls two unique glasses out and places them on the counter before pouring the roseate liquid in them, topping it off with a few cherries. The color, though lighter, ignites that newfound hunger in me. I turn my attention away and back to Cole, who is still stuck in memories.

The expression on his face and the use of past tense in his story gave me an odd feeling. I watch him for a moment more before asking, my voice soft, "Did something happen to him?"

His eyes falter as they return to mine. He nods grimly. "One day, quite recently, his home was broken into by a group of Brais. Practically an army." He pauses a moment, eyes rolling to the wall on his left.

I want to reach out and comfort him, but I keep my hands busy by holding my burger.

"They were led by the Brais King himself, clad in his legendary black armor. They killed him with hopes of destroying the Essites' ability to continue the war." Sadness looms in his eyes as they return to meet mine. "Many Essites joined him after that."

"I'm sorry." I truly am. My heart aches for his grief. I can't help but wonder if Sarah or her coven know about the King's death. I don't say anything else, waiting for him to speak, as I continue eating. The flavor of all the spices cooked with the burger mingle with the saltiness of the cheese. Onion, garlic, a bit of cayenne. They dance on my tongue like I am tasting them for the first time.

Cole lifts a shoulder and says, "It's life, I suppose." We both stare at each other in silence for a moment, a quiet understanding of the experience of heartbreak and loss.

"Who is the Brais King?"

"A shadow," he whispers. "Few have actually seen him, and when they do, they only see him in that black armor. Not a soul has seen his face. His powers are absolutely devastating," he shrugs, "or so I have heard. He only fought the Essites King with a sword."

I swallow a nervous breath. "His element is fire, I'm assuming."

"Yes. He is said to be the oldest vampire."

Great.

Another reason to crawl into a hole. What can I do that no other Essite has been able to do before? If the King of the Essites was killed, there is no way that I could do anything. The sounds of the restaurant dulls, like everyone else is holding their breath, waiting for an answer. I keep my voice gently as I say, "So, what does any of this have to do with my turning?"

After a few beats of looming silence, he continues, "We need all the help we can get. Before the Essites King had died, he ordered me and a few others to find people of strength and turn them."

"You turned me because you think I'm strong?" I ask through a mouthful of food. I don't know how that would make him appear selfish.

"Yes and no. That is only half the reason why." I watch him take another deep breath, his movements shaky. "The first time I saw you was at a bar in town. You were there with a few friends, all drinking a lot of alcohol." A corner of his lips curve upward slightly. "You had come up to the bar beside me to get another round when a guy you didn't know started hitting on you."

"I don't remember this night at all," I say, shaking my head.

Cole leans inward, his hands clasped on the table. His smokey eyes glimmer under the light of the restaurant. There is some blue mixed in with the gray. "I'll get to that. When I saw him bothering you, I was going to be a cliché valiant knight who helps a damsel in distress."

An unfiltered laugh escapes my lips and I close my mouth, grinning. "I'm sorry for laughing."

Now I see that dashing, full smile of his again. "I'm sure you are," he laughs, though something other than amusement mixes in his tone. "Anyway, I stood and walked to the two of you, and before I could do anything you started to tell him off. The guy proceeded to grab you. You took his hand and literally twisted his arm. It looked painful."

My father's teachings came in handy after all.

Cole chuckles, the sound is a ray of sun on a cold winter's day. "He left you alone after that, and so did every other guy."

I smile and shrug. "Go me."

"After that, you just turned to the bartender and continued on like nothing had happened. I went back to sit down, bummed that I had missed my chance to talk to you." He leans back against the wall and crosses his arms.

"You could have, you know. I wouldn't have done anything if you were being nice," I tease, playing with my fries. A loud clanging to my left jolts me from the conversation. I look to see a customer stationed at the host podium picking up their cellphone that fell onto the floor. The dial on my hearing turns up again, the voices a discord of notes. I turn back to Cole, who is watching me, and take a few breaths.

Looking into the calm storm in his eyes is more comforting than the back of my eyelids.

I don't want to know why I think that.

My body relaxes as the voices quiet and my ears focus only on the small space of our table.

Cole continues, "I guess I was nervous." We both laugh. He clears his throat, his expression hardening. "But at that moment, you were on my radar for being turned." He watches me intently, "After that, I did what any vampire would do. I followed you."

"You mean stalked?" I retort, flinching at the harshness in my tone. It is like a switch was flipped. Anger slips into curiosity.

Cole tilts his head, unaffected by my words. "Yes, basically. I was conflicted about it actually. I wanted to keep you safe, but being a vampire, I also wanted to kill you."

I shudder as my heart jumps in my chest. "Well, I'm thankful you had control."

"As am I," he agreed. "For a long time, I kept hidden from your awareness." A subtle tint of pink blooms on his cheeks. "I even followed you as you traveled." A shudder travels down my spine. All that time, and I never even noticed. "You stopped in a coffee shop the other day, and I followed you in." His voice lowers. "I tried to keep my distance from you actually, but I found it hard. So, I said, 'screw it', and decided to introduce myself. I started up a conversation with you and we actually talked for hours."

I chuckle. "Really? I don't remember speaking to each other." I push myself to the edge of the booth, eager to hear more. I watch Cole tell his story as if I were watching a movie. A part of me tingles as he speaks, like a forgotten page of an ancient text that holds crucial information. "What did we talk about?"

"Random stuff really. You mentioned your blog and I talked about traveling. We left the café together. You invited me into your trailer." He stops his speech, most likely because he sensed I would have a comment for that.

And he is right. "Did I really? No way, I would never." Even as the words left my lips, I knew that what he spoke was truth. A speck of some distant memory covered in a suffocating blanket of mist screams inside my mind to remember. I try to fight past the veil that covers the memories only to be met with a grinding headache.

A corner of his lips turn up. "You did."

I must have been really into him or just super trusting of strangers that night. Probably the former.

"I agreed, though I was actually super nervous. I didn't want to lose control and do something I would regret."

"Well, clearly you didn't, because I'm still here."

He frowns. "Actually, I did. We talked longer and got to know each other a bit more. We were telling stories and laughing. Your cat, Helios?"

"Yes," I affirm with wide eyes.

"He leapt onto my lap and fell asleep. Usually, cats hate vampires, but he seemed to relish in my attention. So, I savored in his affection. By the time that he awoke and ran off into the back of the trailer, we were on a sort of flirty conversation." A flush of heat creeps up my neck and cheeks. "At one point, we kind of just started kissing."

My eyebrows shoot up. "Oh my gosh, did we really?" I rub the space between my brows, hiding the embarrassment of not just my actions that night, but the image of my lips on his. They tingle pleasantly at the thought. Like they have the audacity to remember when my mind cannot. "Is that why you compelled me to forget?"

His jaw clenches. "No. It's actually because of what happened next. I lost control. I bit you without any kind of compulsion. And you were very terrified."

A shudder runs down my spine and a subtle sharp pain throbs in my neck. It is like my body remembers the scene, but my mind is still blind, shielded by that same misty shroud.

Behind our table, someone opens the shades of a window, illuminating the back of the restaurant. The sun's late afternoon golden glow reflects off a picture frame and beams into Cole's face. The blue in his eyes shines brighter in the soft sunlight. He squints and shifts in his seat to escape the light. "Once I realized what I had done, I stopped. You looked at me with such terror... you tried to escape." He swallows hard and leans his head back against the wall, looking at the ceiling before exhaling sharply. "But I didn't let you. So yeah, I erased your memory and cleaned the blood from your trailer," his voice is tinged with regret.

"Why didn't you just turn me then?"

"After what I had done..." his eyes fall to the table, boring a whole into the chipped wood. His body is tense. When his gaze returns to me, there is a piercing resolve in it. "I couldn't fathom hurting you again."

I point with my finger, not at anything in particular, as the memory resurfaces. Or, rather, as the memory of the images resurface. "I remember stopping at a coffee shop to post my blog while on the road back to town. I can't remember anything specific about that stop. One minute I was there and the next I was driving home. Other than that, I only recall images which made no sense at the time." I furrow my brows as Cole lifts his.

"What images did you see?"

I chew on the inside of my lip. "Gray eyes," my gaze flutters to his, "*your* eyes." His expression gives away nothing, so I continue. "A purple flower and a crimson teardrop stone on silver paper." I tap the table with my fingertips. "I don't think the stone was a stone at all, nor was it on silver paper. I think it was my blood and my silver trailer."

Cole contemplates for a moment before shrugging. "Possibly."

"But I don't understand the purple flower," I say before he finishes his sentence.

"It could be something insignificant. Visions are rarely to be interpreted at face value. And they rarely are anything to be concerned about. Strange though."

"What is?"

The corner of his lip lifts. "You were a human then. Humans don't tend to receive visions linked with time or the supernatural."

I stare at the coffee mug, not empty and cold in my hands. "Maybe I had magic before," I muse. A piece of the mug's bottom is chipped in a round shape with a miniscule crack going upward, catching my attention. I trace the imperfection as Cole says something across the table, though I don't hear him.

Remember.

The mug.

"What?" Cole asks. I must have said that revelation out loud.

"The latte I had at the coffee shop was lavender and in a purple mug. I remember because lavenders are one of my favorite flowers." Letting go of the mug, I return my hands to my lap and rub them on my pants. My mind didn't forget about the incident with Cole. It fought against his compulsion and created a series of images to try and help me remember.

Cole shakes his head. "You are just a box of mysteries, Thea."

"How so?"

He gives me a look that said, 'Do you really need to ask?' Holding up a finger, he states, "Your rare fire ability, which gives you protection from the sun. And vampiric compulsion is fairly ineffective to you as a human." He lifts another finger.

"I remembered some images, but I still couldn't recall any events," I observe.

"And that is more than ninety-nine percent of humans. There was another time that we met, before you graduated. Do you remember anything about that time?" A strand of his dark hair flutters in a light, imperceivable wind, resting just above his eyebrows.

A curious expression slips onto my face. "When?"

"We ran into each other by your college. It was at that little public restaurant on the campus." The café that students ran. It was always busy and had the most delicious coffee and eggs.

I chew the inside of my lip, trying to recall any memories. The only ones arising are the countless times I ate there with Sarah or alone before class. "I don't remember this. Did you know that I went there?"

"Yes, I knew that you attended that school, but I've been to that place to eat plenty of times before and have never seen you." He leans forward, resting his chin on his clasped fingers, elbows on the table.

"Maybe you just didn't notice me before," I tease, tucking some of my hair behind an ear. Cole watches the movement.

Without hesitation, he responds, "I would have noticed." My fingers stop mindlessly playing with my hair as I stare at him, his face impassive. "Of course you had no idea who I was when our eyes met. But our eyes kept meeting, and every time we would either look away or smile at each other."

His lips curve slightly at that. "So, as you finished with your meal, you got up, stopped at my table and, again, asked me if we knew each other."

Some distant part of my mind hums at that. The red and brown benches, a man sitting in one, and my uncharacteristic courage to talk to him. "I vaguely remember that. Images mostly."

He breathes deeply. "That is when I actually made my decision to turn you. For some reason, my compulsion was either wearing off, or didn't work completely, which is very strange. But I couldn't take the risk that you would remember." Cole reaches in his pocket to grab his wallet, placing some cash in the middle of the table. "Well, that, and I still couldn't stop thinking about you." Cue the annoying blushing. "The next time you saw me was at the coffee shop then when I turned you."

I involuntarily bring my fingers up to the spot on my neck where he bit me. Cole leans forward and puts his hands on mine, startling me with his quickness. "Thea, I know I have already said it, but I am so very sorry for not being able to ask for your permission first."

I bring one of my hands out from under his grasp and put it on top. "I know you are," I smile. "Stop worrying about it so much." Regardless of my reassurance, I can still see the worry in his eyes, masked by the upward curve of his lips. In hopes of changing his mood, I bring us back to the conversation beforehand. "So, out of curiosity, is there any way that you can restore my memories from my trailer? It would only be fair, considering you remember our kiss and I don't."

An enchanting smile curves his lips. "We could always make a new memory." Heat floods my body and Cole laughs. "I'm not sure if I could actually. I haven't ever tried, but I would suggest giving it a go when we are somewhere private. I just don't know what kind of emotions it'll bring on considering there were many different ones being experienced that night." He removes his hands from mine and stands. "Are you ready to go? If you have any more questions, I can answer them as we walk."

"Yeah, I'm ready." I follow suit and stand, shaking out my sweaty hands. "Thanks for lunch." We make our way toward the exit.

"Anytime," Cole responds, holding the door open for me. We are greeted with a slight summer breeze.

The afternoon sunlight caresses me like a silk wrap as we walk across the street, its warmth soaking into my cells. It shines endlessly in a clear blue sky. Children flutter around the park, chasing each other in and out of the tree line, their laughter contagious. Overhead, a pair of geese fly, their constant babbling filling the background. Cheery—that is the word I would use to describe this green space. It invokes the emotion when you enter it, rinsing away tightness that sits in your bones.

I calm my mind, searching for any questions I might not have gotten an answer for. "So, what is the deal with our magic? I get there is the elemental part, but what about the secondary abilities? What can other vampires do?" We cross the bridge again, this time toward the inviting forest. The smell of crisp leaves filter out of the conifer trees lined to indicate the start of the wooded area. The young couple is no longer sitting along the edge of the bridge.

"Well, psychic abilities, like I have, is a pretty common one. I've honed my skills, however, which most don't bother doing."

"Why? How have you honed them?" I mindlessly kick a stone out of the path and it splashes into the pond, sending ripples outward and scaring the fish.

He shrugs. "It is hard work." He looks around before picking up a pinecone and holding it on his open palm. The wind ceases and the forest quiets, like everything is watching. The pinecone shakes and lifts slightly off of his hand, bobbing in the open air.

I close my open mouth. "You're a Jedi." I laugh.

"Far from it." He chuckles as the pinecone soars through the air, landing at the base of a tall maple tree. The pleasant energy of the forest welcomes me again as we continue onward. It hums a sweet melody in my ears, mollifying the lurking fear and anxiety that swirls deep within my cage of emotions. My body relaxes a little when we cross the threshold.

"Just remember," he continues, "using our beta abilities takes its toll on us. There is a fine balance between using them and becoming exhausted and training them to be stronger." He raises his arm and runs his fingers along the smooth silver bark of a beech tree.

Mental note taken. "So, it is like a muscle." I watch him as he keeps brushing each tree that we pass, his touch gentle.

He shrugs. "I guess that's one way to think of it."

"Interesting," I say as I step over a small log covered in white mushrooms. "So, other than psychic abilities, and whatever mine is, what else is there?"

"Well, I'm not exactly sure what your abilities are yet. You healed a tree. That could just be a branch off of a different category of abilities. Pun intended."

I roll my eyes at his corny joke, a smile tugging at my lips.

"Some vampires can turn invisible for a brief moment of time, some can track sources of magic. I've known one who could make you see illusions as if they were real life and one who can read minds." He pauses for a moment, as if remembering the vampires who belong to these powers. "And I even knew a vampire who could turn into a bat." He grins and looks at me sidelong.

My eyes widen in amazement. "Really?"

A laugh rumbles from his chest. "No, not really." I punch his arm for testing my gullibility. "He could, however, jump so high that one would think he could fly."

"That would be cool." As a child, I would find myself observing birds, often losing track of time as I get lost in their dance with the wind and sky. I always imagined jumping into the air and being able to travel with them to new places, going wherever I wanted.

Cole nods in agreement as we continue walking. "So, I actually have some errands to run. I'll walk you to your apartment, then I'll head out."

I ignore the need to know what those errands entail.

"I can walk to my place alone. I don't mind." Cole opens his mouth to say something, but I interrupt. "Really, the walk alone would be good for me. I'll stay on the path." I need time to myself to digest all the information I have learned today.

He rubs his neck. "I don't know, Thea. It might not be safe."

"Do you sense anyone?"

He takes a moment to answer. "No."

I incline my head. "Then I should be fine. Plus, you are going to leave me alone in my apartment. What is the difference?"

He narrows his eyes. "That isn't helping."

"What is so terrifying about the Brais that I can't be alone out here anymore?" I open my palms to the trees and shrubs around us. The hum of the forest vibrates merrily through my body. Tendrils of pleasant warmth wrap around my skin. In the back of my awareness, I can sense the presence of that tree I healed. Its love radiates from the direction of my apartment, slithering across the distance in all the creatures who flock and scurry toward us. Little mammal feet plod against the leaf litter in all directions. Insect and bird wings flutter above and below. I feel a bond between everything and myself, like the forest and her creatures want to protect me.

He exhales roughly. "The Brais live by a code of mercilessness. Wherever they walk, death and destruction follow, damning anyone who stands in their way. To be a Brais means allowing those heavy and controlling emotions to rule over your actions and mind. They kill, Thea."

I shiver at his words. Just the thought of ending anyone's life, even by accident, is terrifying. Hunger stirs in my gut, but I shove it away with a deep breath of pine. The crisp, fresh air clears out the jumbled mess of emotions and sensations in my mind. I would never join the Brais.

Cole's dark hair is brushed away from his brow by a wind that I can't feel. He swallows hard before lifting his swirling eyes from the ground to mine. "Vampires they seek out either join them and kill others, or they refuse and are killed themselves."

I clench my jaw and search his face, taking a step toward him. "I will be okay." His gaze on me is intense, sending miniscule electric tendrils spreading across my body. I curl my toes and take a step back. It does nothing to release those sensations. "You don't sense anyone. I can feel the forest declare the same. There are no Brais out here."

He lifts his brow at that but loosens his shoulders. "Okay. Call me if you need me."

"Okay," I respond as I start to turn around.

"And Thea?"

"Yes?"

"If a Brais comes after you, do not hesitate to release your magic. Promise me." Though he is trusting my ability, his words are laced with unease.

"I promise," I confirm with unwavering confidence, despite the shakiness in my hands. I keep them clenched at my sides. The forest will keep me safe, I am sure of it.

I walk away from Cole, fighting the urge to turn around and have him accompany me again. I feel his warm gaze on me as I continue on, fading away only when I descend a small hill.

The journey back was quicker than I thought it would be. My feet unconsciously followed the dirt path while my mind roamed between thoughts of the distressing Brais and the comforting presence of the forest's aliveness. The setting sun has cast long shadows in the woods, broken up by bits of glowing, tawny light filtering through the leaves. As I approach the exit, a suffocating heaviness pours over me. Horrible and frightening.

Dread.

The hairs on the back of my neck tingle. The sensation briefly morphs into a thin line of pulsing pain before fizzling into a shudder down my spine. I hesitate before stepping out onto the cut grass that runs alongside the secluded parking lot of my apartment and pull my phone out of my pocket.

Leaves rustle behind me and I whirl around to see the auburn fur of a fox as he emerges from the dogwood bush. I blink at him as his golden eyes stare up at me and he sits.

The forest is watching over me. The unease from the parking lot fades away. I bow my head to the fox as I make my way to the tall brick building.

"Hello, Thea," says a smooth, unfamiliar voice from my left. I look and see a lithe woman dressed in black with tall boots. Her wavy shoulder-length pale hair is tucked behind her ears, a contrast to her dark skin. A wicked smile cuts across her cheeks. "The Brais send their regards."

Chapter 10

Frozen in place with my hand gripping the knob of the side door to the building, my heartbeat thunders in my chest. It echoes in the sudden silence of the forest. Her ruby eyes burn in the light of the setting sun. My body screams to move—to do something. Instead, I stand still.

The woman laughs as she takes a few more steps closer. "Struck by awe or by fear?" She sniffs the air, her smile broadening. "Fear." She glances down and jerks her head. "Your hands want your attention."

I follow her gaze, noticing the heat before I see the smoke. There is no fire, but my hands are melting the metal of the handle. I release my hold and see the charred mark of where it gripped the silver. I fumble back a step, returning my attention toward the vampire. She has gotten significantly closer and I suck in a gasp, inhaling her scent of the sea.

"What do you want?" I breathe.

"She speaks." Her voice is smooth. "I am here to offer you the chance to walk the path of power." She lifts a manicured brow. "I am Julietta. I would like to help you step into your true magical path. To become one with your element and to control it before it can control you." Her teeth shine as she smirks. "You have felt it's rising desire to let loose, no?"

"No."

She huffs. "So you haven't been battling any strong emotions, then?"

As she finishes her sentence, that gilded cage rumbles in my chest. Those emotions snarl as I give thought to them. I curl my hands into fists.

Her smile widens. "Join the Brais. We can help you control them. And you will never have to experience that fear again." Her hand motions to the doorknob.

I swallow hard. "No," I respond through clenched teeth.

Her nostrils flare and the smile on her lips falter. "There are no second chances with us."

"I will not join you," I say firmly.

"You choose death then."

I instinctively step back as she lifts her hands. Flames form around her palms and she throws them at me. I manage to twist my body so that the fireball only skims my arm. It grazes my skin like a nail. Only my body is steel. It leaves no mark, only tingles as its heat soaks into my body. I look up to see her dart forward with a sharp piece of wood in her hands.

A voice yells from the building. "Thea!" The vampire is forced backward by an invisible force. She lands on her back, skidding along the pavement. Sarah stands in the double glass doorway that leads to the lobby. She rushes to me, placing herself between the Brais vampire and myself. "Are you okay?"

I manage a nod.

"A witch?" the woman sneers as she stands.

Sarah's back straightens and she holds out a hand. In her palm is a circular talisman and herbs. The vampire stiffens and stops encroaching on us. "You know what this is. Leave and don't ever think about coming back for her. She will never join you."

"The King will not allow her to live then. She must join her own kind or it's the death penalty for her."

"I can join who I want." Fire sizzles underneath my palms.

Sarah lifts her hand higher and the vampire flinches. Her lips curl in rage as she slowly stands.

Behind us, I hear the scuffle of shoes on pavement stopping abruptly. I spin and see a man staring at us, his mouth agape. I recognize him as a neighbor who lives a floor down from me.

I open my mouth to yell for him to run but am too slow. The Brais vampire speeds to him and rips into his throat. Blood pours out of his neck. The cellphone he held and grocery bag crash onto the pavement. Crimson liquid runs down his teal cotton shirt like a waterfall. A gurgling sound escapes his lips.

Sarah says something, but I don't hear her. All I know is the blood of that man. Its enticing spicy aroma rumbles the volcano hidden deep within my body. A thread of tight wire forms between the human and I. My feet are pulled in that direction. Too slowly.

I need to feed.

A warm hand on my arm pulls me back as I take a step forward. I look down and follow the maple toned arm.

Sarah.

Family.

My teeth recede and the driving anger of hunger follows. It lingers though, forced to retreat and hide within that gilded cage.

Her honey eyes are unyielding as she focuses her raw power on the Brais. A chill runs down my spine as a ferocious wind blows from behind us. Sarah's arm stretches toward the vampire. The talisman and herbs radiate a pure white glow.

The vampire writhes and releases the man, who falls to the ground. She looks at Sarah with such hatred, her irises the color of blood. "You will die too if you choose to protect her." She snarls before latching onto the unmoving man with claw-like hands and darting into the forest at inhuman speed.

"No!" Sarah yells, reaching out as if she could grab the innocent human. A witch's speed does not compare to that of a vampire. The vampire is gone.

And so is the man. His belongings are scattered on the pavement. An apple had rolled out of the brown grocery bag.

Sarah bows her head into her hand. She turns and scans my body before wrapping her arms around me. "Are you sure you are okay?" Black curls are tied back in a messy bun that rests on top of her head. A few strands stick out in a wild fashion.

"Yes. Thank you." I lower my head, ashamed of not protecting myself or my neighbor. "I was frozen. I couldn't move. And when I saw his blood..."

"The Brais can pull those debilitating fears out of us," she says grimly. "And for you, they want to exploit your hunger. It is how the King controls his kind. They give in to the bloodlust and want only to consume more."

I sigh. Feelings of hopelessness blooming in my chest.

"It is not your fault," she assures, though her voice is sad.

I look to my friend and see plumes of pearl and cedar swirling around her in a dancing aura. I blink and they are gone. "He was a nice guy." I lower my head, guilt creeping in. "I didn't know him too well, but we had a few conversations. I haven't seen him since I left on my trip."

Sarah clenches her fists. "The Brais..."

When she doesn't finish her sentence, I look to her. Her face twists with both anger and grief.

"They need to be stopped," she whispers into the fading wind.

I remain silent with my head bowed. A frightening yet invigorating thought crosses my mind. I could fight them. Join Cole in the war he thrust me into. Obliterate the plague that is the Brais and their pension for destruction and death. A blooming heat rises in my hands as if in agreement.

A moment of silence passes between us. "What was that in your hand?" I ask solemnly.

She holds the items out in her open palm. A thin, golden coin rests in her palm. Similar to Cole's, except where his was rough and bordered by letters, hers is smooth and contains a leaf in the center. A dried herb with needle-like leaves sits beside it. "It is a talisman. All witches in the Minuit Coven possess one. With them, we can channel the power of all the coven witches. Most vampires would drop dead if we chose to use it against them."

My eyes round. "That is..."

She places a hand on my shoulder. "You don't have to worry about it."

"I was going to say that is awesomely terrifying. But thanks for putting that in my head." I rub my hands on my pants. Birds and crickets resume their songs in the trees, calming my nerves.

Sarah puts her things back in the small cross-body satchel strapped around her neck. "Sorry. You are part of my family. My mother and I wouldn't let them touch you."

I snap my head to her. "Did you tell Valeria about me?"

An apologetic look crosses her face. "I'm sorry. I came here to check on you again and your apartment was trashed so I got nervous."

"My apartment is what?" Before she can repeat herself, I dart toward the side building and up the stairs as fast as I can, my heart beating as loudly as my feet pound the dusty stairs. The Brais are making themselves very known. Get the weak newborns before they become too strong. The thought sends a new wave of panic down my spine.

"Please let Helios be okay," I pray out loud as I exit the staircase on the sixth floor. I approach my apartment at the end of the hall and feel the presence of my scared pet. His terror burns my nose as I open the door.

Nothing is where it should be. Most of the plants are knocked over, the dark colored soil spilling on the white rug and chestnut wood floor. The contents of my backpack are poured on the floor by the couch. Notebooks and papers thrown about, some torn. The doors to the refrigerator are left open, the bottom drawer pulled forward, stopping them from closing. I continue to scan the first floor. "Helios?" I call out with a shaky voice.

A tiny meow toward the living room drags me out of my fear. Helios crawls out from under the couch. He sees me and runs over, placing his front feet on my leg. I crouch and he jumps onto my lap, his eyes wide as he looks at me.

"I'm so sorry," I say into his tan fur as I hug him. Tears of both relief and sorrow well in my eyes. He rubs his head on my cheek and purrs. The vibrations meld into my body, settling my lingering worried nerves.

Footsteps from the hallway put me on alert and I stand, clutching my cat. Sarah opens the door and I huff out a relieved sigh. "My goddess you can run fast, Thea. I barely saw you take off," she pants. Her eyes fall on Helios. "I'm glad he is all right. I couldn't find him."

I put him down on the floor and he sits by ankle. The more I scan my apartment, the more things I see broken or turned upright. "What happened? Can you close the door?"

"Sorry," she repeats. She closes the door and takes a few steps back, inspecting the mess. "Well, we were supposed to hang out today, remember? And after I called a million times without an answer," she turns and glares at me, "I got really worried and came over. It was like this when I got here."

I roll my head back and rub my hands on my face. "That's wonderful." I tread to the door and lock it before turning to the coat rack, now lying on the floor, and restore it to an upright position. This was one of the first gifts I received when moving into my own place.

I glance to the balcony door and check that lock as well. Cole's mention of a vampire who could jump extremely high crosses my mind and suddenly, having so many windows in my house is disturbing. Any one of these floor-to-ceiling windows could be smashed and used to enter my apartment.

They would have to know exactly where my apartment is and jump from the busy street in front, I say to calm myself, pushing the anxiety away.

I clench my jaw as sweat beads down my back.

A roiling pain emerges in my stomach.

Hunger.

Sarah's still thumping heartbeat bounces in my ears and rumbles down to my abdomen. I feel the sharp points of my teeth poking at my bottom lip. I close my eyes and take a deep breath, trying to calm that part of me.

"So, you were outside today?" Her soft voice dances in the air, instantly easing the hunger that prods at my senses.

Family. She is family.

I clear my throat and walk to the refrigerator, hoping to find a blood bag inside. "Yes."

"How?" Her voice is laced with disbelief.

Unfortunately, there are no bags of red liquid inside the appliance. "I don't know. I just was," I huff, closing the drawer and door a little too hard. I look up to see her standing across the island counter, her arms crossed at her chest.

She narrows her eyes. "But the sun..."

"It didn't do anything," I snap. The anger spilled into my words before I could rope them back. I wince as I say, "I'm sorry."

She offers a sympathetic smile. "Don't apologize." Helios jumps up on the counter and presses his face against her arm. "How did you know you could go out in the sun?"

I run my fingers through my long hair. "By forgetting that the shades over there are broken. A stream of sunlight was shining into my bedroom and I stepped into it."

"That could have been really bad, Thea," she says, echoing Cole's warnings earlier.

"I know." I let out another sigh as I pick up a broken ceramic mug next to the sink. It was the red one I received from a friend last Christmas.

"That's a rare trait."

I blow out a breath. "Yeah, I also learned that my magic is fire based." I look sheepishly away. "I kind of exploded a dead log in the forest."

Sarah's head whips to mine, brows furrowed, and teeth clenched. "That's dangerous, Thea."

"I know."

She shakes her head. "No, you don't." I have never seen her this perturbed before. "It isn't dangerous because you could start a forest fire. It's dangerous because that is the element of the Brais." Her hand forms a fist as it lightly pounds on the counter, startling Helios. "They can smell your magic from miles away. You need to keep a low profile. So get your emotions in order!"

My eyes drift to the side, away from the scolding. "I will."

"Good." I peer over and see her in mid-motion of picking up the torn remnants of a notepad, her brows furrowed. "I'm sorry, Thea."

"For what?" I round the counter.

She picks at a clump of cat hair on her floral blouse, the golden colors matching her maple skin flawlessly. "Everything. The turning. The Brais..." The paper in her hand crinkles under her tightening grip.

"You have nothing to apologize for, Sarah."

She smiles sadly at that before resuming the notepad cleanup. Helios sits at the edge of the counter watching her, his tail flapping against the marble. "Did any other abilities manifest?"

I shrug before returning a rose plant to its wicker stand. "I healed a tree. Its branch was withering, and I poured magic into it and then it was lush again."

"What?" She rubs her fingers on her chin, glancing at the snake plant in front of her. "Are you sure?"

"Yes, why?"

"That sounds like energy manipulation," she chimes in wonder. "Almost like a witch's magic." There is a sparkle in her blue eyes.

"Energy manipulation allows healing?" I ask.

"Yeah. All bodies can heal themselves. You can just speed that process up. A witch's magic is similar, though we use incantations and objects for channeling."

Huh. "Interesting," I mutter, looking at my palms. This whole time I was worried that my fire magic would mean that I am destined for a life of destruction. But that is not always the case. Forests need fires to regrow, to heal, and to help seek out invading species.

Afterward, they help each other heal and start anew. The magic inside me tingles as if it is happy with this realization.

"That's pretty amazing, Thea."

I open my mouth to agree, but the smell of blood fills my nose. So subtle, it could have been easy to miss. I freeze, trying to locate the scent in my home.

"Thea? What's wrong?" Sarah's worry breaks my distracted mind.

I slowly turn, scanning the living area and kitchen. "Did you go upstairs?"

"Yeah, briefly," she answers with confusion. "Why?"

"Because I smell blood." She stiffens, her eyes widening with worry. I make my way toward the stairs with Sarah close behind. My jade plant is tipped over and I quickly assess it for any broken parts. *You can heal it, remember?* I remind myself. That would have been helpful with a few troublesome plants that I have had in the past.

At the bottom of the staircase, I swallow hard, pulling all the nerves in my body to continue onward. Sarah places a reassuring hand on my back. The bedroom is dark since no lights are on, and the shades are closed. I can see fine, but I wonder how Sarah manages in a lightless area. All the furniture, decorations, and miscellaneous things appear to be in their rightful places. "I wonder why downstairs is a mess, but up here is untouched."

Sarah shrugs. "Minus the smell of blood?" She remains protectively close as we move the few feet to the bathroom door. It is intact, just like the bedroom. The smell becomes less prominent.

I shake my head. "It is definitely coming from that side of the room." I scan the area as we trudge to the other side of the bed. Something feels off. Putting my detective glasses on—as Sarah used to call it, because I could always find missing items when we were younger—I look from the bed, to the nightstand, and finally to the window. I cock my head, realizing that the blinds are open a few more inches than where I left them. "Did you open those blinds when you came up here?" My voice lowers to a whisper, as if someone could be hiding behind them. I shudder at the thought.

"No," she grimaces, her heartbeat quickening. It echoes in the silence, my own beating equally as fast.

"I left that closed before I left." We creep closer, still wary about someone popping out. I think back to Cole's joke earlier about a vampire who could turn into a bat. Then my horrible brain thinks about those who could turn invisible.

Nope. Will not allow myself to entertain that thought anymore.

"This is definitely where the smell is strongest," I murmur, pulling the string down. The setting sun gleams through the top of the windowpane. Blood, used as ink, stains the glass in a symbol. It is painted in the shape of a Swiss shield—an oval with three points at the top and one on the bottom. In the center it is signed with the letter 'B'. A cold shiver slides down my spine. Sarah gasps and we both step back.

"That's the symbol for the Brais," Sarah says gravely. "It means they're coming."

Chapter 11

I take a deep breath to calm my growing nerves. I haven't even let the fact of the Brais' existence sink in yet, and here they were. At my home. Destroying my things. Or perhaps looking for something. Or for me. A shiver runs down my spine and I shrug the terrifying thought away.

Cole needs to know about this—it was only a matter of time before they knew about each other. "Sarah," I say, sighing. "I'm sorry, but I have one final secret to fess up about."

"What is it?" she asks.

I tell her everything. From the events this morning to our lunch this afternoon. She remains calm, her face soft during my story.

"Who is he?" There is no anger in her voice. Sometimes I manage to forget how understanding and full of love she can be.

I clench my jaw. "His name is Cole," I say, tapping my fingers to keep my nerves busy. I could have sworn I saw her body tense slightly. "I know you told me to be careful, just in case the one who turned me is a Brais, but I really don't believe that he is." I pause, letting the information sink in. "I should really call him about this." I wave at the blood and gesture to the mess downstairs.

She puts her hands in her pockets. "I agree. If you trust him, then I will try as well. But I do want to meet him, and don't expect me to be kind to him. He saved you, yes. And I am so grateful for that. But he also brought you into the vampire world during the worst time in history."

I consider challenging her but refrain. Her words are not comforting in the slightest. A reminder of my current life issues was not necessary. "Thanks," I mutter.

We plod downstairs and I grab my phone from the kitchen counter, dialing his number.

He answers after the first ring. "Missed me already?" I hear his smirk over the phone as he chuckles.

"Cole, something happened."

"What's wrong?" he asks, his voice a mixture of worry and intrigue.

"The Brais have contacted me in more than one way. I met Julietta. And they have been to my apartment. It's trashed." We stand in silence for a moment. The only sound on his end is the faint murmur of voices, like a busy city block, though he stands a distance away. When he doesn't answer, I say, "Cole?"

"Don't leave. They may be waiting outside. I'll be right there." He hangs up before I can ask him about his own safety.

"He's on his way," I say, putting my phone back down. I glance at her and see that she is trying to fight a smile but fails, a light twitch at the corners of her lips. "What?"

"You know you blushed when you spoke to him?"

I clear my throat and turn away, sitting down in one of the chairs at the island counter. One of the few items I recovered from the estate sale at my family's home. These and the bedframe upstairs. "You know, this morning he informed me that he and I have met before." A detail I left out of the story earlier.

"Really? When?" She sits in the chair next to me.

I caught her up on my unmemorable history with Cole while we waited for him to arrive. Helios sits by the small window by the stairs, soaking in the last of the sun's light.

"The Essites King does not permit humans to know about vampires," she says grimly, picking at a crumb on the counter, after I mentioned Cole finally deciding to turn me. "He doesn't like to take chances either. Unless they plan to go through the transition, that is."

"He did try to compel me. But I guess it didn't totally work."

She casts her eyes downward. "They don't *allow* humans to know about vampires, Thea. They either turn or are killed. He put you in danger!" Her hand on the counter tightens in a fist.

A shiver creeps down my spine. "God, I know. But he also saved me from the accident."

She closes her eyes momentarily, the sound of her heart is a steady rhythm in the quiet of the apartment. "I guess thinking of the situation this way makes me glad that he turned you instead of the alternative." Her gaze drifts blankly like her mind is far away. The haunting of a future that could have been.

"Cole told me that the Essites King was killed recently."

"What?" She snaps her head and stiffens. "I overheard my mom mention that they lost touch with him. Not that he died." A knock on the door interrupts her and she snaps her mouth shut.

I put a reassuring hand on her shoulder as I get off the chair and make my way to the door. Cole smiles slightly as I gesture for him to enter. He wears a new set of clothes, not the blood-stained shirt and stolen sweatshirt from the hiker. A gray light jacket covers his torso. His short onyx hair is curled outward in a mess, indication that he may have ran here.

"I didn't think you even knew how to knock," I tease. He snorts, his mouth opening to retaliate but refrains once his eyes meet Sarah's. "Cole, this is Sarah, my best friend." I gesture my hands between them, "Sarah, this is Cole."

Neither of them move to shake hands. The room is suddenly filled with a heavy awkward silence as a thick red curtain of tension wraps around both of them. I blink and the color is gone, leaving me wondering if I imagined it.

After a moment, Sarah stands from her chair and leans an elbow on the counter, her face twisted in a scowl. "The vampire who ended my best friend's life."

Cole blinks at her, surprise written on his face. He recovers smoothly, his stiff back loosening slightly. "Yes, well, I truly am sorry. And—"

"And he already apologized to me," I interrupt, my eyes like slits toward Sarah. I don't want to have this conversation again with either of them. "What's done is done." Cole's expression softens, but Sarah's remains hard, her glare still fixed on him. "Cole, I'm sorry, I told her everything," I add sheepishly, as if I should be embarrassed for confiding in her. "I couldn't keep anything from her anymore. And Sarah is..."

"A witch," she finishes with eyes like fire.

He huffs quietly and clenches his jaw, assessing her. "I see. I sensed some magic around you."

Her narrowed, hazel eyes scan him. A muscle feathers in her lips like she wishes to scowl at him but knows that I am watching. "Then you would be wise to do all you can to keep her safe. *Safer.*"

Cole opens his mouth, but I step between them and he shuts it. "Sarah, please." Her hard expression falters as I stand in her eyesight. I look to Cole. "Can we move past this for now?"

"Right. All is well," Cole says shortly before Sarah can respond. "I did bring you something this time." I watch as he reaches into the inside pocket of his jacket and pulls out a small bag filled with the red liquid I have come to love. My eyes settle on the bag, igniting that roaring in hunger. That familiar, gnawing raw tightness spreads into my limbs. Eagerness seeps into my movements as I take the bag from him.

I turn to Sarah, ripping my gaze from the contents of the bag. "If you're not comfortable with me drinking this in front of you, I can wait." *No, you can't. You need this now*, my subconscious whines. I push the thought away, desperately willing it not to come back. As much as I want to tear into the bag now, I refrain.

She pulls away from her one-man-stare down with Cole and turns to me, her expression kind. "No, I don't mind, Thea. You can drink it now if you need it."

If you need it. I always *need it.*

Sarah walks to the fridge and pulls out a glass bottle of iced tea. The cap pops as she twists it open while I pull off the top of the blood bag and take a small sip, closing my eyes as I swallow—as if blocking the sight of what I am consuming will help with my control. A buzz of energy hums throughout my entire body, responding to the nutrients.

I lower my hands, not wanting to give Sarah a bad impression about my self-control. It takes every ounce of that control to not devour the contents.

"So, you said the Brais were in your apartment?" Cole breaks the silence, his expression serious, though I can see the concern behind them. He knew that I would appreciate the distraction.

"Aside from the place being a complete mess—" I gesture to the apartment.

Cole lets out a low whistle as he scans the area.

"There is blood on my window upstairs." I point to the bedroom. "Sarah says it is the symbol for the Brais."

Cole turns to the stairs to assess the window. He stops walking, pauses for a brief moment, and swivels back to look at Sarah. "How would *you* know what the Brais' symbol looks like?" His voice is laced with a subtle poison. "Witches usually keep to themselves." He cocks his head slightly, taking a few careful steps forward.

Sarah pushes off the fridge into a standing position as if she was waiting for a fight. I flick my eyes between the two of them, ready to stop one if needed.

"You mean you don't see a resemblance?" She snorts at him. "You know my mother."

Cole stares at her for a moment, his eyes narrow. The moment he realizes who she is, they widen. "Valeria." He lets out a barely audible laugh as he brings his attention down to his feet. "You are Valeria's daughter," he adds, his eyes once again meeting hers.

She smiles coldly at him. "Yep, I sure am."

As if her being Valeria's daughter has anything to do with her knowing the Brais. Something I intend to ask her about when Cole isn't around. A stranger in the room would be able to tell that a history exists behind their words. Not a good one either. The air is dense with unpleasant emotions. Someone needs to break this stare down before it gets out of hand.

"Can we just put the unhappy reunion aside for one minute and figure out what the Brais were doing in my home?" I say, glancing at both of them. Sarah's demeanor is calm and collective, which only adds to Cole's defensiveness.

He is the first to break eye contact as he turns to me.

"Yes, I suppose that would be best." His voice sounds odd, like a different person. I make a mental note to find out what happened between Cole and Valeria, so I can try and remedy the problem. I can't have these two at each other's throats. I need both of their help.

Sarah finally breaks her gaze from Cole and looks to me. "Sounds like a smart idea." She offers an apologetic smile, knowing that I did not enjoy that little exchange of words in the slightest. She straightens and pulls her black hair out from the scrunchie. It falls past her shoulders, framing her round face.

"I'll go take a look at the symbol," Cole says as he quickly turns on his heels and walks up the stairs.

I look to Sarah who is still standing near the island counter by the fridge. "So you two know each other?" I ask, taking another sip from the blood bag.

Sarah watches me take the sip, unfazed. She shrugs. "I'm sorry, but he and my mom have known each other for a long time, and they don't exactly like each other." She looks away, as if declaring the end to the conversation.

I, however, am not done. I continue drinking, slowly draining the contents of the bag. I keep my gaze on Sarah, encouraging her to keep explaining.

"Listen," she continues, "I promise we will talk about it. I just don't think that now, with all that's happening, is the best time." She motions her hands wildly at my mess of an apartment.

"I think we both can be civilized enough and talk to her about it." Cole chimes in as he comes down the stairs and strolls into the kitchen area. We both turn to look at him as he puts his phone back into the pocket of his jeans. "I took a few pictures and sent them to Juan, a trusted friend of mine. He will be able to tell which *lackey* of the Brais King wrote the symbol."

One of Sarah's eyebrows raise. "How so? Isn't there just one symbol for the Brais?"

Cole tilts his head from side to side. "Essentially, yes. But to the trained eye, each of the King's Generals has their own little twist on the symbol. It's hard to tell, but this friend of mine managed to learn all their trademarks." He stops at the island counter, resting a hand on the granite, his demeanor more relaxed than it was a few moments ago.

"That sure sounds like a fascinating hobby," Sarah replies. They both laugh in response, sharing a bemused look. Sarah clears her throat. "So what will figuring out who wrote it have to do with why they were here?"

Cole frowns. "The Brais believe that all fire users are obligated to be within their ranks. We need to know who is trying to recruit her into the Brais. Each tracker has their own method, some more sinister than others." His fingers tighten in a fist, nails digging into skin. He looks to me. "I told you before that vampires can sense the unlocking of a Kindria's magic. They sensed you as a fire wielder. Probably a strong one too, because it didn't take long for them to show their motives."

"Why'd they come here? Why not just go straight for her?" All of Sarah's anger toward Cole vanishes, replaced by concern for me. If concern for my safety is what gets them to behave, then so be it.

Cole takes off his jacket and places it on the back of a chair at the counter. He wears a short-sleeved cream-colored shirt that exposes his muscled arms and the whirls of a tattoo on his bicep. "The Brais like to frighten their targets. Some trackers have more advanced abilities than others. By the looks of it, this one may have traced where you've been prior to igniting the log."

My mind races to every place that I have recently been to, every person that I have been with. Valeria's house is the only place in town after arriving from my trip. Witnessing Sarah's ability to ward off that Brais earlier soothes a bit of the nerves growing at the thought of them going after Valeria. Still...

Cole's voice breaks into my worried thoughts. "They found you quickly, so he or she also has to be a strong wielder."

"Why do I get the sense that being strong is not always as fun as it would be in the movies?" I hold my breath, hoping that what I am thinking doesn't come out of Cole's mouth.

He sighs. "Because in their eyes, if you are strong, they either recruit you or mark you as an enemy."

Dammit.

I swallow back a nervous gulp. "And I'm assuming they don't particularly like their enemies living, right?" Cole nods, confirming my fear.

Double dammit.

When I was little, I feared death. I feared it to the point that I would wake up from nightmares screaming. After the car accident that took my parents' lives, I begged for death. I was devastated and wanted to be with them again.

Sarah steps up to the island counter, her eyes narrow in determination. "But we both are here to make sure that doesn't happen." She balls her hands into fists, one on the counter and the other at her side. She looks to Cole. "Right?"

He meets her stare. "Of course." When he looks to me, I see a kind warmth in his eyes. It reminds me of those moments he appeared in my dreams. "I would never let anything happen to you, Thea." I smile back at him, my stomach fluttering.

The fluttering morphs into a tinge of dizziness that spreads to my head. "I'm exhausted," I say as I lean against the counter. The setting sun behind me casts long shadows in my apartment. Our humanoid figures contort against the white tile of the front wall and oak kitchen cabinets.

"You spent a lot of energy today," Cole states. "No matter which vampire is after you, I don't think it would be very safe to stay here tonight." He takes his phone out of his pocket and checks the screen. Unsatisfied, he looks at Sarah, "She would be safe at your house for a while."

My friend shakes her head, sadness looming over her eyes. "I'm sorry, Thea. Vampires are not allowed in my house. My mom ensured that by placing sigils around it that prevent them from entering. It would take days to change or nullify it." She looks frustrated with the thought. "You know I wouldn't hesitate if I could help."

I finish the bag of blood and drop it into the trash can next to the fridge, offering her a smile as I return to the counter. "I know, it's okay." She manages a weak smile in return. I look to Cole, who's facial expression is unreadable. "Want a new roommate for a bit?" I say with a bit too much eagerness.

A corner of his lips quirk up. "I would be delighted." He playfully bows his head.

My cheeks flush. "The pleasure is all mine."

Sarah clears her throat.

I turn to her, my cheeks heating. "Will you come, too?" I don't bother looking to Cole for permission.

"Absolutely. I will never leave you." She turns to face Cole and inhales loudly. "I'm sorry I acted the way I did earlier. I've known Thea almost my entire life and couldn't bear the thought of a vampire taking advantage of her." She takes a few steps toward him and offers a hand. "I believe your intentions with her are not corrupt and I don't carry the grudges of my mother. Truce?"

Cole extends his hand and shakes hers. "Truce." He smiles. "Trust me, I will do everything in my power to not let anything else happen to her." I look out to the balcony, the burning sensation of a reddening face making itself known. The setting sun produces bright auburn and rosy colors that dance across the sky.

"All right, let's go. We shouldn't stay here too long, it doesn't feel safe." I turn back to face them and nod at her warning.

"Agreed. Just let me grab a pack quickly."

"Don't forget the totem I gave you," she calls as I run to my bedroom.

"I won't." At the top of the stairs, I pull out the blue duffel bag that I keep under my desk, proceeding to stuff it with a few t-shirts, a couple pairs of jeans and the necessities from the bathroom. I examine myself in the mirror, noting how just the other day I was human, doing the same thing. Nothing looks different on the outside. My straight, long brown hair still falls around my pale cheeks and reaches my chest. My hazel eyes still a beautiful mix of brown and green. I force my vampiric features out, my pulse quickening as they appear. Colors become more defined and vibrant. No longer are my eyes a mix of my favorite colors, instead they are a deep currant shimmering in the light. The lethal fangs are hard to miss as they stick out from my upper lip. I close my eyes and feel them retract. My human-looking self stares back at me when I open my eyes.

The blinds on the window by my bed are fully open, the symbol taunting me. Luckily, there are no other buildings high enough to see it on this side of the street. Only the forest below has witness to the new threats in my life. My mind races to everyone who could be in danger because of me: my driver, Valeria, and of course Sarah and Cole. What if the Brais gets to them in order to get to me? I shake my head, pushing those thoughts away.

I stash my emergency bag of money into the duffle bag and grab my mother's pendant. I'm not sure how long I will be at Cole's house, but I don't want to take the chance of losing the necklace. I stare at the beautiful azure lapis lazuli stone carved into a crescent moon. When she gave it to me, I was young and couldn't care less about the piece of jewelry. Now that I am older, and she's gone, I cherish it.

"Do you need help?" I hear Cole yell from the kitchen.

"Nope, I'm ready," I call back as I return to him and Sarah. When I waltz into the kitchen, Sarah is looking at her phone by the door and Cole is examining the photos on my fridge. Most of the pictures are memories of Sarah and I during our annual music festival trips. A photo of my parents on their wedding day is plastered at eye level, their wide smiles and twinkling eyes melts my heart. I place Helios in his carrier and walk to the door with him and my bag. "All right, let's go."

After Cole closes the door behind us, I pull out my keys and lock it. He looks at me with one eyebrow arched. "What? I know this won't keep the Brais out, but you never know who else might try to break it."

He shrugs, offering to take the cat carrier, as we begin our descent to the lobby. "I get it. It's just funny because I do the same thing."

The lobby is quiet. The only sound inside comes from the buzz of the elevator. "I'll drive," Cole offers.

"No, let's walk," I suggest. "If that is okay with you two." In truth, since that first car accident, I have always been a little fearful of vehicles. This recent one has just solidified that fear.

"Sure, Thea," Sarah says.

"It could be dangerous," Cole states as we exit the building. Outside, the stars poke through the dimming sky. Vehicles are parked in almost every spot. "The Brais could be waiting."

"I think between the three of us, we could take them," Sarah boasts.

Cole snorts. "That's ignorant thinking." He looks to me and closes his mouth. Whatever expression I had on my face must have made him change his mind because he says, "Let's walk. But be on alert." He grabs my bag from my shoulder, adjusting his hold on Helios. "I can carry this for you too."

"Thank you, it's not that heavy though."

Slipping the bag over his shoulder, he says, "Yeah, but I don't mind. It's the least I could do." The forest that we trudged through earlier today stands dark in the descending sunlight. Cole turns to the right and walks on the sidewalk of the narrow street that leads away from the town. Even walking parallel to the forest, I can feel the energy it emits. I feel like it is calling me into the trees, whispering dark, enthralling words. I step closer to Sarah, wary of all the emotions it is sending me. This morning I felt peace and life coming from the woods. Now there are other feelings—sinister, menacing ones—creeping through.

"Everything okay?" she asks.

I shrug. "I'm not sure. This morning the forest felt pleasant, but now it feels obscure somehow. I follow closely as he crosses a quiet street onto another one. A few houses are spread sporadically along the road. I notice Cole's eyes are up and scanning our surroundings.

"It could be the Brais' magic," he points out. "They poison anything good, leaving only misery and death." His voice is quiet, causing a chill to run down my spine. We continue to walk in silence, both consumed by our frightful thoughts. The farther we get from the part of the forest by my apartment, the better I feel, which doesn't ease my soul as much as I'd like it to. Cole turns onto a dead-end street that leads into the woods and stops. "Are you okay to continue? My house isn't that far into the forest."

"I'm fine. The feeling has lessened quite a bit, actually."

He frowns. "I was afraid of that. I don't think they were too far from your house. Probably just waiting for the sun to set completely."

"Do they not have sun totems?" I shudder at the thought.

"The Brais has a hierarchy and only gift sun totems to those who are higher up on the command chain," he answers. "Come, we are almost there." He walks again, down the shady street. I'm grateful for my vampire sight, otherwise he would have a hard time dragging me farther, because it soon became very dark. The sun's last rays have a hard time penetrating the tall, full coniferous trees.

"Sarah, can you see in this?" I turn to look at her and startle backward at a green glow in her eyes.

"Yes, I have a spell that allows me to see in the dark. Sorry, I should have warned you."

"That's cool," I say after a laugh.

We finally reach a small clearing about a mile past the end of the street. Sitting comfortably under the open canopy is Cole's small, one story, square log cabin complete with a wrap-around porch. What appears to be a vehicle is covered underneath a blue tarp. Stones are gathered to keep it from blowing away. A stack of dried logs is piled high against the south side of the house.

Sarah huffs. "This is a nice space."

"Thanks," he replies softly. "It isn't much, but I like it." We walk toward the front of the house that faces east. A green door sits to the right of the wall which he unlocks and pushes open. With a brief loud squeak, the door opens, revealing the familiar interior. Cole closes the door behind us and places my bag on the couch and Helios on the floor.

I bend to open his carrier and he darts out, his fluffy tail out straight behind him. "Sorry I keep shuffling you around, boy." He ignores me and tentatively sniffs surfaces around the house.

"This is a lot cozier this time around," I say to Cole in appreciation. I could definitely get used to staying here. The thought of living with Cole excites my childish feelings as butterflies dance in my stomach. I shift away before he notices.

He winces. "Sorry... and thanks. Let me show you where everything is, Sarah."

I follow behind Sarah as Cole leads her through his space. The kitchenette consists of a few feet of counter space, a sink, an oven, and a small fridge. The wooden floor from the living room turns into a tan tile as we enter the new room. "So, this is obviously the kitchen. I don't really cook that much, so the size is perfect."

The L-shaped open floor plan ends with a small dining room to the left of the kitchen. A simple, two-person table with chairs sits in the corner by the back door. "And someone who doesn't cook much has no real need for a big dining table, either." He looks around the room and shrugs. "That's the bathroom." A door sits across from the kitchen. "It is also a small room."

"I sense a theme here. Small house, small rooms. Do you spend a lot of time here?" I tease.

"Not particularly. I enjoy my place, but I prefer to be outside." Another door off the dining room sits across from the one leading to the backyard. "That's my bedroom," Cole adds, walking over and opening the door for us to peek in. A queen-sized, wooden bed sits against the wall that separates this room from the living room. As with the rest of his décor style, the bed has a cherry frame with a green comforter sitting atop it. "You two can sleep in here." Across from the bed is a small dresser covered in books, cologne, and a gun.

Sarah sits on the bed, running her hand along the comforter. "I'm going to use the restroom before bed," she says through a yawn.

"Okay." I watch her remove her satchel and place it on the bed before exiting. "A gun?" I ask Cole as he returns to the room with my bag. Helios followed him in and jumps on the mattress and curls up.

"Just precautions. I like to be prepared for anything, you know?" He walks to the dresser, grabs the gun, and places it in the top drawer. "It has wooden bullets."

I tilt my head back in understanding, even though I'm not sure that I do.

Cole stands against his dresser, watching me with a longing stare. I hold his gaze, ignoring the quickening pulse in my chest. I admire the way his obsidian hair falls into his face, half covering his smokey eyes. A bit of stubble texturizes his features, and I picture myself tracing his chin with my fingers. His alluring gaze slowly traces the length of my body before returning to mine, a sexy half grin on his face. A muscle feathers in my cheek, not wanting to give in to the tension.

He lets out a slow, deep breath. When he speaks, his voice is husky, "You should get some rest. We can get out first thing in the morning and train some more." He starts toward the door. When he walks past me, I can sense his desire, mixed with the soothing scent of earth and cedar.

No, no, no. I can't think of him in a romantic way. There is too much going on right now.

The shower is turned on.

And Sarah is here.

I nod, keeping my lips closed. I'm not sure what would come out if I opened them.

"Goodnight, Thea."

"Goodnight, Cole."

At the click of the closed door, I let out the breath that is lodged in my throat. This man is absolutely stunning. He seems like a character from a romantic storybook, too perfect. Perfect is something I don't usually trust.

But it is hard to fight the desire inside me. The flame that yearns for the wind, desperate for a forward leap. One that consumes all in its path, destruction and rebirth in one fearless bound.

Why did the fire choose me? I am not fearless. Images of the tree I healed flash in front of me. I gave that tree a new start, a fresh beginning, free from the disease that ensnared it.

A rebirth.

I stare at the ceiling, wrapping my brain around life. Around *my* life.

I am fire. Destruction and chaos.

I am life. Healing and renewing.

I fall asleep before Sarah returns from the bathroom. Images of fire, a burning sun, and a devilish grin float in my sleeping mind.

Chapter 12

*W*arm, glistening rays of the morning's sun shines into the bedroom. My eyes slowly peel open. I fell asleep on the farthest side of the bed, closest to the window that peers into the front yard. Outside, a blue sky stretches far, promising a clear day. I focus on my ears, listening for Cole to no avail. Either my vampiric hearing hasn't woken up yet or he is silent. I roll over to check on Sarah. There is only an empty side. Still in my clothing from yesterday, I saunter across the cold floor around the bed to my duffle bag. I pull out my favorite loose oatmeal-colored tank and a pair of distressed jeans. My eyes catch the full body mirror by the door.

Yikes.

Strands of my long brown hair are sticking out in each direction. I reach into my bag in search for my hairbrush before cursing to myself. It was on my nightstand back home and I have forgotten to grab it. I huff as I run my fingers through the untamed locks. I guess it was only a matter of time before Cole saw my crazy morning hairdo.

"Cole? Sarah?" I shrug, wondering where they are, as I make my way to his fridge. When I lived with Sarah, she would often wake up early, find a spot outside and watch the sun rise.

I need blood. I clutch my rumbling stomach and search the contents of the shelves, sighing at their emptiness. Only apples, grapes, water bottles, and bread are inside. As I close the door to the fridge, the front door opens, and I turn to see Cole walking into his home. He smiles when he sees me.

"Good morning," he grins. "I like your hair."

I embarrassingly brush it again with my fingers.

He laughs. "Stop, it looks fine."

I scowl at him. "Where is Sarah?" I look around, noting the absence of my friend and cat. The couch is bare, save for the folded green plaid blanket on the back. Burnt logs rest in the stone fireplace next to it. "And Helios?"

At the mention of his name, I hear four little feet thump on the floor behind me. Helios waltzes out of the bathroom licking his lips. "I'm sorry. I never got you a bowl of water."

"I actually already did that," Cole chimes in as I grab a small ceramic bowl from the counter. "Food and water. But he kept trying to drink from the faucet in the bathroom."

"Oh," I respond, putting the bowl back, before turning to Cole with a grateful smile. "Thank you." My eyes flicker to the still open front door. "What are you doing, inviting the forest creatures into your home?" I giggle.

He returns the laugh and shakes his head. "Nope, I've got a present for you. I figured you would be hungry, and I finished the last blood bag this morning that I had stored here, so I went out to get you something."

My eyebrows raise, intrigued. The rumbling in my stomach turns into a subtle stabbing pain and I clench my jaw.

Cole turns his attention out the door and gestures to the living room with his hand. A short, bulky man wearing a blue heavy flannel, jeans, and hiking boots cautiously walks into his house. The man's piercing blue eyes are filled with fear when they meet mine, which have already changed to a darker, redder color. Everything around me blurs as I concentrate on the man walking in to the living room, his tanned skin vibrant against the bright hues of his clothes.

Cole's voice breaks into the honed focus my senses hold on the human. "I had to compel him to come in here, too frightened otherwise."

"I couldn't fathom why," I say, sympathizing with the man. I try to hold on to that emotion as the smell of fear and the sound of his heartbeat fill my senses.

"Walk over to her," Cole commands. The hiker does as he says, taking short, slow steps in my direction. When the hiker stops in front of me, I can hear his heart pounding against his ribcage. His eyes never leave mine, they fill with a fear so intense that it overwhelms the sound of his pulse, which only makes me hungrier. My teeth slowly elongate, pushing against my lower lip. The man's eyes widen even more as he takes in the face of a dangerous being.

I hold his arm with my right hand and pull his head slightly with my left, exposing his neck. My heartbeat matches his as I try to take control of my ravaging hunger. My body urges to lunge, but I ignore it as I bring my teeth closer to him. He smells of the freshness of a forest and the crisp morning air. I feel him wince underneath my grasp as I break the skin on his neck. The euphoria from the nutrients fill my body and I close my eyes to embrace it. The grip I have on his arm remains loose, letting Cole know that I have not given in to the dangerous bloodlust. The pains in my stomach dissolve the more I drink. After a few moments of bliss, I feel my throat close. Pins and needles stab at me from all over. Immediately, I release the man's arm and start coughing.

Cole rushes over and steadies my wobbling body. "What's wrong?"

I look at him with fright and point to my throat, unable to speak. The searing pain flows to my stomach, rivaling that of hunger. My legs tremble as their strength gives out. Cole slowly brings me to the floor, his warm hands on my back an anchor to consciousness. He glances at my neck and a worried expression fills his face. My throat feels like it is closing, and I gasp for air. He bites his wrist, blood trickles from his wound.

"Drink, it should heal whatever you ingested." His voice shakes as he places his wrist to my mouth. I look at him with uncertainty before doing as he says. Only a couple gulps manage to get down before I feel it coming back up. As I turn my head to the side, I choke as his blood splatters on the cold floor.

The hiker stands at my feet, watching as I struggle to breathe. No longer are his eyes laced with fear. Instead, he glares at me with power before turning his attention to Cole. "Your blood will not save her here."

Cole jumped when the stranger spoke. He turns to the hiker, anger consuming his body. Slowly, he rises to meet his gaze and motions to grab him in a deadly grapple.

Before Cole has a chance to do anything, the hiker says in a mechanical tone, "Killing me will only kill her."

Cole freezes.

"A Joining spell. If I die, so does she."

"Get away from her!" Cole yells. The hiker doesn't even flinch. Instead, he turns as if on a dial and marches to the couch. Cole turns his attention back to me as I shake and grab my throat, as if that will unblock whatever is preventing my airflow. As he kneels beside me, grabbing his phone out of his pocket and dials a number.

"*Allo*," an unfamiliar female's voice answers.

"It's Cole. I need to cash in on that favor you owe me." His gray eyes don't leave mine as he places my head on his leg. Darkness seeps into the edges of my vision and my breathing staggers.

"When?"

"Right now. Come to my house, the door is open." He hangs up. "Please stay with me, Thea."

I cling to the sound of his voice and the touch of his hands as they brush a lock of hair from my face. The air around me grows thick. My eyelids are so heavy, fighting their inevitable close becomes tiresome.

"Thea!" Cole's voice startles me back to the present. "Don't close your eyes. Help will be here."

As if on cue, the front door squeaks open. A tall, square-faced, burgundy-haired woman enters the kitchen area. She wears a velvety, long claret coat with knee-high, glossy black boots. Gesturing to me, she says, "Is this your problem?" A strong Russian accent envelope her words.

"Yes. She fed off a human with a Joining spell and had a reaction." His gaze moves to my neck and chest. "These lines look like some sort of dark magic."

The mysterious woman peers at me, her silver-blue eyes holding some unreadable emotion. "*Da*. This is what you want to use your favor on?"

"Yes."

The room feels as though it sits in the arctic. I shiver as my body shakes. Nausea threatens me and I try to curl up. Cole's strong grip prevents me from moving. I focus on the warmth of his body and the fading sound of his voice.

Her ruby lips press into a thin line as she pulls off her black leather gloves. She reaches her hands above my face and I feel a pleasant, tingling energy wash over me. A strange mix of words and sounds vibrate from her mouth. Suddenly, my vision clears and the air around me lightens. The pain in my stomach vanishes as her hands move down my body, finishing at my feet. When she stands, I feel the last bit of poison leave my body. It floats away and evaporates into nothingness.

I would feel infinitely better if it were not for this pounding headache. Or the heaviness in my eyelids. Exhaustion hits me and I close my eyes.

"Thea? Are you okay?"

~

I'm startled awake by a loud noise. Lifting my head off the plump pillow, I grimace. A throbbing pain circling my head reminds me that what happened wasn't a dream. I let my feet dangle from the bed and rub my face with my hands gently before getting up. Wandering into the dining room, I see Cole placing things into his fridge. He wears a forest green t-shirt with indigo jeans. His obsidian hair is messier than usual.

"Hey," my voice cracks. Speaking sends a wave of sharp pains into my head.

Cole smiles at me. Before he can say anything, I bring my index finger to my lips while closing my eyes and pointing to my head. He appears to get the idea because he keeps quiet and pulls something out of his appliance. I watch as he ambles in my direction and pulls the top of the nutrient packed meal that he is about to hand me. Graciously, I take the blood bag from his hand and drink the liquid. This time, I take no issue with consuming the pack's entire contents at once. The hammering in my head subsides before I finish half of it.

"Thank you," I whisper. "My head was pounding."

He nods. "It is probably a side effect of both the poison and Natalya's magic."

"Who's that?" *That's the first thing you ask?* My subconscious sneers.

A toothy grin cuts across his chiseled features. "She's an old friend who owed me a favor. Nothing more." Cole's front door opens with its infamous squeak. In unison, we look to see a panicking Sarah entering the cabin, her eyes wild and curly hair poorly wrapped in a lavender bandana. Cole waves at her and looks back at me. "I found your phone on the floor in my bedroom and saw a few missed calls from her."

"Yeah, it seems to be a theme these past few days," Sarah says under her breath. She hugs me gently. "I'm sorry I wasn't here. Are you okay?"

"I'm fine. Where were you?"

She looks to the wooden floor of the dining room. "There was an issue with the Coven that I had to take part of." She turns to Cole. "How did something like this happen?"

I brace myself for Sarah to explode on Cole, blaming him for my predicament that occurred under his roof. To my surprise, she keeps most of her calm, the only fire leaking through her narrowed eyes.

"Well," Cole says grimly as he sighs and pulls his phone from his pocket. "I finally heard back from my friend Juan. The vampire who is after you and your power is indeed a tracker. His name is Amaund. He's probably one of the most feared Generals the Brais King has. He works directly under the Commander, who works side by side with the King." He places his phone on the counter next to him.

Sarah runs a hand through her hair, pulling the loose bandana out as she does so. "But that doesn't explain him knowing where she lives and knowing that she was here."

Cole tightens his jaw. "Unfortunately, it does. Amaund, like the majority of the Brais, specializes in fire."

Right. I imagine all the big bad Brais surrounded in fire auras, which is terrifying.

"He is also a very strong tracker. Chances are, he was able to feel Thea awaken her elemental magic." He rubs the space between his eyes. "And," he pauses. Whether because he doesn't want his theory to be true or for dramatic effect, I'm not sure. "I believe that Amaund has marked Thea's soul."

My eyebrows shoot up in disbelief. "I'm sorry, what? How would we know?"

Cole clenches his jaw. The sleeves of his shirt pull up slightly as he crosses his arms, revealing a series of connecting triple spirals tattooed on his right bicep. Underneath are the swirls of black ink that I peeked at earlier. They border the spirals. "Have you had any aches recently?"

I cock my head at him, my eyes like slits. "Of course I have." Since my turning, there has been a sleuth of pains, hunger being the main cause.

"Any subtle ones that come and go?"

I arch a brow at him. "I—" Before I can finish the sentence, a piercing throb emerges at the base of my skull and I wince. "My neck," I rasp as tendrils of sharp electricity reach down to my back.

"Since when?" Cole asks with a worried expression, moving as if to take a look but stopping after only a step.

I shake my head, irritation rising in my chest at all the questions. "I don't remember. Maybe since we were at the restaurant?"

"Can I take a look?" He drops his arms to his side.

I rub the back of my neck and pull the loose strands of my long hair messily onto the top of my head. Cole steps toward my left and I turn so he can look. I hear a sharp intake of breath. "What?" I let my hair fall behind my shoulders as I spin to face him.

"There is a thin red line down your neck."

"A tracker's mark," Sarah interrupts. Both Cole and I look to her with confusion. "My grandmother told me a story once about how she tried to help a vampire whose soul was marked." I picture her sweet-tempered grandmother. She was always smiling when I saw her, gray silky hair falling below her shoulders or tied in a neat bun. Now, I can't help but imagine her with a pointy hat and a cauldron.

"I don't like that you used the word 'tried'."

Cole releases a ragged breath. "She tried because there are only two options to break a mark."

A loud sigh escapes me as I grab one of the dining chairs and take a seat, still feeling a bit unwell. I have a sense that I will need to sit down for this conversation. "What options do we have?"

"Well, trackers who are able to mark a person's soul do so because they generally have a goal in mind. Amaund is a Brais General. One of their tasks include expanding the army that serves the Brais King. He marked you because that is what he wants. Or, rather what the Brais King wants. So, one way to be free of the mark is to do as he wishes."

"That will not happen." Sarah steps forward defiantly, shaking her head. "I will not allow Thea to become one of them." She pulls out the other chair and sits next to me, placing a hand on mine.

"I agree," Cole adds.

"Then what is the other option?"

A lingering silence hangs in the air before he answers. "Death is the other option. If either you or Amaund die, the magic binding your soul to his dispels."

Fear crashes with anxiety, leaving me stunned for a moment. Sarah and Cole remain silent, allowing me to sort through my emotions. I almost died once. Cole saved me, offering a second chance. I didn't decide to go through with his offer and live this immortal life just to give up and die at the hand of an evil vampire. Becoming a Brais is also not on my list of things to do, although I would rather that than cease to exist, I think. A barely audible laugh vibrates in my throat.

I look solemnly to Cole. "When you turned me, I could have refused to feed. I could have chosen to die despite the second chance you gave me." I pause for a moment, letting the sound of Sarah's steady heartbeat calm me. "I almost did choose that path." Cole stills at the declaration. Without looking at Sarah, I know the admission saddens her. A wave of stagnant energy flitters from her toward me. "But I chose to cling to this beautiful world and those I love." I look to Sarah then. Tears well in her honey eyes. "I didn't choose life just to die."

Sarah squeezes my hand for comfort.

"Or to become a captive," I add. If they captured me, could I resist their way of life? Giving into those strong emotions and debilitating memories buried deep in that gilded, rusting cage within me... I shudder. They claw at the bars, snarling and hissing to be let free. When I feed, a small wisp of their influence infuses into my hunger, driving for that desire to kill. The Brais would probably encourage that.

"Killing him won't be easy," Cole says gruffly, pulling me out of my thoughts. "But I agree. It should be our first attempt to get this resolved."

"I agree. I think the first thing we should do is get her more trained in her powers," Sarah offers. "Aren't both of her abilities rare as far as vampire magic is concerned?"

"Very much so," Cole answers.

"That doesn't please me very much," I say. They both smile sympathetically. While I definitely was not a shy person growing up, I never enjoyed being the center of attention, nor did I like anything that made me stand out.

Sarah taps her chin with two fingers. "I think I could create a dome barrier spell of some sort that, while inside the dome, will block the communication that whatever-his-name-is receives when she practices. But..."

"But what?" Cole asks.

"But... I will definitely need the help of my mother." Sarah's gaze meets mine. "I know she will be willing to help you, Thea. But," she moves to Cole, "she'll be less willing to help you."

"Of course," Cole responds dryly. "This spell would be solely to help Thea. You can tell her that."

Sarah bows her head. "I'll call her now." She walks outside, confirmed by the squeak of the door as she opens and closes it.

"How are you feeling? Physically, I mean." Cole asks, worry in his voice.

"Most of the pain is gone."

"Do you want more blood?"

I swallow and wince from a dry throat. That tense gnawing bubbles in my stomach. "Yes, please."

He goes to his fridge and grabs a bag, popping the top off for me. "Thank you." I take a sip, relishing in the nutrients. When the scratchiness in my throat subsides, I ask him the question that has been bothering me. "How did that hiker's blood poison me?"

Cole leans against the counter, pushing aside a roll of paper towels and shoving his hands in the pockets of his jeans. "The Brais relish in exploiting other's dark desires. They have a few witches under their control who use magic to harm people. There was a Joining spell linking you and the hiker."

"A Joining spell?"

He clears his throat. "If a witch wants to harm a person without getting close to them, they use that spell. It links two people for," he lifts a shoulder and knits his brows together, "an hour, maybe two." He shakes his head. "Witch's magic is strange to me," he mumbles, pinching the bridge of his nose. "Even though he was human, because you two were linked, it was like you were drinking your own vampire blood when you bit him. The spell caused a toxic reaction in your body."

I grimace. "And you're sure that the Brais sent him?"

His nostrils flare. "I know it. He was very chatty after you passed out and the spell wore off." Cole's eyes flashed to their scarlet color.

"You mean you went into his mind." I shake my head, knowing the answer. "Why would Amaund send that hiker in instead of just coming in himself? Not that I want him here, though." A burst of icy fear runs through my blood at the thought.

Cole shrugs, his eyes returning to swirling smoke. "He might not know who turned you, so he doesn't know what arsenal you have—mostly, he's testing you. Like I said, the Brais enjoy taunting their targets. But I can't be sure that he was solely targeting you, either.

Most vampires who sire someone protects them for a time, until they can protect themselves. He might have tried to get you alone."

The thought of Cole being the one who ingested the poison sends a paralyzing shiver down my spine. "If that spell joined the hiker and I, would it have affected you if you drank from him?"

"Possibly. They would have needed something of mine that could connect me with the hiker, but it is possible. From what little I know about the spell, a witch can connect multiple people at once."

If something like that happened to him, I'm not sure how I would handle it. I push those concerning thoughts aside and change the subject. "I always thought vampires were more like lone-wolves."

"Quite the opposite, rather. Because we live such long lives, virtually forever, living with our own kind gives us a sense of family or purpose. Also..."

I raise a curious eyebrow. "What?"

"Well... when we create a new vampire, we are giving them a part of us, a part of our magic. Due to that, we are weakened for quite a number of years. We can keep our strength if we stick close to the one who we turned for that duration." He holds his breath, anticipating my response. His tapping finger giving away his nerves.

For a moment, I sit there dumbfounded. Cole sacrificed a piece of himself in order to turn me into a vampire. He did it for the war. What if I didn't go through with it? Or what if I wasn't who he thought I was and joined the Brais? *Maybe that's the only reason he keeps me close.* My insolent inner critic screams in my head. I remember the story he told me about our past. Surely, that was not a one-sided moment. I still would like to remember that night. One head spinning thing at a time, though. "That..."

Cole remains silent, allowing me to soak in the information, though he appears eager for words. His fingers continue drumming at his sides silently.

An unsettling thought bounces in my head and I sit up straight, listening. "Did you hear Sarah outside on the phone at all?"

Cole stills as he listens. He furrows his brows and shakes his head. Without a word, he starts toward the front door and I follow behind. My hearing is still new to me, but even a human would have been able to hear a person on the other side of the door. With a squeak of the wood, we look out onto the green of Cole's forested front yard.

My eyes frantically search for my best friend. The only thing we find is the tarp by the house and typical forest plants—everything, untouched, that was here yesterday. Terror floods my body with each passing second of no Sarah. All the worst scenarios flicker in my mind, most of which involve Amaund. I look to Cole, who had trudged around the cabin and was making his way back to the front. He shakes his head gravely. Hot tears pool in my eyes as a pang of guilt pulls at my heart. What if Amaund was waiting for someone to leave this house? What if he took Sarah to get to me?

Chapter 13

The snap of a branch behind me grabs my attention and I swing around hastily, adrenaline flowing. My hands warm as the energy of fire swirls within my palms.

Relief pours over me as Sarah appears out of nowhere from the tree line. She is looking down at her phone, not even noticing when I run to her for an embrace, almost knocking her over.

After the shock of the surprise hug, she wraps her arms around me in return. I soak up the warmth of her embrace. "What is this for?"

"I thought something bad happened to you." We release each other. "We didn't hear anything after you shut the door and became worried."

The corners of her lips turn down. "I'm sorry, Thea. I didn't mean to worry you. When I talk to my mom about anything Coven or magic related, I just like to make sure no one can overhear the conversation."

My expression softens. "Noted. Next time, a little warning, please?" Cole slowly makes his way over to us.

"Definitely," she vows.

"Did you do a cloaking spell?" Cole asks, intrigued.

She turns her attention to him, excitement gleaming in her eyes. "Pretty much."

"Interesting."

Sarah holds up her phone. "My mom said she will help us. She loves you, Thea—even as a vampire." She places a comforting hand on my arm. "She wanted me to make sure you know that. She knows how you worry."

I sniff back the tears that still lingered, threatening to break loose. Of all the things that were changing, losing Valeria's love would have crushed me. Other than Sarah, Valeria was my rock after my parents died. Without hesitation, she took me under her wing. "Thank you."

Sarah smiles gently. Her expression hardens as she fixes her gaze on Cole. "She also mentioned that the *only* reason, other than her love for Thea, that she helps is that she despises the Brais more than she despises you."

I let out a low whistle. "What exactly happened between you two?"

Sarah's eyes pierce Cole with an expectant look. When he doesn't immediately answer, she raises an eyebrow and stretches her neck forward.

Cole sighs and takes a deep breath as he turns and paces in a slow circle. He looks to Sarah before turning his conflicted and guilt-ridden attention to me. "Valeria and I have a history that goes back about forty years."

"What?" I look from Cole to Sarah. "I thought your mom was that age?"

She twirls a lock of her black hair around a finger. "Witches live longer than a typical human. Though we can be just as vulnerable if we aren't trained or careful." Come to think of it, Valeria never really seemed to age. She looks almost exactly as she did from all of our elementary school photos.

"So, are you..."

She shakes her head. "I'm as old as you know I am."

I sigh with relief. At least that's something. Sarah and I were born only a few days apart, twenty-two years ago in the same hospital. We have always joked that we were hospital siblings, meant to be in each other's lives.

Cole clenches his jaw and releases a weary breath, anxiety written all over his face. "First, I should mention that I am most definitely not the same vampire that I was back then."

I nod. Hopefully he knows that I trust him.

He runs a hand through his hair, closing his eyes briefly, his movements stiff. His past must really be bad if he is this nervous to share it.

My empathy gets the best of me. "Cole, you don't need to share your past yet if you aren't ready."

The flattened grass gratefully lifts itself back toward the sky as he stops pacing. "No, no. You should know."

I walk to him and place a gentle hand on his arm. I want him to feel relaxed and comfortable to talk about what is painful for him. A warm, tingle spreads through my arm and into his body. I close my eyes and inhale the scent of the forest. When I open them, I see our energies mix in an elaborate waltz. The energy that surrounds him, gray in color, is full of anxiety and worry. For calmness, I focus on the color of the sky, of the beautiful morning glory and hydrangea that bloom in the summertime. I send those images to him, focusing on the comforting blue. I watch as he takes a slow, deep breath before opening his own eyes.

He looks at me with curiosity. "Did you just... calm me down?"

"I think so." I hesitate, removing my hand from his arm. The tingle slowly recedes from my palms until it diminishes. For a brief moment, I can feel the energy swirling in my body, eager to be explored and understood.

"Well," Cole says, shaking out his hands, "Thea, you should know that when I was turned—which was about 163 years ago—I was in with a bad crowd."

I had assumed that Cole wasn't exactly young, regardless of his looks. But I wasn't quite expecting him to have that many years under his timeline. Not that it—or anything that he has said—changes how I feel about him.

"At that time, I was still living in Italy, and there were some big riots and heavy criminal activity occurring. I met someone who I became... *infatuated* with." He grimaces, his words dripping with regret and disdain. "She turned out to be a vampire. A *Brais*. Over time, she and the other vampires in her clan fed me false facts about the Essites, as well as other supernatural species." A bitter laugh escapes his lips. "I'm embarrassed to say that I soaked in everything that they taught me."

A cool wind blows, rustling the trees around his yard. The sun has already begun to make its decent in the sky, casting long shadows on the ground. Sarah shivers with the caressing wind. I look to Cole who is staring intently down at the grass, lost in his past. "Let's go inside and talk more. Sarah, you look cold."

"Sorry, my fault," Cole states. "I've buried this bit of my past behind thick walls. I lose control of my magic sometimes when opening up about it."

I soften my expression. We make our way back into his cabin. Once inside, Cole lights a fire while Sarah and I make ourselves comfortable on his couch. We sit, a foot away from each other, consumed by our own thoughts. Sarah knows Cole's story. She knows what it is that makes him ashamed. I'm thankful for her being quiet and caring.

"I did some things that I am not proud of," he continues. "For decades, I gave into the addiction of bloodlust and I used my powers for ill purpose. I..." The smell of a fresh fire and the sound of crackling logs fills the silence in between words. The energy from the flames dance on my skin, tickling as it spreads. "I've killed so many. Humans, vampires, witches." He glances shyly at Sarah, who is staring into the dancing wisps of heat. "Eventually, others started fighting back."

"My Coven," she says impassively without averting her eyes.

Cole nods. "Your mother killed the vampire who turned me. She was going to kill me as well but didn't. She saw some good in me." He lets out a sigh. "It didn't take too long for me to betray that trust and change her opinion."

"What happened?" I ask gingerly. One of the logs crackles loudly, bringing all of our gazes to the mesmerizing flames. They call to me, whispering for more power. I resist the urge to put my hand into them.

"I was still under the influence of the Brais King."

Whoa. "You knew the King?"

He shakes his head. "I've never met him directly. I was never important enough, I suppose." He shrugs. "The Brais convinced me to get close to Valeria and end her. The King thought that one day she would become the High Priestess of the Minuit Coven and wanted her dealt with."

"Well, she's still alive, so you didn't succeed, right?"

A harsh burst of air exhales from his lungs. "No, I didn't kill her. I got close to her, as they pushed me to do. Valeria was supposed to be in the greenhouse that day, so I planted a bomb." He lets out a snort. "I was too much of a coward to do it with my own hands. Little did I know that she and her best friend had switched shifts."

I suck in air, surprised at his story. He said he was a different person—er, vampire—then. My heart breaks for both Valeria losing her friend and for Cole. A swirl of black clings to his consciousness—regret. The desire to ease his pain wakes up the tingling sensation in my hands. I refrain and rub them on my jeans instead.

An awkward silence hangs in the air. Even the fire paused its spitting. Sarah keeps her attention to her torn jeans, playing with the frayed strings. Cole, who is now leaning against the wall, is staring out the northern window. I look between the two of them, noting the discomfort radiating off both of their bodies.

A few agonizing minutes pass before Cole turns to look at Sarah, water forming in his eyes. "I am truly sorry for my past actions. I don't deserve your mother's forgiveness. I just needed to say that."

Sarah stands and puts her hand on his upper arm. "I believe you," she says, a kind smile on her lips. "For what it's worth, I forgive you."

He smiles. "Thank you."

A knock on the front door startles all three of us. We do not move to open it. "It's me," says Valeria in a muffled, orotund tone.

Sarah moves before Cole can and lets her mother inside. "Hi, Mom."

Chapter 14

Valeria steps inside Cole's cabin, the space suddenly feeling too small. She wears a loose ashen blouse, stained with fresh powder of a maroon incense. The shirt is tucked into black pants. Her chestnut skin is dusted with golden sparkles on her cheeks and her dark brown hair is tied into a braided crown atop her head. She hugs her daughter, "Hi sweetie." Her gaze softens as it lands on mine. She releases Sarah and walks over to me with open arms. I stand and melt into her kind embrace. "How are you doing, love?" Her familiar, modulated voice soothes the nagging nerves that were growing since early this afternoon. She releases the hug, still holding onto my shoulders as her eyes scan my face.

"I'm doing okay," I say. The weak smile on my lips is genuine, which startles me a bit. After everything that happened today, I'm quite surprised that I didn't collapse into a lachrymose mess at the sight of this strong, loving woman in front of me. The shakiness of my limbs betrays my face, and she takes my hands in hers and plasters a sympathetic smile on her lips.

Her hazel eyes flick to the corners, to behind her where Cole stands. Her back straightens, her hands falling to her side. Cole stands still, not cowering while she penetrates her glare onto him. Her eyes narrow like slits as she crosses her arms. "Nicolai."

I raise an eyebrow at him from behind Valeria. He peers at me quickly before turning his fixed look back to his old enemy. Friend? Lover?

"Valeria." He bobs his head sharply at her. "I go by Cole now."

She throws her head back in an exaggerated movement. "Well, *Cole*," his name a hiss in her mouth, "I'm only here to help Thea. My daughter who you murdered."

"*Mom*," Sarah exclaims.

Valeria continues, ignoring her actual daughter. "I almost wish she was part of the Coven. If she were, we would have no choice but to hunt—"

"Valeria, please." I place a pleading hand on her arm and step out from behind her shielding stance. Since she took me in, I know Valeria considered me a daughter. She only mentions it when she was being her usual protective self.

At the touch of my hand, she relaxes and takes a sidestep back. "I'm sorry." She clenches her jaw. "I planned on staying neutral." A soft laugh bubbles from her chest. Kindness now swirls in her eyes, crinkling at the corners. "I want to hear about your magic, dear. But first, let's get this barrier up."

"Since we now know that Amaund can locate you wherever you are, we need to create a placement barrier that can't be broken through. Thea, we need something of yours to bind the spell to you," Sarah adds. "Something personal with meaning. The more personal it is, the stronger the barrier."

The necklace from my mom is the only object that comes to mind. I quickly stride to the bedroom and retrieve the jewelry, placing it in her outstretched arm.

She immediately recognizes the piece. "Once we get this situation fixed, you can have the necklace back." Turning to Cole, she says, "And we need something that can represent your home. It will bind the spell to this location."

He pushes off from the windowsill and walks past us toward the back door. I notice Valeria watching him as he crosses the tile floor. I would look into her emotions, but it feels invasive with her, with this.

Cole returns with a skeleton key. "The first key to this house. A bit outdated now." Sarah takes the key, examines it quickly, then nods in approval.

"I thought that was just a decoration," I jest.

"Nope, the OG key." Cole meets my gaze and returns the soft smile.

Valeria shuffles uncomfortably around the coffee table. "We are going to make a mojo bag to hang on the door. Don't remove it. We will also place some of the pre-made bags around the property." She pulls a handful of small, velvety green bags from her purse. "There is just some herbs and crystals inside. They will create the barrier while the one on the door will hold it." She hands a larger, black bag to Sarah, who places the key and necklace inside. At least my mom's jewelry will be safe inside the barrier.

"You two can wait inside, it won't take long," Sarah states as they walk outside, closing the door behind them. Silence hangs in the air.

"Well, that was interesting."

"Indeed," Cole agrees.

I take a few steps closer to him. "Have any more blood bags, *Nicolai*?" A devilish grin spreads wide across my face.

A sincere chortle escapes his mouth. "Ah, yes. I cringed a bit when she said my old name." I follow behind him as he enters the kitchen. "I always hated that name."

"Oh, I don't know. I kind of like it," I say as I reach for the meal. Cole's outstretched hand retreats teasingly with the bag.

The corners of his mouth raise sharply along with an eyebrow.

"Okay, okay. Just Cole." He chuckles, hands me my prize, and grabs a bag for himself.

I close my eyes briefly, taking in the glorious, rejuvenating sensations. "Thank you, by the way," I mutter after a few generous sips.

"For what?"

"For saving me. I don't think I said it before." My face warms, a redness blooming in my cheeks.

He takes a step forward. "No need to thank me." The space between us bristles with a magnetic pull. His eyes fall to my lips and he lifts a finger to it, wiping gently. A quiver of pleasure tickles down my back at his touch. A small drop of blood is smeared on his fingertip when he pulls it away.

For a moment, I forget everything around us. I forget the two witches outside the house, casting a spell. I forget the scary vampire hunting me. I even forget the bag of red liquid in my left hand. My heart pounds in my chest as he slowly brings his face to mine, the electric butterflies bouncing dramatically in my gut.

The sound of the front door opening pulls us apart. My lips ache to feel his against them. Cole takes a step back as Valeria opens the door, her eyes shifting between the two of us. Sarah follows behind her mother and notes the silence. Clearly, we can't hide our actions nor the blooming cheeks. She clears her throat. "Everything is set."

I place the blood bag on the counter behind me without turning around. Sarah may be okay with watching me drink, but I don't want to push Valeria. "So, it's safe to be outside now?"

"Yes," Valeria answers shortly. "The spell created a dome around the house that only those in this room and people you invite in can pass through. At its edge, you will see a clear wall that will shimmer in the sunlight. Sarah tells me she thinks you can manipulate energy." She changes the subject in a single breath.

"I healed a tree. And I was able to influence Cole's emotions earlier." When he told his story. Sadness still tugs at my heart for him. And Valeria.

A curious expression replaces her edgy one. "Can you show me?" She holds out her arm.

"I can try." I walk to her and take hold of her arm, mimicking what I did to Cole. The sensation of my magic is pulled forward, igniting my hands in the now familiar tingle. Valeria's emotions churn with a mix of Tuscany yellow, raven black, and fuchsia. I push that same calming powder blue from my body to hers. Under my touch, her body loosens. Soft blues replace the black and mixes with the other colors. She exhales softly, releasing the stress that clung to her.

I watch as she opens her eyes, searching for Cole's. She parts her lips as if to say something but quickly shuts it again and changes her posture. I release my grip and step back. I know in my gut that she wants to forgive him. Decades of holding a grudge has weighed down on her. After all this time, both her and Cole are different now, better and stronger.

"Good." She straightens her gray blouse. "Definitely an energy manipulator." She clears her throat. "I should get going." Before turning to leave, she places a hand on my face and smiles. "I am glad you are doing okay, Thea. I worry about you sometimes. This new life will be far from easy, but," she glances at Cole, "you are in good hands." With that, she turns away, puts a loving hand on Sarah's shoulder briefly before exiting the house.

I turn my attention to Cole, who is standing stunned, staring at the closed door. He holds the bag still in his hand, too distracted to remember. Although not an outright statement of forgiveness, Valeria's words were as close as one could hope from her. The tenseness in his shoulders release a bit.

"Cole are you okay?" I creep closer to him.

His awareness returns. "Yes, I'm fine."

"So, let's get to some magic, shall we?" Sarah interrupts, clapping her hands together.

I jump at the noise, pulling my attention from Cole to her. "Sure. I'm just going to drink this really quick." I go back to the blood bag I left on the counter and drain it. Cole remains silent, doing the same with the one he still holds. I can't help but wonder what he is thinking.

Outside, the sapphire sky melts into shades magenta and orange as the sun sets. Cole turns on his outdoor lights, illuminating his front yard. Darkness sets in beyond the tree line. I inhale a deep, welcoming breath of fresh air, enveloped by the scent of the earth. A pleasant energy emanates from the surrounding landscape. Whether the barrier is the reason, I am not sure. Relief floods my body every second that goes by without the suffocating feeling of the Brais.

~

We practice well after the sun disappears. In the center of the yard, Cole put together a fire pit. With my magic, I started a controlled, warming blaze. Embers float around us while I enlarge the flames. Cole and I work together to bring height to the fire. His air magic feeds oxygen to the hungry flames as I keep them contained within the pit. The sensations of our magic mingling together is just as intoxicating as his physical touch. His air weaves around my flame, like the eternal dance of the elements. When our eyes meet in a sultry gaze, a different kind of fire ignites within my body, pooling in my center. I do all I can to ignore the buzz in my heart and keep my body rooted on the cool grass beneath my bare feet.

Per my request, Sarah shows me small witch spells, using branches and grasses around the cabin as anchors. Healing spells, destructive spells, and illuminating spells. Depending on the specific incantation, rainbows of colors seep from her hands in wisps and swirls.

Tonight, I focus on my fire magic. It comes easily, eager to be used. Cole uses his magic to snuff out any flame that clings to the surrounding plants.

With each practicing motion, I feel more confident in the ability to control my magic. The eager buzz from deep within me is a bit frightening, a lingering fear of destruction bubbling. Alongside the confidence, I feel the strength of my magic's desire to let loose. That is what most frightens me.

Chapter 15

Over the next four weeks, Cole, Sarah, and I continue to train. Sarah decided she would stay with me at Cole's cabin to help, which I am grateful for. After putting up the barrier, she gave her mom some needed time alone. She said she planned on going for a mini vacation to recharge, visiting family members in Canada. I think Valeria would prefer Sarah to be within the safety of the barrier as well.

During the night, Sarah and I—and Helios, who has taken to sleeping on my legs—share Cole's bedroom as he sleeps on the couch. Some nights, I find myself lying awake, listening to his steady breath through the wall. The sound is a comfort, lulling me to a deep sleep when I find it difficult. My brain often races to all things that could turn bad, like Amaund breaking through the protection barrier, or the Brais King coming for me himself.

Some mornings, upon waking, Cole is in the kitchen cooking breakfast. Before she left for vacation, Valeria was kind and dropped off a large supply of blood bags, which we drink plenty of to keep our stamina up. It also keeps our hunger away from being enticed by Sarah. Valeria told us not to ask where she got the bags from. For Sarah, her mom brought plenty of various human food items.

Since the incident with the hiker, I've been strictly using blood bags to keep me sustained. Just the thought of drinking directly from a person reignites the pain from the poison.

There has been no further attempts at my life, nor that of any of my closest friends. With each day in the clear, I worry that Amaund is planning something worse. At least, I am also getting stronger with both my magic as well as some combat skills. Cole knows some advanced martial combat moves, which he insists will come in handy if I ever find myself in the grasp of the Brais. Sometimes, while we are taking a break from the excursion of training, it is easy to forget. During bits of laughter, I get lost in the happiness that I forget all about the dangerous world outside this little clearing in the forest. Occasionally, we spend more time laughing and reminiscing that it is also easy to forget me being a vampire.

Sweat beads down my forehead as I kneel over a dead goldenrod flower. A tingling warmth spreads from my arms down to my palms as my energy manipulation ability roars to life. Inky black dots slither around the plant, consuming the buttery petals of the plant. I envision a perked flower catching the rays of the sun during a warm autumn day. From my hand, cottony amber tones swirl, latching onto the stalk of the flower. The buzzing energy eats away the smudges of black until there is nothing left. I am panting when I pull my hands away.

The goldenrod sways happily along the edge of the pines.

"Nice, Thea!" Sarah enthuses. The plant was the poor victim of an out-of-control fireball. Luckily, it wasn't large enough to cause too much damage to anything else. Bringing the little plant back to full health, however, severely drained me of energy. I fight the heaviness to my eyelids that so desperately want to close and rest. Winded, I sit down on the early autumn grass, admiring its deep color. A dull ache sits in my body.

"You know, there is one thing I've been wondering," I say as I pluck a blade from the ground and mindlessly tie it into knots.

"What's up?" Cole answers as he sits down next to me, his arm brushing against mine. During these couple weeks, he and I have been slowly playing with fire—figuratively and literally. Stolen moments of hand grazing and lingering eye contact has severely tested my ability to refrain.

"Well, I know that the barrier prevents Amaund from both tracking me and getting into my head, but he must know that I am here, right? Why hasn't he come?" I drop the grass and put up my hands. "Not that I want him to ever come here, or anywhere near me or you guys."

Cole and Sarah exchange glances. "Not to frighten you, Thea, but he probably has come by and saw the barrier." Sarah plops down across from us, caressing the grass like a pet. I know she sees the closeness that has grown between Cole and I these past few weeks. I am grateful that she hasn't said anything yet, letting me sort through my own emotions. "This spell my mom and I set was not easy, especially considering how big we made it."

Cole leans back on his hands and stretches out his legs. "He probably saw it and retreated for a different strategy. He's a patient, old vampire who knows how witch magic works. It showed him how strong your allies are." He nudges me reassuringly with his shoulder.

Twirling my fingers in the greenery, I clench my teeth. "That sort of doesn't make me feel any better." Silence lingers with the acknowledgement that danger is always lurking. Sure, I know in the back of my mind that Amaund doesn't give up, but I almost convince myself that he will.

Dark storm clouds roll in, blocking the warm sunlight. The petrichor of a distant rain closing in hugs me. I take a deep breath to calm my growing nerves. I've learned the hard way during training that nerves and fire magic do not mix well. The impending storm reminds me of a time long ago when my mother and I would sit on our porch listening to the heavy drops hit the metal roof above us. We would sit in silence, waiting for the purple-white flash of lightning and the following roll of thunder, appreciating mother nature's roar.

"Let's head inside before the rain comes," Cole says as he stands up and brushes the dirt from his pants.

"Actually, I am going to head home."

I whip my head to Sarah with confusion. "You're leaving?"

She offers a comforting expression. "I'll be back tomorrow. My mom should be back by now and I just want to check in with her."

Prickly nerves climb up my spine. "Is it safe to leave?"

"I'll be fine. Trust me." She comes to me and gives me a reassuring hug.

I fight back the urge to argue with her to stay. I often underestimate her abilities as a witch, though am usually reminded once we begin training. If she trusts herself to be able to fend off a vampire, then I should too.

Worrying is just natural, right?

"I'll call you once I get home, okay?"

A worrisome sensation gnaws within my gut. "Okay," I say, forcing a smile. A phone call in an hour or so is better than having to wait until tomorrow when she returns. "If you need anything before then, call me, please."

She hears my layered plea and nods. "I will." A lie, easy to miss. If I hadn't worked on honing my senses over the past weeks, I would have missed that subtle change in her tone. If something happens to her, she will not call. She won't risk my safety.

She looks to Cole, bobs her head and turns to leave. We watch her as she disappears into the trees. Far away, the beginning of the storm announces its presence with a low clap of thunder. Hopefully it holds back long enough for her to get to her car that Valeria graciously had left at the edge of the woods.

"I wish we escorted her at least to the edge of the forest," I say as we walk inside, my nerves growing ever stronger. I pull my phone out of my pocket and turn the volume up high so as to not miss her call. My lips quirk up at the thought of her getting home and calling me, only for me to miss it as usual. She might storm back here and give me an earful.

What I would give for a guarantee of that timeline happening.

"Now that would have been a bad idea." Cole grabs two bags from his refrigerator and hands me one. Our hands touch momentarily, and intoxicating sparks are left behind. "If Amaund attacked Sarah, he would have the wrath of the Coven to deal with. She is safe."

The tiny amount of worry in his last sentence was almost easy to miss. He's trying to convince himself just as much as he is trying to convince me.

"Regardless, there is nothing to do now but wait for her phone call," he says after a moment of deafening silence. "She will call, Thea."

To pass the anxiety-ridden waiting game, Cole and I pull out a deck of cards for an attempt at normalcy. I teach him how to play a game called "Spit", which I have perfected over the many times playing with Sarah, or so I thought. He is a quick learner and I find myself losing more than winning. While we play, we bring a bit of class to our choice of nutrient packed drink by using crystal rock glasses, occasionally speaking in accents to add to the façade.

We finish the sixth game, which happens to be my fifth miserable loss, and I'm ready to swipe the cards from the table. Cole holds up one of the King cards then points to himself, a smug look on his face.

I wipe my hands across the table, clearing it of all the atrocious pieces of rectangular paper.

There is a thud at the door.

Cole and I freeze.

We stand and silently make our way to the front door. The sweet scent of blood wafts in from underneath. Cole pales and steps in front of me as he takes a deep breath before swinging the door open.

A severed head stares at us from his doorstep. Drops of blood pool around the torn neck. My hand flies to my mouth.

"James," I breathe, my voice shaky. Sarah's cousin's boyfriend. Despite the fragrant aroma, I feel as though I am going to vomit.

"Hello, Thea." A strange, gruff male voice comes from the other side of the yard. Cole and I snap our heads forward.

A pair of menacing, red-gold eyes stare at us from the tree line. Just outside the barrier. They glint in the light of Cole's porch lamp. Behind him sits a veil of darkness. A hush falls upon the forest that surrounds the cabin.

"It is good to finally be able to speak with you."

I clench my fists, fury erupting in my chest. A fearsome heat sizzles under my skin. Time slows as I take a step forward. I feel Cole's cool hand brush against my arm as he tries to grab a hold of me. In a whir of unrestrained anger, I run at those eyes.

Something slams against my chest before I reach the edge of the barrier. I look down, ready to tear it away. Cole's arm is stretched out across my chest, his immense strength pushing me back.

He glares at the vampire in front of us.

"Amaund," I hiss.

A smirk tugs at his lips. His amber skin glows in the silver beams of the rising moonlight. Long onyx hair is pulled back from his angular face. "Impressive," he says.

"What do you want?" I fume.

His expression remains amused. "It's not what I want, it's probably what you want. At least that's what I hope." Sharp teeth poke from behind his upper lip. He tosses a golden coin at me. It lands in the grass at my feet, the imprint of a leaf on its surface. "The black-haired witch will remain in my possession until you decide to fulfill your duty as a fire wielder and join the Brais."

Hot, angry tears threaten to break free as everything around me spins. "Where is she?" I seethe. I push back the regret seeping into my mind for not seeing Sarah off to safety. Cole's words repeat in my head. It would have been too dangerous. But maybe Sarah would be okay. I hope she is still.

She has to be.

He lets out a short maniacal laugh. "What is even more impressive," he evades, "is your circle of allies." He stretches a muscular arm out and his hand presses flat against the barrier. He jerks his chin at Cole. "Is this your sire?" Amaund's beady gaze roams over him as if memorizing his features.

I lunge at Amaund.

Cole grabs my arm.

"Let me go," I snarl at him.

"If you walk out there, he will not hesitate to snatch you."

Amaund snorts. "Yes, we wouldn't want your precious sire to be out of reach," he says to Cole.

I forgot about the magic bond between Cole and me.

Still, if I can save Sarah... I rip my arm from Cole and set my burning gaze on the Brais. The symbol of their shield is engraved on a silver medallion in the center of his chest, fastened to the cloak hanging on his back. "Is that what you want? To weaken—" I snap my mouth shut before saying Cole's name.

A sinister grin cuts across Amaund's face. Slowly, he says, "You want to know what I want? I want you, my dear." My breathing hitches. This entire time, we were living in a fantasy of safety, nestled inside this magical barrier. Amaund was waiting to snatch Sarah the entire time. Waiting for one of us to leave and to soften our guard. Cole said he was patient. Patient, indeed. "I want to help you reach your full, powerful potential."

I scoff. "You want my power for the Brais."

"One in the same, is it not?"

I clench teeth so hard that a pain erupts in my jaw. "I will *never* join you."

One moment, Amaund is standing unnaturally still, his face a blank expression and the next he is thrusting his long, silver sword through the barrier. His speed is beyond anything I have witnessed before.

There is no time to react and my body embraces for the sting of his blade.

Except it never comes.

Something pushes me backward, knocking me off balance. I open my eyes and am stricken with horror. The tip of the blade is plunged through Cole's abdomen, crimson liquid dripping onto the soft grass. My hand flies to my mouth. "Cole..."

He grunts. "I said I wouldn't let anything else happen to you." His words are garbled in quiet staggering sounds. "I meant it."

Amaund rips his sword out of Cole, who then collapses. I manage to catch him before he hits the cold ground.

"I will give you twenty-four hours to decide if your friend's life is worth yours." Amaund cocks his head, golden eyes flicking to the cabin. "Enjoy your gift."

Wrath explodes in my chest. Forgetting my rational self, I leap forward after him. But he is gone. The forest resumes its mellow songs.

Movement from Cole brings me back, the volcanic emotions lessening. "Cole, why did you do that?" I examine his wound, which he had lifted his shirt in order to look at it himself. Stupidly, my body freezes at the sight of his body underneath his clothing, a heat having nothing to do with my magic rumbles in my center. I shake it away and drop to my knees. The wound has already closed. "Do you need my blood?"

His dark gaze moves to me, irises flickering from ruby to gray. He drops his shirt. "No. I'll be fine."

"Why did you do that?"

He snorts. "A thank you would suffice." He sighs and wipes his bloodied hands on his soiled shirt. "I already told you."

I hold out a hand and help him to his feet. "What if it had been poisoned?"

"I thought it could be," he says in a quiet voice.

Silence falls around us as I stare at him. "Cole..."

A half grin forms on his lips. "Then I would have gladly taken your blood." He lifts a hand and glides soft fingers along my neck. "Right here." I shiver at his intoxicating touch. Too quickly, he drops his hand away, my body mindlessly following. I catch myself before my feet have a chance to move closer to him, clearing my throat.

Had there been poison on the sword and Amaund somehow taken me after stabbing Cole... How could we let this happen? I knew in my gut that she shouldn't have left the dome surrounding the cabin. If we just pushed, she might have stayed.

I scoff at myself. Sarah, the ever-stubborn witch, would not have stayed, I tell myself. The tears I held at bay stream down my cheek. I pluck Sarah's coin from the grass and turn toward Cole's cabin. I keep my eyes forward, wincing as I walk by the body part of my driver on the front stair. Equally ignoring the guilt that comes with my actions. I collapse on the hard floor. Cole appears next to me a few minutes later and drapes an arm around my shoulders, pulling my head to his chest. "I'm so sorry."

Quietly, I sit there, staring at the cards spread out on the floor, unable to feel sad. The tears ceased as soon as they came, replaced by an anger bubbling in my stomach, creeping all the way to my warming hands. I stand up abruptly, leaving a cold, aching spot where Cole's arm was. I clench my fist, holding back the budding flames. My magic swirls angrily in my chest, responding to my strong emotions.

"What are you doing, Thea?" Cole follows suit and stands. He looks at my hands, understanding spreading across his face. "No, you can't. Thea, this is a trap."

I glare at him. "Yes, I can. I need to save her."

He takes a step back, blocking the front door. "You can't just waltz into the forest and expect him to give up Sarah. He won't give up his leverage that easily. She is a member of the Minuet Coven, an evasive enemy of the Brais."

He found them because of me. I led him right to her. The intrusive, harsh thought slams into me, knocking the air from my lungs. I press a hand to my shuddering chest. The world around me is pressing in. Sounds of the insects outdoors scream in my ears. Cole's hammering heartbeat echoes like thunder rumbling through my chest. I gasp for air and stumble backward.

"Thea?" Cole's worry pierces my heart.

I catch myself against the cool wall. Sarah is out there. I need her. "I have to save her, Cole!" I exclaim, my voice cracking. "I have no choice. She's my best friend, my family!" She would do the same. The tears come back, though they don't break free. "I need her to be safe." It is a plea more than anything—a prayer to whoever is listening in the universe. The anger in my chest slowly diminishes as his words sink in and I realize he is right. Overwhelmed, I drop to my knees. A loud, unflattering sob escapes my mouth. Cole kneels beside me.

"We will figure this out, okay? He puts a hand on my shoulder while the other brings my face up to meet his unwavering gaze. "We won't leave her a captive. We will make a plan."

My watery eyes flick between his before he pulls me into an embrace. We sit, holding each other in our emotions for a while.

A thunderstorm rolls in and roars its might at us. The soothing sound of pounding water on the house fills the painful silence. I'm not sure how long we sit on the floor, but once he moves, it doesn't feel like it has been long enough. I take a deep breath to collect myself. "I should call Valeria."

After pacing back and forth a handful of times, I finally get the nerve to call Sarah's mom. Even dialing her number, sweat trickles on my back as I continue wearing a short path on Cole's floor as I keep pacing. By the fifth ring, I stop and look at Cole worriedly.

Please, no. Not Valeria too.

Five more rings with no answer.

She *always* answers her phone.

I give up and hyperventilate.

Cole directs me to the couch and grabs a blood bag. "Drink," he commands with concern.

I do as he says. His comforting hand on my back and the blood soothes my jitters. "Thank you," I mutter. I hand him the bag and he takes it graciously. "Wouldn't he have gloated about having Valeria as well? If he does… I don't know how we can save them." I rest my head in my hands.

"We will figure it out," he repeats as he drains the rest of the bag. He lets out a sigh and his muscles loosen softly. I realize then that I am so consumed in my own feelings that I don't even notice he is tense. "We just need to plan. It would be easier if we had an idea of where he was keeping them."

A wheel churns in my head. "We can find out." Cole looks at me with an arched brow. "Sarah gave me a talisman. She told me witches use it for protection. And with it, she said we will always know where each other is."

He shrugs. "How does it work?"

"I have no idea." With that, I stand and run into the bedroom. I rummage through my bag, shoving folded clothes to the sides in a heap. When I can't find it, I tear everything out of the bag. Shortly after temporarily moving in, Cole suggests I use a drawer in his dresser. Stupidly, I tell him that my bag is fine, and I continue to wear slightly wrinkled clothes. I don't want to take up residence in his space.

"What's wrong?" Cole asks, standing in the doorway.

Shaking my head with frustration, I say, "I can't find it!" The magic in me swells again, heating my palms. "Ugh!" The fire on my fingertips burn a hole through the duffle bag. "And my stupid fire is acting up!"

"Thea." I feel his consoling hands on my shoulders. "Deep breaths. Let me look." I scoot away from my belongings.

With hot hands, I close my eyes, focusing on my boiling magic. Instead of thoughts of suppression, I push my magic down with a promise. I promise to unleash all the fire on Amaund. And the Brais. They will not harm my family, lest they get burned.

"It isn't here, Thea." Cole's voice pulls me from my meditation. "Did you pack it?"

My eyes widen as I picture the talisman that I placed safely in the back of my nightstand drawer. "We have to get to my apartment."

Chapter 16

"It is our only chance at finding them." I force assertiveness into my voice. I run a hand through my disheveled hair as I pace in front of Cole's bed. My foot catches something on the floor, sending it flying across the room and into the far wall.

While I paced around nervously, Cole managed to neatly place all my clothes back into my duffle bag. I'm too shaken and full of adrenaline to think about all the garments that he has touched. "You are sure that it is back at your place?" He gently puts my bag on his dresser, subtly hinting at using the empty drawer beneath it, before leaning against the wall with crossed arms.

"Yes." I think back to how the Brais broke into my home and ransacked the place. What are the chances that they looked inside the nightstand and knew what they were looking at? Slim, I hope.

Cole sighs. "Well, I might have a way to get us there. Though, it might put us both in the debt of a witch." A look of worry crosses his features.

"Your witch friend who helped me? What was her name?"

"Natalya. She is kind-hearted, though she enjoys doing shady business deals. It may not always be in your favor to owe her a debt."

I press my lips together. "Do we have another option?"

He takes a deep breath and shakes his head. "None that can guarantee as much safety as she can."

"Not that I don't trust you, but how can she guarantee us safety? She's a witch, just like Sarah and Valeria." My words drip with trepidation. I've learned quite a bit of head spinning information during our little four-week isolation. Sarah was very talkative once she got started. And from what I have absorbed about the Minuet Coven, if Valeria, the strongest witch of one of the oldest and most powerful covens, got captured, then how could any other witch help us?

"Natalya is," he pauses, searching for the right word, "unusual."

Everything about life is unusual these days.

My right eyebrow lifts. "Oh?"

"She is not part of a coven, and therefore, has less limitations on how she can practice her craft." He doesn't say any more, as though that was all the explanation that I needed in order to know what he meant.

"Yeah, that didn't explain anything."

He chuckles. "Right, sorry." He leans away from the wall and places a palm down on his dresser. "Covens bring stability and the light to the magic that flows into witches. Black magic is always lingering, whispering to those without a support system."

"Like the dark side of the Force?" I quip, snuffing out a laugh.

"Actually, yes." He smirks back when my eyes enlarge. "From what I hear anyway." An amused rumble escapes his lips. "Natalya has been practicing with black magic for decades. She has managed to keep most of her sanity as well, which is rare. I don't fully trust her, and neither should you."

"So, let's weigh our options." I hold out my left hand, palm up. "One choice is to ask Natalya for help and possible owe her down the road."

"*Definitely* owe her down the road," Cole corrects.

I raise my other hand. "Another choice is to risk getting there on our own two feet and possibly run into Amaund—"

Cole interrupts, "Do you want to risk being left exposed to Amaund and his soldiers?"

"In which case," I resume my thought, "we won't be of any help to Sarah and her mom." I lift and lower each hand, as if each option had weight.

I chew on my bottom lip. "Could the Brais be waiting at my apartment for me to go there?"

He thinks about it, his eyes darting around. "They could be. Natalya could help us defend against any that are there. We would only need to buy time for you to grab the totem then teleport back here."

"Sounds easy," I huff.

"This could be dangerous, Thea. Perhaps we should find a different way to—"

"No." I bite back the bitterness in my voice. "This is our best chance at finding them."

Cole runs a hand through his hair. "But we don't even know how to use the totem."

"Then we ask your friend." He looks at me with an exasperated expression. "If you don't call her, I am going to walk to my apartment."

His jaw clenches, gray eyes piercing. Without a word, he pulls his phone out of his pocket and dials the witch's number.

~

"So, let me get this straight. You want my help to teleport you to your old apartment to search for some *totem* that you are not even sure is still there?" Natalya snorts. Where she is bursting of pleasantries with Cole, she is full of sharpness with me, her lean face twisting and snarling. It makes her look older.

Not that I would say that to her face.

"That *totem*," I copy her disdain, "will help me locate my friend and adoptive mother who are—"

"Who are most likely being held by Amaund," Cole interrupts, his hand on my back. Natalya glares suspiciously between the gesture and our faces, her silver-blue eyes narrowing. With a sidelong glance at his expression, I understand that she does not need to know about Sarah and Valeria being witches. Or maybe just them being part of their coven is a need-to-know fact. I wonder how black magic practitioners and those in covens feel about each other.

We give her a moment to think it over, though I don't know why she would need to. We offered to help her in the future, which Cole said would greatly pique her interest. Perhaps going against the Brais is too much of a risk. She slowly sips at her cup of tea, seated at Cole's dining table with her long legs crossed regally. Her mahogany hair is tied back into a tight bun, not a thread sticking out. Outside, the storm has long passed, and the rising moon beams through holes in the clouds.

"So?" I ask unable to keep patient. The longer we take, the longer he has them. I have absolutely no idea what to do after we get the totem and somehow find their whereabouts. But I am going to do everything in my power to save them.

I have to.

Natalya gently places the ceramic cup down onto the saucer, her crimson lips pursed. Hiding my emotions is not one of my strong suits and she is well aware of my impatience. "*Da*, I will help," she answers, turning her greedy eyes on mine. "I will bring you, and you alone."

Cole steps forward defiantly. "No, we will both go."

The witch shakes her head. "I can only transport myself and one other person. Unless you can spare a half day for me to rest in between jumps?" she responds, her piercing eyes penetrating Cole's. The thought of being alone with her is unsettling, especially after Cole mentioned his distrust of her.

"Then I'll go," he adds.

I put my hand on his shoulder. "Cole, I can go." This is my home and my family, after all.

Natalya scoffs and stands. "It can only be her. She is the owner of this home, no? It has to be the owner."

He dips his head in defeat before turning to me. "Please, be careful."

"Of course." We clasp hands in a promise. At this closeness, his scent of cedar floats around me, a grounding and comforting scent. A promise of return. I step away from Cole, our fingers the last to say goodbye. The moment we are no longer intertwined, Natalya puts a cold hand on my shoulder and the world spins violently around me.

My body separates into its elements, twisting and swirling with the molecules of space. It is impossible to tell the difference between a leg and an arm. All that I know of myself is melding together like metal under a torch. When we land in the entryway of my apartment, I double over with nausea. "Thanks for the warning," I seethe, staring at the hardwood floor of the entryway. The familiar earthy scent of my home soothes most of my spinning head. I take a few moments to steel myself before standing upright. Everything is still a mess. I clench my fists, nails digging into my palms and bite back rising anger. I haven't been back here since Sarah and I found the symbol.

I look to Natalya, whose face twists in disgust at my disaster of a home. "Why couldn't Cole come here if you can teleport me to his place?" I ask apprehensively.

"I have left a ward—a sigil—on his home. It allows me to teleport there at will," she chides, stepping away from a pile of dirt at her feet as if it were something disgusting.

I scrunch my nose at the ward. Does Cole know? I let out an audible sigh before walking farther into my home. A strange feeling washes over my body and I survey my belongings. Though everything was a mess before, it is even more so now, as if the intruders came a second time. The spilled dirt from the tipped plants are more spread out, like someone new has walked through them. The trash can in the kitchen is knocked over, garbage spilling out. The more I look, the more I notice. In the living room, my television on the stand is crooked and the couch cushion is upside down—the stain from a full cup of coffee is out from hiding.

Unease fills my thoughts, my pulse quickening.

Something is wrong.

I turn to the witch. She stands like a statue in the center of the entry space, her legs apart and hands steepled in front of her. "How did you know where to teleport us?"

A cynical grin spreads slowly across her lips. "I was wondering if you would ask me."

Chapter 17

Natalya takes a menacing step forward. The heels of her boots click slowly on the wood with each step. "I'll admit, I expected it to take you longer."

Adrenaline courses through my veins in the form of fire. It makes its way to my hands as I rush toward the stairs. I need to get the totem. In the past weeks, my magic isn't the only thing that got stronger. My speed rivals Cole's now. With my sudden speed as a distraction, I throw my hand up to send a fireball at her once I reach the far side of the living area. She reacts by lifting her arm as well.

A splitting headache explodes within me—incapacitating torment. I let out a loud groan and drop to the floor, the agony persisting and growing. It feels as though daggers are shoved into my skull then ripped out repeatedly. Nausea washes over me again as I continue to clutch at my head, unable to move. I fight the pain and look up, wincing. Natalya creeps over to me, her arm still outstretched with claw like fingers.

She sneers at me. "There is a bounty for you, *durak*." The Russian accent on her words are heavy. "Do you know what I can get by handing you over to the Brais?" The pounding sound of her heels on the floor as she prowls forward sends excruciating shockwaves into my skull.

The closer she gets, the more intense the torment ravaging my brain becomes. "S-s..." Words can't take shape on my tongue. Darkness slips in and out of my vision.

I can't give in.

"I know your friends are of the Minuet Coven. I looked for something I could use to find them in this garbage pit." She gestures to my things. "They have been hunting me for decades, chasing me to no end. By giving you to the Brais, I get their heads."

She stands a foot away now. She wants harm to come to my family. To the two people who have been a constant in my life. Who kept me grounded during the toughest lessons life can deal out. The skin under my hands burn as the fire beckons to let loose. When I look at her again, something causes her to startle. She stumbles a half-step backward, worry plastered on her face. In that moment, the torture she inflicts lessens just a little. Enough for me to gain control. I call forth all the flames that dance on my skin. With a roar, I extend my hands toward her. Amber and scarlet hues flare angrily from my palms, shooting directly at her.

The fire is all-consuming.

Unforgiving.

Flames engulf her body. She opens her mouth to scream but sucks in the extreme heat of the smoke. Like a block, she drops to the floor, motionless. I keep my eyes on her, waiting for a twitch of the hands. The fire continues, burning away at her flesh and spreading onto the rug underneath her body. The smell is horrid. When I am sure that she won't be standing, I lower my eyes, palms on the floor and scrape my nails along the wood.

I heave a heavy, ragged sigh.

I just killed someone.

But she was going to hand me over to Amaund. All so she could kill my family. My eyes widen in fear.

I used my fire magic.

Outside the barrier. I've exposed myself.

Quickly, I rise to my feet. I need to get the totem and return to Cole's cabin before the Brais arrive. It could be minutes before they track my fire magic. I swipe at a tickling sensation in my ear and pull away to see dried blood. My lip curls at the witch's body. I never want to go through that again.

My body buzzes with energy from the fight as I rush to my bedroom, praying that what I seek is still there. When I reach the upstairs, however, my heart sinks. The last time I was here, my bedroom was untouched. Now, it is just as much of a disaster as the rest of the place. The doors to my wardrobe are ripped off the hinges, clothes spread everywhere. I can see the curtain of my shower sticking in the doorway. When my eyes catch my torn apart bed, I gasp sharply.

I swallow a lump forming in my throat and run to the nightstand where I left the totem. Furious, I pull the drawer hard and it falls out onto the floor. Only a few pens sit inside. I shake out my crumpled sheets, waiting to hear a thud on the floor. I peek beneath the spotless underside of my bed, under the rug, and all my clothes.

The totem is gone.

I sink to the floor in defeat.

They took it. They stole the totem.

I really am the reason he was able to find them.

Like before, fire burns underneath my skin. But instead of it simply concentrating in my hands, it pools in each of my limbs and torso. My nostrils flare as wrath consumes me, my fire letting loose once again in a thunderous howl. It rips apart my furniture, clawing at the walls. I hear the beep of the fire alarm begin before it falls to the floor in silence. The banister explodes, tumbling to the first floor. The windows in my bedroom and bathroom shatter.

I sit there, listening to the destruction of my fire, the crackling is soothing somehow. An unmeasurable amount of time passes as I remain unmoved. As the flames dissipate, I contemplate waiting until Amaund arrives. Then, Cole's face flashes in my mind. He is home, waiting.

Shakily, I stand. Pillows of black smoke float to the ceiling. I look over the charred and broken banister to see its ruins aflame on the couch. The sound of my door opening freezes me in place.

"Thea? Thea!" Cole's voice bellows from downstairs.

"I'm up here," I say with a trembling voice. I barely finish the sentence before he stands at the top of the stairs. His face hardens as he scans the charred remains of my second level.

"Thea." He strides over to me, his arms encircling my tense body. "I saw a body..." I tremble in his embrace. "What the hell happened?" Smoke fills the second floor as the fire consumes more of my home.

My eyes fall on the burning ivy plant that hung next to the bathroom door. I close my eyes as salty tears of grief pour down my cheeks.

"Let's get out of here. We can talk on the way back," he says, pulling me out of the embrace. His eyes scan my face.

I don't move, despite his tug. I can't bring myself to look at his face when I speak. "The totem is gone." I clench my jaw and squeeze my eyes shut. The image of Natalya's burning corpse has etched itself onto the back of my lids, forever taunting me. "She planned to give me to Amaund." His muscles tense, but he quickly moves to my side and puts my head on his chest. "You should leave," I whisper.

"Why would I do that?"

"I used my magic. He knows where I am."

He exhales. "Then I will fight by your side."

~

Cole all but carries me out of the building. My limbs feel like lead weights. Flashing lights from the fire department shine into the forest shortly after we enter. When I ask about the body, Cole assures me that there are numerous Essites who work within the police department who would help keep our involvement clear. I am too fatigued to ask more.

By the time we reach his cabin, the moon is high in the dark sky. The comforting forest emits a soothing energy that takes some of the edge away. Though we took the same path as we did that first night, it felt infinitely longer this time. Consumed with exhaustion and defeat, my pace was slow. Cole did not leave my side as we trudged mostly in silence.

I had to ask what made him come to my place anyway. He said we were taking too long, and it unnerved him.

I winced as we passed the small bag on the birch tree that marked the boundary of the barrier.

"Let me get you something to drink," Cole offers as I sit down on his couch. Helios nudges my leg gently before sitting in front of the fireplace.

I nod in response as I yank the soft throw blanket from the basket and wrap it around myself. It smells of firewood and pine. Cole returns with a glass half full of the only liquid that will heal my tired body. Next to me, he plops down and sighs, his own glass clutched in his hands.

My mind races back to what I did in my apartment, unable to move to something else. Natalya's broken, charred body remains visible to my closed eye. The scariest part is that I don't even feel any remorse. By threatening me—threatening my family—she brought it upon herself.

No one will hurt them.

I will not allow it.

I've done enough, and now, I must fix my mistakes.

"It isn't your fault, you know," Cole whispers, his eyes fixed on his fingers. I don't even know to which situation he means. The stolen totem is my fault without a doubt. Leaving it behind was stupid. Sarah entrusted me with it, an object from her Coven. I let her down. I let Valeria down.

I exhale, shaking my head slowly. "I shouldn't have left it behind."

The touch of his hand on my arm is comforting and warm. "Life was chaotic. It still is. You can't put fault on yourself when you were just thrown into the path of danger." His voice shakes, and I bring my eyes to meet his and see sadness and regret behind them.

"Cole, this is not your fault, either." I place my hand on top of his, the familiar buzz of my second ability forming at my fingertips. "Even if you asked me for permission before turning me…Knowing about what is going on in the world? I would agree to it." My own words surprise me. These thoughts I have never put into fruition before. "These past few weeks," I resume, peering out the window, "have been some of the most enjoyable and authentic I have ever had. Spending them with you and Sarah…" I choke out her name, pausing for a second as Cole's hand squeezes my mine. "I could never wish them away."

His hand curls lightly around my chin, bringing my attention back to him. Garnet dances with the gray in his eyes, revealing the desire he holds. His comforting scent of cedar mixes with something floral and sweet. Jasmine. Without any words, he leans closer, his face inches away from mine, stopping too soon. We gaze into each other's eyes, wanting to close the gap but neither of us moving.

Helios jumps on the couch between us, belting out a long meow.

We pull away from each other. I glance down at my cat with a reddening face.

Cole rubs the back of his neck before clearing his throat and standing. "We should brainstorm," he murmurs.

"Right." I run a hand down the soft, tan fur on my cat's back as I take a deep breath. I make my way to the dining room where Cole is staring at his phone.

"I think I might know where Amaund is."

I furrow my brows. "How? Where?"

"Actually, Juan figured it out."

I lift a brow.

"My friend, the one who figured out that it was Amaund who was tracking you. He is very skilled at finding people." He crosses the floor to the kitchen sink, placing an empty glass down inside. "There is an old, moss-covered brick manor by the Lewen Lake about ten minutes south from here. That's where he thinks Amaund is hiding with Sarah and Valeria."

I freeze, overcome by dread. "Did you say, Lewen Lake?" Out of all the bodies of water in this city.

"Yeah, why? Does that place sound familiar?"

The manor, sitting comfortably away from the road on a hill, faces the lake so that the setting sun reflects beautifully into the large, stained windows above the front porch. In the expansive back yard, a tree swing dangles from a low hanging willow branch. One of the ropes are frayed from years of use, held together with faded sparkle glue. "My family used to own that house." I haven't set foot near that place since I moved out and into Sarah's house.

Cole's jaw tightens. "It must be him, then."

"How? How did he know that place was part of my past?" I just want this nightmare to end. I want it to end with Amaund's head rolling. He chose the wrong vampire to hunt. The fire in my hands agrees, responding with such intense heat that I shake my hands as I stand.

"I don't know. There's no way that it is a coincidence, though. He either did his research, or..."

"Or what?"

He contemplates for a moment. "Or he got the information out of Sarah or Valeria." Cole watches me intently, his eyes fixing on my clenched fists and reddening face. "I don't know if we should go there, Thea."

"What?" I snap. "If there is even a small chance that they are being held there, I'm going." I start toward the bedroom. I need a more comfortable outfit for this excursion, I think. "If Amaund is there, then all the better."

Cole follows me, stopping in the doorway when he sees me changing. "My friend found his hiding place because he trailed him, Thea. There is no way that Amaund would have let him know where he is if he doesn't want to be found."

"If that's true, why did your friend even risk following him?" I change into my black yoga pants and a long-sleeved, black shirt that belongs to Cole. I ignore the comforting smell that hugs the fabric.

"Amaund is good at not being found, and Juan took that as a challenge. He was stupid to do that." I walk toward the doorway, but he remains fixed in place. "Amaund is ruthless," he whispers, a plead for me to reconsider.

It would work, but all I can see are the faces of my friend and her mother. I narrow my eyes. "You seem to know an awful lot about him." A low blow. I fight the urge to wince at my own harsh words.

Cole's eyes fall, concern replaced by hurt, and he steps back, allowing me to pass. "I was once a Brais, remember?"

I move past him, not wanting to see the damage my words have caused. That surfacing anger took over again. Anger at Amaund for taking my family and for desecrating my childhood home. I swallow it back before I can cause permanent damage. "Cole," I sigh, "I'm going to the manor, even if I have to go alone."

The lack of response hangs in the air. He is quiet for long enough that I look up from tying my shoes. "You will never be alone, Thea," he says. His hand twitches, as if he wants to touch my arm but was able to hold himself back. I ignore the guilt at being the cause for that hesitation. He continues, "I brought you into this mess and I will follow it through to the end with you."

Tears prick my eyes and I stifle them back. The only emotion I need right now is the heated rage that fuels my fire. Cole still hangs on to the regret of his decision to turn me. Even with my assurance from earlier, he holds that weight. I nod sharply, "How much time do we have?"

He looks at his watch. "Fifteen hours."

I wince. "Let's get going, then."

Chapter 18

We set off on the path to my parent's manor, taking the trek by foot through the woods. This route is a risk, but it is also quicker compared to the roads that would take us there. Amaund has extremely good hearing, even for vampire standards, and we can better conceal our footsteps than the tires of a car. Cole grabbed his gun from his dresser before we left and tucked it into the holster underneath his light jacket. The best way to get there without raising any alarms is through the woods, leading to the back of the house. From there, we plan to use the dark cover of the tree line to make our way to the back door. Sarah and Valeria could be anywhere in the house, though I suspect them to be either in the basement or the large family room. Neither will be easy to get to without alerting someone. We are both hoping that Amaund is either alone or with only a few comrades.

Above, the sky is black, devoid of a moon. Stars pinprick the sheet of endless darkness. The new moon helps us immensely, aiding our mission of stealth. We both don black clothing for increased chances of going unseen. Cole's obsidian hair sticks out from the hat he wears, giving him a criminal look. I smile to myself, masked by the night, picturing us as characters from a medieval game, breaking into a palace for a treasure.

Somewhere, a lone great-horned owl hoots into the crisp night air. The wind picks up around us, ruffling leaves. I don't know if that is of Cole's doing or if it just genuinely windy tonight. Regardless, it creates both an eerie feel to our mission and a cover for any sounds we might make. In front of us is a thinning maze of trees, indicating the open yard behind the house.

We stop before the yard begins, clouded by the secrets of the forest. No matter how good a vampire's sight may be, they can't penetrate the thick understory of these woods. Cole taps my arm twice, indicating that he doesn't see or hear anyone. We decided to make this a no talking mission so as to not compromise our silence.

With the confirmation, I lead us toward the side of the yard. A fence stands on the sides of the property, not allowing us to keep to the trees. We made a plan for this which involves creeping behind the shed before darting to the deck where we will hopefully be able to enter through a basement window. I've done this path countless times in the past, sneaking out to the shed to meet my only neighbors.

From behind the shed, we glance around again. Another two taps on my shoulder and we make our way for the deck, keeping to the grass for quiet steps. I don't see any lights on in the house, though the shades and curtains could be closed.

The rectangular basement window sits where it has always been underneath the deck. It opens nicely, without any resistance. The moment it does, a waft of mixed aromas assaults my nose. Out of the musty stench of mold, basement, and dust, one smell in particular stands out.

Blood.

I freeze, my body beginning to shake with both terror and anger. A strange combination.

Cole grabs my arm, but I wring free and jump straight into the basement, my feet making a thud onto the cement floor. I hear Cole land behind me as I push forward. The smell becomes intense and I struggle not to drop everything and make a beeline for food. The familiar dull throb of hunger mingles in my emotions. If someone is down here with us, I'll need my sense of smell and hearing to notice because it is pitch dark.

"Thea." Cole's voice startles me. I want to tell him to be quiet, but I realize there is nothing to hear us.

There is only silence.

There is no one alive here but us.

I don't know which outcome I would have preferred.

I open my palm and a small flame appears, offering some light in this depressing place. That's when I trip over something solid. Cole grabs my shoulder to keep me from falling over. I stifle a gasp.

"Mr. Esposito?" I whisper, voice shaking. My fire-loving professor. The one whose lessons taught me control of my own power over his favorite element. There is a leaf-covered stake protruding from his chest. My mind spins, unable to process that my favorite, caring professor was a vampire.

Cole kneels beside the body, his head in his hand. "Dammit, Juan."

Mr. Esposito's short brown hair is caked with drying blood. His once sparkling chocolate eyes stare blankly at the ceiling. I remember how he always smiled during lectures. "H-how?"

Cole closes Mr. Esposito's eyelids. "I told him he was risking too much."

"How do you know him?" The anger that resides permanently in my mind masks the confusion and sadness.

Cole flinches at my tone, his brows knitted together. "He was my friend. My ally when I was a Brais." His shoulders slump. "He was a spy for the Essites. He risked too much," he repeats.

Nausea ripples through me. "He was my college professor." The words come out strained.

I straighten and shake away the pain of his death. I clutch Cole's shoulder, offering support. I know he's in the midst of grieving, but right now I need to focus on finding my family. And Amaund. He will die tonight for hurting those I care about.

I will have to grieve my professor later.

"Now we know that he was here." The question is, was Sarah and Valeria here as well?

Cole stands. "Let's keep going," he says, his voice hard. "Maybe we will find a clue to his whereabouts."

We walk to the wooden stairs. An open wall panel around the corner catches my eye. It rests on the floor, just barely sticking out behind the furnace. A crease forms between my brows and I cautiously creep to it.

"What's wrong?" Cole whispers from behind me. Despite the silence from the rest of the house, his voice is hushed.

I don't respond as I continue on, shifting the flame in my palm to the hand farthest from the furnace. I don't think blowing up this house would help our investigation. Nor would it help my fragile emotions. It is the only piece of my parents left. And it is slowly being tainted.

The flickering light of the flames shines upon the open section of paneled wall. A stunned gasp leaves my lips when I behold the inside. Old looking crossbows and daggers worn away from time locked away hang from rusty hooks and nails. Stained papers, their inside edges uneven from being torn, lay on a wooden shelf next to crossbow bolts. A vial rests on its side beside them, whatever contents it had once long vanished.

Cole stills next to me, a light movement of air causing my fire to dance nervously.

I take a step back. "What... what is this?" My words come out in staggered sounds. When he doesn't answer, I whirl on him, the flames in my palm intensifying. "What is this?"

His eyes flicker to mine. "I have no idea." His tone is a baffled murmur. My fingers curl, nails digging into flesh. The fire engulfs my fist. Cole hardly takes notice as he looks back to the exposed wall section. "Did anyone own this house after your parents?"

"No," my voice is hard. "It is technically still mine."

Cole swallows. "Your family..." he runs a hand through his hair. "Your family were vampire hunters," he says, his voice distant.

"No," I repeat, taking more steps away. Away from a hidden truth. I shake my head. "There is no way."

Cole picks up one of the perforated papers, his gray eyes scanning. "This is barely legible, but it is addressed to a Connor, signed by an Adam Knight."

I clutch my shirt. "My grandfather to my father," my voice trembles. The last piece of my normal life comes crashing down in an explosion of chaos. My family. The weight of their kept secrets bubbles in my chest. The emotion—whatever it is—mingles with those that have leaked from the cage, inciting my magic to a destructive force.

Cole places a hand on my arm. "Thea, I'm sorry."

I look to him, my vision red with fury. "Do you think—"

A soft thud from upstairs stifles the words from leaving my lips. We look from the stairs to each other before simultaneously making our way up to the first floor.

I always hated the basement of this house. For some reason, it had always made me uneasy. Now, the image of the hidden compartment and the body of Mr. Esposito will taint any remaining memories of this place.

Once upstairs, the metallic aroma of blood becomes overwhelming, filling my senses. My hunger returns, fueling my magic that is already raging inside with anger. The smell invokes worry. I was hoping that it all had come from the basement, but that doesn't seem to be the case.

My heart pounds, echoing in my head, the only sound I hear. There is no one here but us.

I am terrified of what we might find. Memories of family dinners resurface as we make our way from the kitchen to the dining room. The house is a skeleton of what it used to be, empty counters lay against the tiled walls with layers of dust collected on their marble surface. The walls in the dining room are stained and cracked from years of being unkempt. The old dining table that we used to use for our formal meals is pushed out from the center of the room, complete with worn wooden chairs.

Somehow, the emotions of my parents' death, long thought released, mix with that of everything else that I am feeling. Every inch of my skin burns, the magic inside whirling fiercely within. The sensation is not unpleasant, but actually strangely intoxicating, like if I gave in to the flames, I could explode with ecstasy.

All the more reason to hope Amaund is close by. For I will give him a show.

Around the corner of the dining room is the family room. Suddenly, a deep-rooted feeling of dread pounds in my gut. As I round the grand archway into the room that once held so much love, my feet stop, and so does time. The world around me shatters like a mirror that met a hammer. Strings that held my life together snap and I feel myself teetering out of control. In the middle of the floor lies a lifeless Valeria. Her blank eyes stare at the ceiling, devoid of color. My legs move toward her and collapse next to her body. She still wears the gray blouse she wore when she made the barrier. The smear of the maroon incense still clinging to the material. The whole time we were enjoying life...has she been a captive?

Her throat is torn, and dried blood is pooled underneath her, staining her beautiful chocolate brown hair. My hand trembles above her body as I reach for her, nausea slicing through me. I want to collapse on her, cry into her shirt like I've done a thousand times before. I stand abruptly, clutching my stomach and mouth to stifle a sob, as I turn away from her body.

Nausea and dizziness threaten to consume me.

In the doorway, Cole stands with his hat in his hand. His eyes are rimmed red. "Thea..." he says softly.

I ignore him and grab hold of the pillar in the doorway to keep my shaky legs upright. My grip is so tight that I feel it crack under the pressure. A few tears fall free from my eyes.

"Thea," Cole says again, taking a step closer. His voice is soft, "Don't get angry. Feel sad, feel the loss. But don't feed the anger." He places a hand on my back but immediately pulls it away.

My skin feels like pure fire. Underneath my grip, the column smokes and burns, a sizzling flame spreading outward from my palm.

"Control yourself, Thea."

My head snaps to him and he takes a step back, eyes wide with surprise. "I can't, Cole. I can't feel anything but wrath," I seethe, releasing the column and running a hand through my hair. The smell of the smoke covers that of Valeria's blood.

"Thea, your eyes." He moves closer again and puts his hands on my face despite the heat. His skin tingles on mine and he winces. I motion to take a step back, but he holds me firmly in place. "He wants you angry, Thea. That's how he'll find you. That is how you give in to the Brais. Don't let him have another win." His eyes frantically dart across mine. "The more you use your magic out of anger, the more it will consume you. You'll be so addicted to the destruction, that you will go with him freely."

My ears hear his words, and they make sense. But my body is rejecting the thought. It is already addicted to the magic. To the incredible feeling of releasing the ravenous, glorious flames.

The release is euphoric.

Pure.

He pulls me into an embrace, my skin still hot. "Thea, please."

Out of the corner of my eyes, I see her again. Her motionless body. The emotions become stronger, hotter.

Cole releases me and steps back.

"Cole, please leave," I say through gritted teeth.

"No."

"Please, Cole." Tears sizzle on my cheeks, evaporating before they reach my chin. "I want to burn this place to the ground. It holds nothing but misery now." Fire engulfs my hands and travels slowly up my arms. "If I don't, I might lose control in the forest." My voice lowers. "I'll do it whether you're here or not."

His eyes hold my gaze for a moment, then without a word, he leaves through the back door. I didn't miss the look of disappointment on his face. Or the slight tinge of his fear in the air.

A loud sob escapes my mouth as I hear the door slam closed. I pinch my eyes shut, embracing the sensation of the flames licking at my skin as they travel up toward my neck and down to my legs. I feel like a bomb heading for the ground, anticipating the explosion. Images float to the forefront of my mind. Of Valeria's smile. Of the dark family secret hidden downstairs. They fuel that last bit of swirling magic deep inside. I scream when I fall to the ground, but the roar of the fire masks it. It sounds like ten fighter jets thundering overhead. And it feels like the release of all the pent up, debilitating heavy emotions leaping off of my shoulders and into the night.

Chapter 19

Amaund

I open my eyes and take a deep inhale of the night's air, a triumphant smile tugs at my lips. The smell of a fresh fire in the distance is comforting, especially considering how it was created. Crippling anger and sorrow flood my senses, but I know that they are not my emotions.

All the sweeter.

The night sky gives away no secrets to the events that occurred just a mile south from where I am now. The stars shine in the endless abyss above as they always do.

"So?"

I turn to see Commander Kael standing underneath the lamppost. His angular face is stoic against the darkness like a perfectly chiseled masterpiece. His jaw is clenched. He expects good news.

I never disappoint.

"You will have her soon," I say calmly, my hands clasped behind my back. "I will be surprised, actually, if she doesn't come willingly." The pull of her emotions is astronomical, all-consuming.

"Good," he responds. "And what of the witch?"

The leader of the filthy coven. "Dead. What better way to egg her along?"

His smile cuts across his face in a sinister way, bordered by dark facial hair. In the lack of light, it appears that he is wearing a mask. It would be hard to argue that he is not if his teeth weren't reflecting the light with his smile. "The King will be very pleased to hear this." His piercing amber eyes shine like a lantern in the darkest of nights. "Do you have a plan?"

A corner of my lips pull up. "Always." I inhale deeply, sorting through her emotions that mingle with mine. "She is already addicted to destruction. I'll remind her of her choices. The King will grind her to the ashes that she creates when she comes."

"Good." He turns to walk away, engulfed in the darkness of the night. "I will meet you at the castle."

Chapter 20

All around me is rubble, piles of brick and wood. Where there once was a family room, there is now a heap of a burnt, old home. Dust and smoke dance like a haze, visible only in the light of the smolders. The only part of the house untouched is where I kneel. The floor directly above me is the only indication that this building once had two stories.

When I stand, my legs feel unstable and I use a broken chair for support. I suck in a deep breath and wince at a sharp throb at the back of my neck. My arms hang at my sides, numb from the spent magic. A throbbing headache blooms behind my eyes. Without taking another look, I walk straight over the debris and out the obliterated wall.

Cole stands at the edge of the forest, his eyes reflecting the light of the dancing flames. I make my way to him slowly, my feet scuffing along the grass. The release of my magic expended a tremendous amount of energy, leaving me tired and dry. Somehow, the clothes I wear were not burnt away. My foot catches on the root of a tree and I almost tumble to the ground, but Cole comes to my side in a flash.

He wraps my arm around his neck and helps me walk away from the burning building.

A loud crack echoes in the silence, making me flinch. We turn and see the last part of the second-floor crumble to the ground.

My family's home is no more, a mere memory, like everything else from my past is beginning to be. Everything that made me who I am is crumbling to ash. I will not share that fate.

I am not the phoenix who rises from the ashes.

I am the inferno who makes them.

Cole and I stand in silence, watching the remainder of the manor burn away. The smell of the smoke is somehow comforting. It is the concrete end to my past life, my human life. It is like starting a painting on a fresh canvas. All creations from the past do not matter, only what goes on now. You can take the lessons learned from those old works of art and forge a new, better piece.

"We should get going," Cole finally says, "before the authorities show up."

"I can walk."

He lets go of my arm without arguing, and we resume our trek back to his cabin. I know he is disappointed in my actions tonight. Part of me feels guilty about that. All of me would choose to do it again.

Our ten-minute walk turns into twenty. Two vampires at full stamina can move a lot faster than when we have one who still is and one who is exhausted. I half expect Cole to continue walking, leaving me to my own pace. Instead, he simply keeps a few feet away, occasionally looking behind his shoulder to make sure that I am still following.

"Is the barrier still intact?" I ask, my voice shaky, when we finally reach his quiet property.

"Yes. So long as Sarah is alive, it will remain up."

We enter his house. Helios is sitting on the couch and I am ready to collapse into a long sleep next to him. But I can't. We still need to make a plan to get Sarah back. That entire excursion took only an hour and a half. We have a little more than eleven hours before Amaund kills Sarah. If he hasn't already.

"I need a drink," I mumble as I trudge to his kitchen. Cole closes his door and remains standing by it, watching me as I help myself to his supply. "Do you want some?"

He just stares, his eyes pinned on me.

I can't tell what thoughts race through his head, though I don't think any of them are cheery.

"Thea, I need to know if you are going to do that every time something angers you." He crosses his arms. I close the door to the refrigerator and put the bag down on the counter. "Because if that is your plan, then you might as well leave and join the Brais because that is where you will end up." He sighs. "Either with them or dead."

I flinch at his words. I wonder to myself how anger has become such a part of my being when I hardly succumbed to it as a human. "I don't know," I admit, my eyes falling to my feet. And I truly do not. There is no way I could promise to not feel the pain and anger with whatever happens in the next ten hours. Amaund may be a fire wielder, but I know mine can beat his. I feel it in my soul. My fire consumes all, even the power of my beta ability, feeding on both my anger and revenge. Those emotions make it strong.

"Thea," he walks to me, lifting my chin so my watery eyes meet his, "I will do what I can to help you from falling onto those paths. But you need to trust me. Listen when I give advice." The coolness of his soft lips tingle on my forehead. The compassionate gesture soothes the buzz of leftover magic in my bones. "I've been at this for a long time. I will not watch you ruin yourself."

I let my eyes close and lean into his chest, breathing in his comforting scent. This man, I can't let go of. In the short time that I have known him, he has morphed into my rock. My stability in this new, chaotic life. "My family..." I let the thought trail away, and he wraps his arms around me tightly.

"We will figure it out. Together," he murmurs into my hair. We stand together, holding each other for a while. I let the pain of everything flow out of me.

My death.

Valeria's death.

My parent's death.

For each one, a sliver of myself broke away, floating in the endlessness of the universe. Standing here with Cole, I realize that he is one of those pieces, transformed. He and Sarah.

And that is why I need to save her.

Even if it means losing myself.

Chapter 21

I stand in the dining room with Cole, who sits at the small table, formulating a new plan. Only ten hours left on the clock. Time is running dangerously low before we lose our leeway. The cabin is still secured by the barrier, despite Valeria being killed. The magic was bound by the bags she and Sarah set up. Only one of them can break it.

"I did my research on Amaund some years ago. He likes being close to his targets, probably hiding in the forest somewhere. Or in another abandoned building."

"Why is he interested in knowing who turned me?" I remember the conversation I had with him. Just the thought of that conversation makes me shiver, my world crashing down in a matter of hours.

Cole looks up from the map laid out in front of him. "They want to know whose magic line you come from."

"They? Magic line?" I ask with a raised eyebrow, leaning against the doorway of the bathroom.

He nods. "They as in the Commander and the King." He clasps his hands together on the table. "Magic lines connect vampires. The older vampires believe that they are entitled to those under their lines."

"Oh," I say, pulling out the chair across from him. "So, whose line am I?"

Cole lifts his shoulders. "I don't know, honestly. I turned you and after that it is a mystery. The vampire who turned me is dead. I never asked when I was turned, and I didn't care to find out afterward."

Sighing, I gaze at the map. The parchment is a little outdated. Some of the segments indicated as a forested area has been destroyed and made into industrial zones. I remember vividly because there were a lot of protests from environmental groups. Sarah and I tagged along with some other friends during one of the protests. It happened to be the only one during that long week that ended without any hostile confrontations. Now, I can't help but wonder if Sarah—or any other witches—were the reason behind the civility of the crowd.

"This area is mostly small factories and warehouses. Would he be there?" I point to the spot on the map, which he circled with a red pen some time ago. The ink is slowly fading, worn out by the sun or some other agent.

He shakes his head. "No, I don't think so. He prefers classier or wilder settings."

A red square indicates where Cole's cabin sits amongst the trees. A couple miles to the east are some older houses where the heart of the city once was. Most of them have been converted into renovated local shops or art studios and galleries. The newest buildings in that neighborhood have been renovated and kept as homes, either for renting permanently or as temporary getaways.

"What about here?" I place my finger on the stretch of renovated buildings.

"I was thinking there too. The secluded homes at the far end could fit his likeness."

"Great, let's get going then," I say a little too eagerly.

Standing from the table, Cole folds the map delicately and places it back in a kitchen drawer. "Before we go, promise me that you'll follow me this time. If I say we continue, then we continue. If I say we turn around, we do so." He stands firmly with his arms crossed.

I swallow a lump forming in my throat. "I promise," the words are like sandpaper on my tongue. If there is any sign of Sarah in trouble, I don't know how I will respond. My magic rumbles in my chest, mirroring my feelings.

He eyes me, perhaps to see if my facial expression will give away any lying intent. "Good," he says finally. "How is your stamina? Do you need blood first?"

I test the responsiveness of my magic, which roars to life immediately. That once secured cage hidden deep within bends, giving space for those buried emotions to seep into my blood. The veins in my hands vibrate. "Nope, I'm good."

"Okay."

We set back out the door, toward our new hopeful destination. Once again, we are covered in dark clothing from head to toe, matching the night sky above. The magic of my energy manipulation has taken a back seat during these twenty-four hours. I feel it in my body, suppressed by that of the fire inside me. It tried to claw its way out at the manor, but by then, the flames were already engulfing my body. That magic reminds me of who I was as a human, who I wish to still be. I used to be good at not holding on to anger.

Now it is the strongest emotion I feel.

"What are you thinking about?" Cole asks, startling me. I shrug, contemplating whether or not to confide in him. "You can tell me, you know."

"I know." I sigh, looking up at the stars above. "I was just wondering how anger has wedged itself so bluntly into my regular emotions." My voice is quiet, like I am afraid to admit it out loud. Maybe I am. In the past, I always prided myself on the calm aura that hummed around me at all times. The human me wouldn't even recognize me as a vampire.

He places a hand on my back. "I get that. Do you remember me telling you about a vampire's heightened senses?"

I shove my hands in to the pockets of my jacket. "Yes, but these are emotions."

"They're one in the same," he responds with a wave of his hand. "Remember, our senses and emotions can be glorious or debilitating. What we perceive in the outside world effects our emotions. We choose how we respond to those triggers. And as vampires, we have a heightened capability of both. As a human, stubbing your toe hurts and might get you mad, but you probably won't punch the furniture or wall. As a vampire, it might not hurt as much, but you could see it as an irritating nuisance and lash out, destroying the object and anything in its path."

His words sink in and I recall the morning that I awoke after the car accident. Vampires feel and experience everything on a higher level, he had said after I fed for the first time. I can't believe I have been dead for over a month already. I chuckle, thinking of the tree that stopped the car all those nights ago.

"What are you laughing about?"

"It's just funny that the one thing that can kill me already has."

Cole huffs a laugh. "Well, it tried back then."

"Right." Technically, the tree almost killed me. Cole was the one who finished the job, though he was ultimately saving me in the end. "A car accident claimed my parent's lives. A car accident almost claimed mine. A plant can kill me, and a plant almost did." Fate. Destiny. I don't know what I would call these. Coincidences, maybe.

One thing is for sure, fire cannot kill me.

So, Amaund's magic is useless.

We walked for almost forty minutes before we reached the neighborhood of old houses. The one we figured Amaund would use is nestled on the farthest plot of land on a dead-end road. It has enough space as a base and is far enough away from any prying eyes or ears. Its gray brick structure is covered heavily with browning vines, slowly giving way to the call of autumn. Outside, there are no vehicles, animals, vampires or humans that we can see. The eerie quiet sets my nerves on end, and my fire magic pools underneath the skin of my palms. Only one light appears to be on in the house, and it is located on the first floor, facing the road.

I shadow Cole as he creeps toward the window, a wooden stake in his hand. He decided to ditch the gun since we were going to a more residential setting. We crouch underneath the window, listening for any sounds from inside. I follow suit and pull out the stake I kept hidden in my jacket pocket. The buzz of the branch's energy vibrates into my cells.

Cole motions with a hand to move around the corner of the house. No noises emanate from these windows, but we hear voices on the other side. We stalk their sounds until we reach the backside of the house. A two-car garage sits behind the home, the door is open wide. Inside, we see two people standing and conversing with each other. They wear black leather, a silver symbol of the Brais etched on their backs. A large brick chimney blocks our bodies from being seen.

"Vampires," Cole mouths as he holds out two fingers. A wind picks up as he stands. This, I know is his doing. The ground is littered with brown, decaying leaves, giving a perfect sound buffer. In the garage, the two vampires continue their conversation, oblivious to us.

Cole takes one large step out from the house. His movement catches the eye of one of the vampires, he turns and notices Cole but is too late. The stake once in Cole's hand is thrown, propelled with lightning speed at the vampire's chest. He collapses in a heap. Cole stretches out his hand and the stake returns to him, dripping with crimson liquid. The other vampire turns, his face red with fury.

The window behind me shatters as another vampire jumps out. I turn to face the new threat, trusting Cole with my backside. He is tall, standing maybe almost a foot in height above me. Fire bursts from his hands, only going as far as his wrists. A corner of my lips lift. This poor fool.

He throws a small fireball at me and I hold my hand up to dispel it. The flames hit me in the palm and crawl up my arm, disappearing in my skin in a glorious frenzy. The vampire's eyes go round, and he falters out of surprise but recovers quickly and pulls his own stake out from behind him.

"Where is Amaund?" I ask demandingly.

He responds with a laugh as he charges forward at me. I have just enough time to dodge his jab toward my stomach.

He's fast.

But I am too. And I had a phenomenal teacher.

As I evade his rebound attack, I fling my fist at my attacker's head and connect with his jaw. This hardly phases him physically, but it sure appears to have made him angry. Apparently, he plans to try fire again. Amber sparks from his fingertips and he moves to grab my neck. I move in time and he latches onto my arm instead. Searing pain breaks my concentration and I look to his hand. Instead of orange flames on his fingers, they are a sickening green. The flames slide around my arm like liquid and I howl in agony.

The vampire smirks and his grip on me tightens. A wave of nausea washes over me quickly, and I fight to remain standing. He is too distracted by his pleasure of causing me pain that he doesn't notice my fist coming up from underneath him. The point of the stake cuts upward into his chest, hitting its mark. The vampire's eyes roll over and he falls to the ground in a thud.

Kneeling, I twist to look at my arm. Burns, green and white, bubble on my skin. It looks like some kind of poison. My attention snaps up towards the back of the house when I hear glass breaking. Fighting through the pain and nausea, I get to my feet and rush to help Cole.

I find Cole and his enemies in the garage, toward the back. One vampire is on the ground, his skin already sunken in. Cole has the other vampire pinned against the wall—his grip tight on his neck. Sharp objects of all sort hang in the air, aimed for the enemy's face.

"Where can we find Amaund and the witch he took?" Cole exclaims.

"Not...here..." the vampire answers, his voice raspy. "Coming...for you."

Cole shoves the vampire against the wall hard enough to crack the cement. "Where?"

The vampire laughs as blood oozes from his lips.

I see Cole's lip twitch before he stabs the vampire in the heart with his stake. The objects in the air drop simultaneously after the body does. I just stare, mouth agape at his abilities. If I didn't want to get on his bad side before, now I definitely don't. I pity anyone who does.

I look around at the destruction. Broken glass, tools, and blood splatter the ground. We struck out again. Sarah is not here.

"We will find her, Thea."

I look at the sky, the colors are lightening from black to navy. "We are running out of time, Cole." The fire inside me boils, anxious to find my best friend. I shake off feelings of unease at thoughts of her possible current shape, beat, broken, and bloody.

Please let her be okay, I plead to anything that may be listening out in the universe.

"Should we check the other houses?"

He shakes his head. "No, it would be a waste of time. He wouldn't have his resources spread out this much." Cole's eyes fall on my arm, a sting still lingering. "What happened?"

I shrug. "I don't know. That vampire grabbed my arm with flames on his fingertips, but they turned green and hurt like hell."

He steps closer, examining the burns. "He has a poison ability." His eyes return to mine. "You are lucky he only grabbed you by the arm. This could have dropped you quickly."

I lift an eyebrow. "How do I fix it?"

Cole's charcoal eyes turn scarlet and his sharp fangs protrude from his mouth. He bites his wrist and offers his blood to me. "This will heal you."

I recoil from his wrist, my mind flashing to the day of the hiker. Vague memories of drinking his blood after getting sick from the hiker's clatter in my mind. "Trust me," he says. "This is nothing like that poison," he adds, reading my thoughts. "This will help."

I look at him skeptically, but heed his advice, taking hold of him. My own teeth elongate and sink into his skin. The sweetness of his blood dances on my tongue like cotton candy. It doesn't satisfy like that of a human. Instead, it ignites a pooling heat in my center. I curl my toes at the intensity of the rising desire. His other hand lands gently on my lower back, sending shivers down my spine.

The magic that binds us together works its miracles. I feel the skin on my arm mend together, the burns nothing but a memory. When I pull away from his wrist, his eyes are a mix of a deep shade of merlot and smoke, reflecting the light from the garage.

"Thank you," I whisper, wiping my lips with my fingers. "That was... oddly sensual."

"For me, as well," he says, a low growl from his throat.

Heat rises from my neck and I clear my throat. "Should we head back?" I peek up at the sky. The sun is brightening the dark sheet above our heads and the stars recede. The moon would have fled a while ago, retreating into the distance beyond the mountains. "We are running out of time," I say again, a bit of panic settling into my tone.

Cole follows my gaze above and lets out a sigh. "We should probably abandon our plan for a surprise advantage. By now, Amaund sensed your power. He hangs his head, his eyes fixed on the gravel beneath his feet. The wind still whips around, though with less fury than it had when we started. It makes me wonder if Cole just incites the force of the phenomenon, then nature carries on with it.

"So, we just sit and wait?" I furrow my brows. That feels like giving up to me. There is no advantage when it comes to getting Sarah back with that plan.

He brings his eyes to mine and shakes his head. "Who said anything about sitting and waiting?" A slight smile tugs on his lips. "I vote we go back to my cabin. Make him come to us on known ground. It will be our last line of surprise."

"What about Sarah?"

"He will bring her. I know it. She is his leverage."

I nod. "Okay. I second that vote then." His eyes light up like a child staring at a toy shop. Butterflies dance in my stomach at his glee. I raise an intrigued eyebrow. "What do you have in mind?"

He walks back in the direction of his home. "Well, I have some fortifications in place around my property. They are mostly audio bombs that I planted a few years ago. I will have to use the rest of our time to tweak them a little, but they should still work."

I cock my head. "Um, audio bombs? I have no idea what those are, but a bomb probably would be a bad idea. Just in case Sarah is with him." Oh, I hope she will be. I need to see with my own eyes that she is alive still.

"They'll be harmless to her but debilitating to Amaund and any other vampire in close proximity."

"What about us?" It seems counterproductive to use a device that would incapacitate us as well.

He shakes his head. "We will be far enough out of range. It will take them a few seconds to get back to their feet, in which we can stake them and get Sarah." A *few* seconds? That doesn't seem like enough time. "I might be able to keep them down longer with my abilities," he adds as if he could sense my doubts. "Their guards will be down, so I think I should be able to get in their heads and keep them down longer. You can get Sarah away to safety then I will stake them."

"That sounds like you are betting on a lot of ifs." *If* he can keep them restrained with his beta ability. *If* he can get the bombs to work.

"It will work, Thea." Something about the confidence in his tone makes me believe that I can trust Sarah's life—our lives—in his hands, even if it is reckless.

We enter the forest. The call of the trees is serene as life stirs with the promise of the rising sun. Birds sing in the far distance.

They are chirping their merry songs, as if it were a time to be merry. I inhale the calming scent of pine and leaves.

"I've been speculating about your beta ability too." Cole nudges my arm as we keep a steady pace.

Curious, I arch an eyebrow. "How so?"

"If you can manipulate a person's emotions to calm them, you could probably do the same for fear. Root your enemies in place, make them afraid to move."

A twinge of my second ability purrs underneath the fire, eager to be used. I gaze at my hands as we walk, the crunch of leaves echoing in the silent woods. "But so far, I have only used it while touching something. I would have to be close to them to use it."

He shrugs. "It is just a speculation. If you find yourself in a dire situation, keep that idea in your mind."

"Okay."

Cole's hand against my chest stops my legs abruptly. I look over to him, his eyes are pinned to our surroundings, searching.

"What?"

He doesn't answer immediately, and my nerves pick up. The call of my fire warms my skin. "Do you hear that?" he asks, his voice barely a whisper.

I look straight down the endless pines, their dark branches shadowing the forest. I concentrate on my ears, straining them. Not a single chirp of a bird, crack of a stick, or groan of a tree. It is as if we have entered another dimension. One where there is no sound, no movement. The wind has ceased as well, not even enough to sway the branches at the canopy. I turn my head to meet Cole's gaze, my eyes wide. "I hear nothing."

Scarlet flashes in his eyes, anger and magic. I watch as he slowly pulls out the stake from his jacket pocket. The wood is still caked with the blood from our earlier combatants, the green inner part barely poking through. "Amaund is here," he growls.

Chapter 22

Vampires step out from behind the trees, as if they were covered by a veil on all sides. We should have been able to hear or sense them, but it is like they appeared out of thin air, hiding behind something only they could see. At least a dozen stand around us, forming a circle. More than half of them have flames dripping from their hands and arms. I fear for Cole. Their fire could kill him.

Cole and I stand with our backs to each other, both of us gripping a wooden stake. Though they greatly outnumber us, no one budges to make the first move. We all stand still, watching each other with hunger in our eyes.

After a few moments, a vampire to my left charges. He pulls water from the ground as he runs, leaving a trail of dried leaves and plants. The water crawls up his arm and freezes into razor sharp edges. Without a thought, I react to him, turning my body to face the danger. I hear movement behind me in response, but Cole twirls to defend my back.

The ice vampire brings his deadly arm up, aiming for my gut. With just enough time, I step to the side and land a blow on his chest. Fire pours out of my fist and spreads over him. He howls as he crumbles to the ground, writhing in pain as the element consumes him. I stare, stunned for a moment. I only meant to punch him, not engulf him with my magic.

The sound of another attacker pulls me back to the fight. I look up just a moment too late and catch a jab to my throat. Thorny vines cling to my neck, tightening with each second. This vampire can control the earth. I drop to the ground, breathless, clutching the plant with my hands. He pulls back for a punch to my head, but I hold out my left hand to block. A large inferno roars from my palm, sending him and two other vampires back fifteen feet. I watch as the flames consume them and the trees around us. The vines around my neck disintegrate in my fiery hand, landing around me in a pile of ash.

Gasping for air, I steal a glance at Cole. Four vampires lie on the ground around his feet, puncture marks on their chest dripping with red liquid. He moves at lightning speed, fending off two at once. One attacker manages to blast a fireball toward Cole's back. A gust of wind releases from him, pushing his forward attacker back. The fireball falters a little but slices at his shoulder as he tries to dodge.

I try to call out to him, forcing myself to a wobbly upright stance. My throat is scratchy, and it feels like a lump is sitting inside of it. Out of the corner of my eye, I see more vampires emerge from the invisible wall.

How many are there?

I peek down at my feet, the stake I was holding lies in waiting. I don't dare reach down to grab it while new enemies approach in all directions. Instead, I call to my fire. I call to the flames that live within my body. They react immediately, sizzling at the surface, my skin hot like glass in the sun. Cole and I turn to face each other simultaneously. Our eyes meet in a wordless understanding. Our minds are one. He drops to the ground, an aura of wind racing tightly around his body.

I roar as I release all the energy building up. Everything around us brightens as the firestorm snarls out of my body, racing toward the vampires seen and unseen. With any luck, this will affect any vampires still hidden behind their invisible safety net. The release is sweet, like letting go of a heavy object that I have been carrying for quite some time. My limbs lighten and tingle as the last bit of flames leave my skin.

The attackers around us had no time to react. Some run at me from all sides but dropped once my flames encircles them. Most don't even have time to scream.

I drop to the ground in exhaustion, nails digging into the dirt. My limbs are heavy and my arms wobble. All around us are burnt, lifeless bodies. The plants and trees suffered too, and I feel a tinge of guilt, of loss, as they burn from the trunk up. Cole lifts himself off the ground, kneeling in the dirt. His eyes are wide as he takes in the damage around us. I watch as he brings his hands outward, palms facing me. A barely visible sphere of some sort closes around my head and I flinch, confused. I see the same thing around his head. Looking up, I see the flames receding from the tall trees. When they are no more, the sphere around my head disappears.

"What did you just do?" I ask as Cole catches himself from face planting onto the ground. His breathing is heavy, indicating the amount of magic he used to do that. Whatever that was.

"I created a vacuum to put out the flames." He pauses, taking in air. "Stole the oxygen from the vicinity." Sweat beads from his forehead and he swipes them away, his hand trembling. He smiles weakly at me. "I'd like to never have to do that again." He leans back on his knees, resting his hands on his thighs and blows out a deep, shaky breath. "It uses a lot of my energy."

A faint smile makes its way to my lips as well. "Noted." Looking around at our mess, I say, "Thank you, though. For clearing the fire and having my back." I swallow, the scratchiness in my throat still prominent.

"Of course, Thea. I know the guilt you would feel if this place burned. I will always have your back."

My face splits into a grin even more, a red heat blooming on my neck and face. I clear my throat and force myself to a standing position. When I see Cole trying to do the same, I lend him a hand. We stand together, a pair of wobbly vampires, holding each other from falling. "Do you think that was all of them?"

I hoped, but I doubted it. There was still no sign of Amaund.

No sign of Sarah.

Cole shakes his head slightly, wincing at an unknown pain. "Unfortunately, I don't think so."

As soon as he finished his sentence, more vampires stepped out of the shadows. Each of them held a large recurve bow with what appeared to be live wooden arrows knocked and aimed for us.

Cole and I separate from each other, readying ourselves for another fight, though I am unsure how we can fend off attackers with these weapons. Especially considering that we both have spent our magic. The fire beneath my skin tingles where once it blazed. It wants to lash out, to help defend, but lacks the energy.

That's when two more figures emerge from the veil. The others part to create a path.

A tower of a man waltzes in from behind a tree, his hand around the neck of a girl with bruises around both eyes and a long gash down her cheek.

But she is alive.

Sarah.

Chapter 23

My heart breaks at the sight of her paled skin and sunken, puffy eyes. A dark, crusty line of crimson stains her neck and dribbles down to her blouse She looks at me with a deep sadness.

She opens her mouth, about to speak, when the nightmare of a vampire shoves her to the ground. The Brais next to them puts his bow down and holds Sarah tightly, a knife to her throat.

My lips curl as I move my attention to that of the man who has haunted me for the last month. Somehow, he is more intimidating in this space than he was at Cole's cabin. His hair, a dark glistening onyx, is slicked back and tied into a braided ponytail. Glowing red-gold irises shine in his eyes, a menacing smile on his lips. A cloak covers his rigid body, the material so inky black that it appears to swallow the light of the rising sun. "Amaund," I hiss.

"Thea, dear."

Bile rises in my throat in response to his voice. To his words. Memories of his visit come crashing to my consciousness. The fear I felt in that moment shakes my body all over again. From behind, a vampire grabs my body, placing me in a tight hold. I fling my arms forward, trying to break free of his grasp. My strength has retreated with my magic. The vampire's grip on me tightens, nails digging into my flesh.

"You are most certainly not what I expected," Amaund says as he stalks toward me. "First, you had that barrier created to keep me out that none of my witches were able to break. Second, you killed the witch I hired to capture you." He places a hand on the hilt of a sword at his hip. The flowing cloak on his back hid the weapon and the steely silver armor he wears, which glistens in the slowly emerging daylight. I wish the sun would reveal itself right now. An emblem with the symbol of the Brais is etched onto the chest plate of his armor. The shield with the letter "B" inside.

"Third," he continues, "you and your sire here," he jerks his head at Cole, "killed many of my men." With a gap of almost six feet, he stops creeping closer. His demeanor is so calm, so unmoving, that he frightens me more than if he was a bottle of pent-up anger. "I must say, that has most definitely surprised me." He leans in a bit. "But what is even more surprising is your magic. Your power of destruction. Capable of destroying a forest," his hands raise, gesturing to our charred surroundings, "or an entire building." A sinister smile pulls his lips upward. "You are a strong Brais."

Memories of Valeria on the floor of my childhood home filter in front of my vision. My nostrils flare as fear recedes and fury resurfaces. "I will *never* be a Brais," I spit. My magic is still dim, but my anger has no limits. It floods my body with immense adrenaline, and I break away from the one who holds me as I twist my arms from his grasp. I fling myself toward Amaund. He doesn't move. He remains a poised statue, watching as I will my power to come forward.

It doesn't. It hides deep within my body.

Still fatigued, I falter and fall to a knee in front of Amaund, gripping the ground. Leaves crumble in my grasp, but there is no smell of them burning. When I needed it most, my fire left.

"Don't let them be another casualty of your selfishness to surrender," Amaund says.

I look up and see Sarah still in the grasp of a vampire who is much stronger than she. The knife at her throat holds firm, a drop of blood trickling from where it is pressed against her skin. My eyes shift to Cole behind me. Two vampires hold him, one on each arm. A third vampire holds a stake to his back. All around us, wooden arrows are pointed to his chest. I clench my jaw and squeeze my eyes shut. Salty tears break away from my lashes and fall down my cheeks. I open my eyes again and meet Cole's unbreaking gaze. He knows what thoughts race in my mind as my gaze sweeps over the two people I care most about.

I cannot lose them.

Turning back to Amaund, I see his hand outstretched toward me. "Come with me. Save them," he says.

"Thea, don't," Cole calls from behind me, his voice faltering. I turn to look at him again. "Please."

I memorize his face, his body. The way his grey eyes pierce mine with intensity whenever the heat of our closeness reaches its peak. The way his soft obsidian, messy hair falls around his face, giving him a dark but intoxicating energy. I etch in my head the color of his lips and the longing I have to taste them. The feel of his hands as they caress my cheek. Of how they fit perfectly in mine. And I memorize the soothing sound of his voice in my ear. Finally, my eyes meet his, and I watch them as they widen, his head sinking in defeat.

Slowly, I face Amaund again. His eyes remain fixed on me, ready for any ill movement. "They will be spared," I grit out.

He nods without hesitation and outstretches his arm. I reach my hand for his—

"Take me instead," Cole's firm voice booms into the silence.

Amaund's gaze flicks behind me to Cole.

"No," I whisper.

The Brais General takes a step toward him, his head cocked. "What do you have that the King would want over her?"

"I'll give you my name." His voice falters. I hear the quiver in his words despite the force he puts behind them.

Amaund studies Cole for a moment. "You have piqued my interest. Go on."

"Swear it. That you will take me in her place." There is a slight tremor to his voice, the words melding together as they spill out of his mouth.

"No," my voice comes out quiet and raspy.

"Okay," Amaund says. "Tell me."

I hear Cole swallow and feel the heat of his intense gaze on me. Something inside my heart cracks at that sensation. I feel as though I could be swallowed up by the earth, broken into pieces and scattered into the wind.

"Nicolai Moretti."

I squeeze my eyes shut and a tear falls down my cheeks.

A short laugh rumble in Amaund's chest. "The Tempest. We thought you had died." He steps back so that he is in front of me once again, though his attention is still on Cole. "The King will want to hear that you are actually alive." He offers Cole a light bow of his head. "Thank you for offering that information."

I feel a cold hand grab my arm and haul me to my feet abruptly. I hear Cole shout, his voice laced with anger and sorrow.

Without a second to spare, Amaund pulls me away.

Away from my best friend.

Away from the man who holds my heart.

And into a world I have come to fear.

Acknowledgements

It feels unreal that I am even writing this section in this book. There are so many people that helped me get to this part in this process. To anyone who is reading this section, welcome. I hope I don't forget anyone! Let's get going!

First, I wanted to express my gratitude to everyone who read my book while it was still in the creation phase. My beta readers, you all are the best! Tara, thank you for offering your time to be my first reader. You not only helped me with the writing and development, but you helped me move past all my internal struggles as well. Nicolette, there are no words that I can use to say how thankful I am for you! You are an absolutely wonderful editor and helped me bring this story to life. You stuck through all the mistakes (and sheesh, there were a lot!) and were so helpful and kind about everything. I adored all the little notes and drawings you included on the manuscript!

To my beloved family, thank you for being the guinea pigs and my very first fans! You helped me stick to the writing and creation of this story and cannot express enough how grateful I am for wanting to read it (especially before the edits were implemented!) Despite all the mistakes, you kept on reading. To my mom, my rock and continued support, who was the first to read my book after the heavy edits I put into it. Your love for Thea and Cole makes me so happy! To my dad who kept on my butt about getting this story finished. Despite not being a fantasy reader, you have continued to support me through this, and it means so much to me that you have read it! To my brothers: you both lent me an incredible amount of support through this and I am teary-eyed just thinking about it!

To all of my fantastic friends who have supported me. To Sienna for helping me realize that this story in my head is worth putting out into the world. You're an amazing friend and I don't know where I would be on this journey without your kind soul! And to Brittany, who was extremely helpful and supportive during my journey despite how crazy some of my questions might have been. I am so grateful for being able to lean on you when I felt lost!

To all the writers, readers, and professionals who have helped me with throughout the process. From Instagram to TikTok, you all mean so much to me and I have learned a lot from your endless wells of knowledge! To Natália Bodišová for creating the absolutely stunning cover art. I can never get enough of it.

To my readers! Gosh, there will never be enough words for you all. Thank you for picking this book up and delving into this world with me. Thea, Cole, Sarah, and the others would not be able to come to life without you all. I hope you stick through with me. Thank you!

About the Author

Arleta Rae

Arleta is from a small town in Massachusetts surrounded by mountains and forests. Her mind has always been wrapped up in a wild fantasy world. When she isn't reading, you can find her out in nature or having a coffee with a friend. She is getting her master's in ecopsychology at Naropa University and is in the process of creating a nature-oriented children's book for her thesis. Rising Ember is her debut novel.

www.ingramcontent.com/pod-product-compliance
Lightning Source LLC
LaVergne TN
LVHW011809060526
838200LV00053B/3712